A Letter to Three Witches

Books by Elizabeth Bass

Miss You Most of All
Wherever Grace Is Needed
The Way Back to Happiness
Life Is Sweet
A Letter to Three Witches

And writing as Liz Ireland

Mrs. Claus and the Santaland Slayings
Mrs. Claus and the Halloween Homicide

Published by Kensington Publishing Corp.

A Letter to Three Witches

ELIZABETH BASS

KENSINGTON
PUBLISHING CORP.

www.kensingtonbooks.com

KENSINGTON BOOKS are published by

Kensington Publishing Corp.
119 West 40th Street
New York, NY 10018

All Kensington titles, imprints, and distributed lines are available at special quantity discounts for bulk purchases for sales promotion, premiums, fund-raising, educational, or institutional use.

This book is a work of fiction. Names, characters, businesses, organizations, places, events, and incidents either are the product of the author's imagination or are used fictitiously. Any resemblance to actual persons, living or dead, events, or locales is entirely coincidental.

To the extent that the image or images on the cover of this book depict a person or persons, such person or persons are merely models, and are not intended to portray any character or characters featured in the book.

Special book excerpts or customized printings can also be created to fit specific needs. For details, write or phone the office of the Kensington Sales Manager: Kensington Publishing Corp., 119 West 40th Street, New York, NY 10018. Attn. Sales Department. Phone: 1-800-221-2647.

The K logo is a trademark of Kensington Publishing Corp.

ISBN-13: 978-1-4967-3433-4 (ebook)
ISBN-13: 978-1-4967-3432-7

First Kensington Trade Paperback Printing: February 2022

10 9 8 7 6 5 4 3 2 1

Printed in the United States of America

A Letter to Three Witches

Chapter 1

Griz

"What is she doing in there?"

Tannith's magic lamp draws her so near the glass that her breath fogs its surface. In her perplexed impatience, she's breathtakingly beautiful. Almond-shaped green eyes reflect like gemstones against the glass, and hair blacker than mine drapes over her shoulders, tantalizing me. Sometimes that hair swings when she moves and I can't take my eyes off it. In bed at night I often reach a paw out to touch its silkiness, though only lightly, careful not to wake her. Nothing angers Tannith more than disturbing her sleep. Seriously. Objects get thrown. She has good aim.

She peers so closely that her nose is almost touching glass. "Why is she just *sitting* there?"

I gaze at the lamp and the woman visible inside it. She's in the front seat of her vehicle, which pulled into her driveway a full minute ago. The image flits and flickers, unstable, but the woman is also in motion.

"She's not just sitting," I point out. Tannith's powers of inference can be woefully lacking, but that's one of her failings that I, a mere feline, am not supposed to acknowledge. As her familiar,

I'm not supposed to acknowledge *any* of her failings. Holding my tongue isn't always easy. "She's moving."

And not even subtly, but in jerky gyrations. From anyone else this might be considered odd behavior, but I know the woman inside that glass. There's nothing graceful or normal about her. Just the sight of her makes my fur bristle.

Tannith's gaze narrows, then she bleats out a joyful laugh. "You're right! The idiot is sitting in the front seat of her car in her driveway, dancing to..." She angles her ear, and her smile widens as she recognizes a tune that means nothing to me. "Oh my God, that's Barry Manilow! 'Copacabana'!" She bends, laughing silently but gleefully. Then she leans forward, almost kissing the glass. "Gwen, you pathetic cheeseball."

I don't care for any of Tannith's relations, but I had the misfortune to be stuck at Gwen's apartment once. Every day was torture. Her smothering attention was unendurable, and the food she served me wasn't worthy for the most pathetic alley cat, which I most definitely am not.

Tannith's delight in Gwen's dancing is short-lived. She drums her long, red-lacquered nails on the table. "Damn, this song goes on forever."

"Why are you watching her at all? You said the others reacted just as you expected them to. What is there to see?"

"I just want to make sure Gwen gets her letter, too." Tannith smirks at my skeptical glance. "Okay, I admit it. I'll relish seeing her devastation more than anybody's."

I want to see it, too.

"Dear Gwen." Tannith barely keeps an eye on the glass now as she engages in jubilant speculation. "First she'll open the letter, then she'll read it—*twice*, just to make sure her eyes aren't deceiving her. She'll have to sit down." Tannith's expression pantomimes every emotion her cousin would be going through. "And then she'll have a little debate with herself. Should she call Daniel? No! That would show *a lack of trust in their relationship.*" Tannith shakes her head, hair shimmering. "Gwen is the type who thinks in dorky phrases like that. You know what she'll do instead of calling Daniel?"

I look up at her, blink slowly. "No . . ."

"She'll run to the other cousins. They'll have an impromptu meeting of their little cupcake coven. Their *un*coven. And it will be nothing but confusion, because they're idiots."

Pleasure purrs through me. Tannith's clever, powerful, and devious, and—God help me—I love her. Sometimes I feel I don't deserve her, and other times it seems she doesn't appreciate me. But moments like this compensate for the bad things.

A flash inside the lamp draws our gazes.

"Oh, look! She's finally getting out of her car. Dressed in lumberjack lite, as usual. And there she goes . . . up to the door . . . checking her box . . ."

The woman in the glass plucks a letter attached to her mailbox and turns it over to examine the address. Suddenly, the angle has changed and her face looms close. It startles me.

Tannith mimics a gasp, pretending to be Gwen. " 'Who could it be from? Why, Cousin Tannith!' "

My nemesis of the inedible dinners stares long and warily at the back of the envelope, her forehead crumpling into deep lines. "She probably wonders why you sent her a letter when you live right across town."

Tannith clucks happily. "Pretty soon she'll be wondering all sorts of other things. Poor Gwen! I've ruined her Manilow high."

With one eye still on the envelope—she can't seem to look away from it—Gwen stabs at the front door's lock with her key, but misses. Tannith smirks as her cousin makes a second try. "Gwendle-bug's already discombobulated."

I yawn. "Are you going to watch that lamp all day?"

Tannith sneers at me. "You're one to talk. I've seen you staring at it for hours."

What's so strange about that? The lamp's bubbles go up and down constantly. Tannith calls it a lava lamp. Occasionally it mesmerizes me. I resent her poking fun at a weakness I can't help.

"You wouldn't want to watch her either if you had my memories. I still can't believe you left me with her."

Tannith clucks at me in disgust. "The least you could have done was a little useful spying."

"How could I spy? I could barely think. I was humiliated and patronized, and I was starving."

She laughs. *Laughs.*

Does she truly have so little empathy for me? Rage grips me and I twitch all over.

"No claws," she warns.

"I had to eat dry food for an entire week. *Pellets!*"

"Give me a break. I've seen you eat bugs." She swings her curtain of hair over one shoulder.

Oh, that hair. I think she does it on purpose. She knows how it affects me. But for once I try not to let her see it. I turn away, tail in the air. "I'll *get over it* as soon as you apologize."

She smiles, and for a split second I bask in her radiance. "Don't hold your breath, hair ball." One manicured hand swats me off the table with surprising force. I go sprawling to the floor, just managing to land on my feet and retain my dignity. Such as it is. I glare at her, but Tannith's forgotten all about me. She's back to peering into her lamp again, completely focused on Gwen.

Chapter 2

Gwen

I was still humming "Copacabana" to myself when I spotted the mint-green envelope clothespinned to the mailbox. The humming stopped when I turned it over and saw the *T* in elaborate foil script on the envelope's flap. *T* for "Tannith."

Give me strength. Not today. I didn't have the energy to deal with Tannith.

It had been a garage-clearing day. Not that I should complain. Garages are the bread and butter of Abracadabra Odd Job Service. Without garages I'd go broke, and I and my two employees would be spending our free time at the unemployment office. And yet . . .

So. Many. Garages. And Mrs. Caputo's had been stuffed to the rafters with boxes accumulated over decades. Boxes of clothes, quilts, and blankets, ancient kitchenware and dishes, household files going back decades. Boxes of abandoned crafts. Broken sports equipment. Most of all, there were Christmas decorations— cartons stacked halfway to the rafters with broken ornaments and tangled strings of long-dead lights. These sat alongside the towers of disintegrating newspapers and dusty stacks of *National Ge-*

ographic, which she said she couldn't throw away because they were her husband's. Her husband died in 1986.

And then there were the shelves of hoarded stuff—jars of rusty hardware, jars of marbles or seashells or pebbles, and sometimes just empty jars; old gardening pots; broken ceramics; yellowing books. For it all, filth was the common denominator. No matter how it was stored, everything was rusty, water stained, or ruined by bugs, mice and other rodents, or birds. A whole day of work, and we'd only managed to clear out enough space to move things to when we tackled Mrs. Caputo's attic. Our next task.

After a day of garage cleaning, all I wanted was a soak in the tub and to relax. A letter from Tannith was not going to relax me.

Tannith, with whom I'd been raised, was all right under controlled conditions and in small doses. But that envelope looked like it contained an invitation, and just the thought of an entire future evening devoured by the self-styled Siren of Zenobia filled me with dread. Not to mention, getting Daniel to go would take wheedling, and I hated to wheedle him. I hated to ask anything of him at all.

Daniel, the man I'd been living with for three months, had stated his dislike of Tannith early on: "She's the kind of woman who can't stand not to be the center of attention."

And to think, I'd been worried about introducing them. Physically Daniel was just the sort of man Tannith cycled through regularly—tall, muscular, brainy, but not necessarily worldly-wise. And sure enough, when she'd met him, Tannith had arched a brow at me as if to say, *You're punching above your class with this one.*

Which made me do a mental fist pump when Daniel had seemed oblivious to Tannith's charms, even though she never failed to turn them on full blast when he was around. I loved him for this . . . yet I didn't quite trust him. How could he not fall at Tannith's feet like every other man I'd ever encountered?

I let myself into the house and wandered to the kitchen, dropping the envelope on the breakfast table to fix myself a cup of coffee from one of the pods Daniel deplored. He kept pushing them and the machine they belonged to toward the back of the cupboard.

"People made coffee for centuries without creating piles of plastic waste," he'd lectured me more than once.

He was right. But my pod machine was so handy. Especially after spending an afternoon in a garage full of dust and mouse poop, when I just needed a quick caffeine pick-me-up to handle whatever my witchy nemesis had in store for me. Good to the last drop of guilt.

Anyway, Daniel was not here to scold. Cupping my steaming mug, I dropped into a chair at the chrome dinette to contemplate the green envelope again. It had to be dealt with. If there was a party, Tannith would expect an RSVP yesterday.

I opened the envelope, unfolded the letter, and scanned the message, printed in a fancy font imitating calligraphy. When I reached the end, I frowned, leaned forward, and read it again.

> *Dearest cousins,*
> *By the time you receive this letter, I'll be gone. (Put away the smelling salts, Trudy. I don't mean suicide.) I'm relocating—heading to the Big Apple to seek fame and fortune and all that jazz. Much as I hate to break up our idyllic little cousin coven, I just can't see moldering away the rest of my life in pokey Zenobia. Strangely, I can envision the rest of you moldering away, which is part of the reason I didn't want a big goodbye scene. I want to remember you all just as you are in my mind right now. I'm guessing that's pretty much how you'll stay forever.*
> *So this is it, friends.*
> *Goodbye, farewell, auf Wiedersehen, etc.,*
> *Tannith*

She'd chosen deep purple ink for her signature. Her handwriting was even larger and more extravagantly loopy than usual. It momentarily distracted me from what came directly after it.

P.S. Oh, I almost forgot. The other reason I didn't want a big goodbye scene is that my new squeeze is follow-ing me to NYC at the end of the week. You know him well—in fact, one of you happens to live with him . . . or did until I charmed him away from you. I'm sorry if it comes as a shock, but as a famous New Yorker once said, the heart wants what it wants. . . .

This was not an invitation. More like a sucker punch.

The "cousins" she'd addressed the letter to were a group of us who all lived in Zenobia. Trudy was the oldest. She was a teacher, a mom, a fabulous baker, and the wife of a history professor at Zenobia College, who was currently on sabbatical. She and Laird had recently become empty nesters when their twin daughters, Molly and Drew, had left for college in California in September. Another cousin in town, Milo, was a year younger than me. He owned his own landscaping design business and lived with his boyfriend, Brett, who was currently running for mayor.

Tannith was a distant relation my parents had adopted, and not a favorite of any of us, but since we'd grown up together, she was included in what we jokingly referred to as our cousin coven—or sometimes the cocktail coven, or the cupcake coven, depending on what we were ingesting. I'd always expected Tan-nith to leave Zenobia, especially after we finished college and she came into an inheritance from her deceased parents. Instead, she'd stayed, bought a little house in town, shopped, took up var-ious hobbies, and continued to hang out as if she were still a col-lege student.

Now she'd finally decided to leave, but she was going in typi-cal Tannith fashion. Causing discord. It had been like this from the beginning. When "my new sister" had appeared in our house, already beautiful and intimidating at eight years old, I tried to make her welcome. My class at school had recently dis-cussed the goodness of sharing, so I'd decided to walk the walk and had handed over half my doll collection to Tannith. For weeks after I would find my poor dolls decapitated in the bathroom sink, buried up to their necks in the yard, or hanging by their tiny ankles from tree branches.

Each time, my parents had reminded me that giving something away meant no longer being in control over what happened to it. Which was easy for them to say. They didn't have to worry about scooping up their favorite Ben & Jerry's Brownie Batter ice cream and finding Barbie's head in the middle of a pint.

Our relationship hadn't improved much by the time we finished high school. On graduation night, someone sneaked into my room and put Krazy glue on the inside of my mortarboard. I'd spent my last summer before college with my hair buzzed off like a marine recruit.

Things had seemed smoother between us of late, but obviously that was wishful thinking on my part. A strange sound echoed around the room. Was that the wind, or a faint laugh? Hair rose on the back of my neck, a spider sense of being watched. *Don't be paranoid.* Causing paranoia was another of Tannith's talents.

Scanning the kitchen, I pinpointed the sound I'd probably heard: a Kit-Kat Klock in shiny chrome and black. It had been a housewarming present from Tannith when I'd moved in with Daniel. He was picky about what stuff from my old apartment I put around—but for some reason he'd taken a liking to that clock. The tail made a swishing sound as it swept out the seconds.

I focused my attention back on the letter. Whom could Tannith be planning to run away with? Daniel? It didn't seem possible. We'd only been living together for a few months. We were still in our period of adjustment—although most of the adjusting was on my part, since this was Daniel's house. He'd lived here all through grad school and for the four years since he got his doctorate and had been teaching and researching at Zenobia College.

But I couldn't imagine Tannith with Trudy's husband, Laird. Trudy and Laird had just celebrated their twentieth anniversary. Milo and Brett had been together less than a year, but they seemed happy. . . .

I was so absorbed by the puzzle created by Tannith's malignant message that my phone's chirping ringtone caused me to shoot about three feet in my chair. I dove for my purse, extracted my phone, and flipped the cover open. *Daniel.*

My stomach somersaulted. Was this the end, then? I braced myself to be dumped over long distance.

"Where are you?" I asked without thinking. My brain had almost settled Daniel in the Big Apple with Tannith. Which was ridiculous. Daniel didn't even like New York City. Or Tannith.

But wasn't mutual dislike the spark of half of all the romances since Shakespeare?

And hadn't half of all my own romances *ended* when my boyfriend got to know Tannith a little better? My first kiss, a wet peck from Josh in eighth grade, had taken place behind the cafeteria at lunch. By three o'clock that afternoon, Josh was walking Tannith home instead of me. In high school, I'd dated Chris Wilson for six weeks before I came back from after-school debate club to discover Chris and Tannith cuddling together on the backyard trampoline. Once a blind date had shown up at the door, seen Tannith standing behind me, and suggested she accompany us. Tannith had, of course, agreed. And then there was the Great Prom Disaster, which was still soul withering to think about. Tannith had stolen my prom date from me during the prom itself, in just the time it took for the DJ to play "Dancing on My Own."

After a moment of distraction on my part and confused hesitation on his, Daniel's dry laugh rumbled in my ear. "Hello to you, too."

He wouldn't be laughing if he'd run away with Tannith, would he?

Unless he was deliriously happy.

"Right. Hi." Angst made my voice airy and doubtful. Through the phone, a car horn blared in the background, along with a lot of chatter noise . . . and maybe some kind of music? "No kidding, where are you?"

"Vermont."

Are you alone? It was on the tip of my tongue to ask. I needed to play it cool, as cool as Tannith would be under the same circumstances. Daniel, an entomologist, was on a trip to—supposedly—investigate spruce beetles. The specific borer that he was interested in, the red-ringed spruce beetle, was native west of the Rockies, but recently one had inexplicably been sighted in Vermont. In the world of entomologists, that bug had set off a firestorm.

"I needed to stop for coffee," he said. "There's a good place here in Brattleboro."

I glanced down at my cup. They wouldn't use plastic pods in Brattleboro . . . if he really was in Brattleboro. How would I know? He could be anywhere. Just because he said he was in Vermont didn't necessarily mean that he wasn't somewhere else. New York City, for example.

"Gwen? Are you okay?"

"Why wouldn't I be?"

"I don't know. You sound strange."

"I, um, have a headache. We cleaned out a garage this afternoon."

He clucked. "You didn't wear a mask, did you."

He was always after me to wear a mask when I cleaned out garages, attics, and abandoned buildings: *You never know what's floating around in the air in those places. Mold alone can make you sick.*

His nagging usually annoyed me, but today I found it reassuring. And not just because it demonstrated an ongoing concern for my well-being, but because it was a good reminder of why Tannith would not have run off with Daniel. Tannith might have flirted with him—mostly to piss me off—and might have been physically attracted to him, but if there was one thing Tannith couldn't stand, it was someone telling her what to do.

More to the point, Tannith wasn't Daniel's type. He'd told me as much.

"She's so obvious," he'd said after the first time the three of us had met for lunch. "She can't stand it if men don't think she's the hottest thing in the room."

Honesty had forced me to point out the depressing truth: "She usually *is* the hottest thing in the room."

"If you like that type."

"What type?"

"Artificial."

"What type do you think I am?"

He made the universal helpless gesture of a guy worried he'd strayed out of his depth. "You know, natural."

I shook my head at the memory. Poor, oblivious dope. Did he really think perfect highlighted streaks appeared in nature? Did he not have an inkling of the amount of moisturizing, plucking, and concealing that went on in the bathroom every morning? Did he think I kept cosmetics around just because I liked to collect little bottles and tubes?

Maybe he did, and I never corrected his misperception that I was some kind of au naturel, cosmetic-shunning purist. *Why disillusion him?* I'd thought at the time.

Now I worried I'd been living a lie. Daniel might accuse Tannith of being fake, but she never hid her artifice. She was a genuine fake person.

"Gwen?"

His voice startled me. "Here!" It sounded like I was answering roll call.

"For a second I thought we were cut off. Seriously, are you okay?"

"Mm."

"You sound odd."

"How?"

"Listless? Monosyllabic? Maybe you should see a doctor. No telling what you inhaled in that garage. You know, bubonic plague is—"

Not plague warnings again. "Have you heard from Tannith?"

There. I'd spoken the dreaded name. Now I awaited his reaction. It was too long in coming for my liking.

"Uh, no, not since . . ." After a pause, he reversed course. "Why?"

"I just got a weird letter from her."

"What other type of letter *would* you get from Tan?"

Tan? He was calling her Tan now? "She's moving. To New York."

Silence ensued.

"Daniel?"

He cleared his throat. "I knew that, actually."

"Since when?" Maybe since he started calling her Tan.

"I think she mentioned it at one of those endless evenings at your cousin Trudy's."

Daniel rarely even went to parties with the cousins. Although, now that I thought about it, he'd been there one evening not too long ago when we all played Clue. Of course Tannith had cheated—she'd been cheating since our Candy Land days—and then Milo had attempted to cheat in retaliation, to the effect that the cards for both Colonel Mustard and Mrs. Peacock ended up in the solution envelope, which caused Trudy's husband, Laird, to have a snit fit, chuck the tiny lead pipe at us all, and stomp off. We'd all laughed and ended up in two chat klatches—Milo, Brett, Trudy, and me . . . and Tannith and Daniel.

Tan and Dan.

That had been back in September.

"She told you about New York?" *Over a month ago?*

"Yeah. We talked about it."

"You mean you were over there having a heart-to-heart with Tannith?" *And I didn't notice?*

"Must have been the appletinis."

Trudy had perfected drink mixing from two decades of faculty dos. Cocktail coven provided her a chance to experiment or revisit favorites. Appletinis were always a hit. Apparently they'd been a good tongue loosener that evening, too. At least for Daniel and *Tan*.

"So you sat there listening to Tannith's life-changing plans?"

"At the time it seemed preferable to hearing Milo talk about the mayoral campaign."

Milo was helping manage Brett's campaign against Karen Morrow for mayor of Zenobia, so the campaign was a natural topic of conversation.

"Did Tannith mention anything else about leaving town? Any pertinent information involving other people, for instance?" When he didn't answer right away, I felt sure he knew something about which of the cousins' partners intended to join Tannith in her New York love nest. Either that or he himself was guiltily planning to do so. I took a deep breath. "You can tell me, Daniel."

"I think she said she was going to put off selling the house for a few months even after she moved. Something about waiting until the market got hotter." His voice sounded befuddled and maybe a little bored, but that didn't surprise me. His enthusiasm and intensity were reserved for insects.

"Why didn't you tell me about this?"

"About the housing market?"

"About Tannith leaving."

"I didn't think you'd care."

"Of course I care." *Especially if she's running off to New York with* you.

"Or maybe I assumed you already knew," he added.

"If I had, I would have told you."

"Right, but I might not have been paying attention, so . . ."

I sucked in a breath. Okay, so now he was saying—implying, at least—that I gabbed at him so much he didn't listen to half of what I said. I shouldn't have been surprised. Daniel always thought it was strange that my cousins and I had such an endless capacity to chatter. If nothing new was happening, we would just retread past events. He laughed at us for finishing one another's sentences and talking in unison.

Tannith was the least gabby of the four cousins. Maybe that

would appeal to strong, silent Daniel. I also recalled a clue she'd dropped in that letter: the word *charmed. . . . Until I charmed him away from you,* she'd written. That indicated that she'd used witchcraft to lure him—whoever it was—away.

Even if she could do that, did she actually think she'd get away with it? Back in 1930 the Grand Council of Witches had issued an edict forbidding any of my great-great-grandfather's descendants from practicing witchcraft. This had been a harsh, almost unprecedented ruling; then again, my great-great-grandfather seemed to have been an especially incompetent witch. Blundering and witchcraft don't make a good combination. Whether intentional or not, his sorcery had resulted in the Dust Bowl, which had ravaged a huge swath of North America. Of course the history books and PBS documentaries don't mention my ancestor—they've come up with all sorts of scientific rationalizations for it—but every witch in the world is taught my family's sad legacy of epic disaster. We are held up as the ultimate example of enchantment gone wrong.

We were lucky not to be expelled from Wiccan society altogether. My great-great-grandfather had nine children and thirty-one grandchildren, so that would have created quite a band of outcasts. Maybe the possibility of a rogue witch clan was what the Grand Council of Witches worried about. Instead, their edict punished our family for one hundred and fifty years. This was year ninety-one so there was still quite a while to go. The Council didn't simply trust that members would follow edicts, either. They sent anonymous snitches called Watchers to ensure we did.

If Tannith was practicing witchcraft, she'd have to be secretive about it. Could she really have progressed to the point that she could successfully cast a love spell? Those were supposed to be difficult.

If Daniel was her victim, it would be an ironic twist. Daniel never believed my talk about my family's supernatural lineage. He considered witchcraft as unscientific as crystals and healing with magnets.

Something odd had happened with our phone connection. Daniel was murmuring to someone as if he were holding his hand over the receiver. No one did that with cell phones, though, so he must simply have been holding the phone away from his body. I strained to hear what was being said—was that a woman who was replying to him? All I could make out was Linda Ronstadt singing in Spanish in the background. Linda Ronstadt's voice could cut through anything.

Was Linda Ronstadt something a coffee shop in Brattleboro would play?

If he actually was in Brattleboro, and not in, say, New York.

"I need to go," Daniel told me. "My sandwich is here."

"Your sandwich." Sure.

Or, like a cigar, maybe a sandwich sometimes really was just a sandwich.

His voice turned more serious. "Gwen, we need to have a talk when I get back."

My stomach felt as if I'd swallowed a bowling ball. "About what?"

"I don't want to discuss it over the phone. It has to do with my future. Yours, too."

And there it was. *His* future. And mine. Not ours.

Damn it. I'd just settled in. I thought I was happy. Why had he asked me to move in if he was just going to go and get enchanted away from me by someone as obvious as Tannith?

Okay, maybe that wasn't fair. He couldn't help being the victim of a love spell . . . if that's truly what had happened. And maybe I'd been more enthusiastic about moving in than he had been. But it was so frustrating. I'd gotten rid of so much stuff from my old apartment. All my furniture, lots of knickknacks, kitchen stuff . . .

I looked up at the Kit-Kat Klock. Tannith's housewarming gift. Its stupid grin was mocking me.

"I'll call you later, okay?" Daniel said. "After I get to the lodge."

After he ended the call, I started to press the icon next to Trudy's name on my contact list. I stopped before my index finger could touch the screen. No doubt Trudy and Milo had received the Tannith letter by now. But on the off chance that Trudy hadn't, maybe I could get to her place in time to save her the agony of opening that mint-green envelope and being blindsided by its poisonous contents.

Chapter 3

The aroma of vanilla that greeted me when Trudy opened the door made me forget momentarily why I was there. I crossed the foyer feeling like one of those old cartoon figures that float through the air sniffing their way toward food by its smell. In this case, the scent originated with the cupcakes sitting on the counter of the open-concept kitchen visible from the front door.

After I got a look at the living room, though, even the draw of freshly baked cupcakes couldn't hold my attention. Trudy lived in a renovated 1920s Craftsman house in one of the older neighborhoods in Zenobia. The décor of the place had always seemed minimalist to me—until tonight.

Gone were Laird's leather chairs and the backbreakingly stiff couch that had been there forever. In their place were a new sofa and two chairs in eye-popping colors, one with a matching puffy ottoman. A bright rug splashed cherry red and yellow across the floor. Although she was the only cousin with children, Trudy's living room had always captured the vibe of a psychiatrist's waiting room. Now, after decades of being in a family home, the room finally looked homey. The couch, a solid green, was strewn with bright tasseled and fringed throw pillows . . . and my cousin Milo. Wearing a BLAIR FOR MAYOR T-shirt, he was huddled against the cushions, shoes off, staring intently at his phone. Trudy's family's pet rabbit, Peaches, was nestled in his lap.

"It's about time you got here," he said.

"Milo's looking up Tannith's profile on Cackle to search for clues," Trudy told me.

So much for warning them. They'd both obviously seen the letter.

Cackle was Twitter's social media equivalent for witches. Participating on it was risky for us because of the Edict. You never really knew whom you were communicating with online.

A mixed drink and a vanilla cupcake with sprinkles sat untouched on the coffee table in front of Milo, though he'd taken the mint sprig out of the highball glass and was feeding it to Peaches the rabbit. "Peaches is my emotional support bunny tonight," he explained.

I was on the verge of asking why *he* needed emotional support, but the living room's appearance sidetracked me. "What happened to your furniture?" I asked Trudy.

"Laird wanted to move some things down to his basement office, so I found these chairs and a sofa to replace the old stuff. The rug was an impulse buy. Isn't it cute?"

I sank into one of their chairs. It was pure bliss compared to the torture chairs that had been there before. "Yes. It all looks great. So—vibrant."

Trudy beamed. "That's what I wanted. Liveliness!"

Milo shook his head at us. "How can you two talk about home décor at a time like this? Don't you care that Brett has left me?"

"Brett hasn't left you," Trudy and I said in unison.

I did a double take at her, but Trudy had gone back to her crystal pitcher to pour a drink for me. From the ingredients on the bar and the looks of Milo's glass, tonight was a purple-haze cocktail night—vodka, cranberry juice, and blackberry liqueur.

And from the purple-haze glaze in her blue eyes, I guessed Trudy had already gotten a head start on us. It wasn't like her to overindulge.

I studied her to see if anything else was out of the ordinary, but she had on her usual baking attire—knit pants and a flowing tunic covered by a pink apron with her Enchanted Cupcakes logo on it, a cupcake whose iced hat had tulle coming off the top like a princess's hennin. Trudy and I were alike in one respect: our business names were the only vestigial signs of the supernatural in our lives.

"How is it that my clothes are the only ones that don't advertise anything?" I wondered aloud as Trudy handed me a drink and placed a cupcake on a plate on the side table by my chair.

Milo quirked an eyebrow over his phone. "Nothing except your need for a new wardrobe."

Ouch. But looking at the old work cardigan I was still wearing, I couldn't argue too strongly. I picked up my cupcake and inhaled half of it. Another thing I could blame Tannith for—a night of stress eating.

"Why would you think Brett's run off with Tannith?" I asked Milo. "Brett's in a race for mayor. He won't leave Zenobia."

"He *has* left Zenobia—on a 'business trip.'" Milo used air quotes. "And he's been totally ignoring my messages."

"He's probably just in a meeting," I said.

"All day? And guess where he is?" Milo didn't wait for us to guess. "New York City."

For heaven's sake. Brett worked in a bank. "New York is a banking center," I pointed out. "And I'm sure bankers can have all-day meetings."

"Forget that. He's been shopping."

"How do you know that if you haven't talked to him?" I asked.

"Because there have been new charges on his credit cards."

"Milo."

He bristled defensively. "Can I help it? His passwords are taped on the keyboard drawer of his desk. That's more than reckless—it's like a cry for help."

"Right." I shook my head at him. "You had no other choice than snooping into his financial data."

"He took off the same day Tannith sent us that note," Milo said, not backing down. "I'm not only his boyfriend, I'm also running his campaign. I need to know if he's bugging out on everything."

"He's not," I said.

"Then who's he buying jewelry for?"

That tidbit brought Trudy and me up short. "Jewelry?" she asked.

"Tiffany's. Eighty-two hundred dollars."

That . . . was a lot of money.

"It might be a present for his mother," I suggested.

"Deceased."

"Or for himself."

"Mr. Frugal, splurge on himself? Or jewelry for anybody? This is the man who for my last birthday gave me a contribution to my IRA."

Oof. "That's worse than Daniel giving me a DivaCup for my birthday."

"No, it's not," Milo and Trudy said at once.

No, it wasn't.

"Believe me," Milo said, "the only reason Brett would spend that much money on something that doesn't pay dividends would be if Tannith put a spell on him."

There it was. Milo suspected an actual love spell, too—and from Trudy's nod, I could tell she did, as well.

No one had to say it, but the idea of Tannith going rogue frightened us all. When she wanted something, she usually got it. She didn't always get to keep it—or even want to keep it once it was in her grasp. But she was clever, and she knew just how to mess with people's heads. That letter, for instance, was a masterstroke. She knew it would be just like poking a stick in an anthill. We were the ants.

"Where would she have learned to cast spells like that?" I wondered aloud. Witches usually apprenticed under other witches. Because of the Edict, we'd all been denied that opportunity.

"Cackle's a good start," Milo said. "Or Witchbook. They've got all sorts of groups even isolated witches can join. And you can find out how to do anything on BrewTube."

"Right, but if any of us started chatting with one of the Council's Watchers, we could wind up in big trouble."

At least, that's what my parents had always warned. Once when my mother had found me levitating my Barbie, I thought she would have a heart attack. As far as I was concerned, I was just doing what came naturally, but my parents acted as if they'd caught me in the middle of something shameful. They were normally so mild mannered that their horrified response startled me. I'd only strayed back toward witchcraft once or twice since. Teenage shenanigans, mostly. Time-savers. Nothing anyone would ever find out about.

I'd assumed Tannith was the same. I should have known better. She'd inherited money from her birth parents' estate when she came of age, and she hadn't had to work. That must have given her a lot of time to dabble in witchcraft on her own. Could she really have honed her powers to such an advanced degree that she could cast a love spell?

"Why is she doing this?" Milo asked.

That was easy to answer. "Because she's Tannith. Causing mayhem and unhappiness is what she excels at. That, and cheating." Cheating at games, cheating at love—it was all the same to her. The Great Prom Disaster leaped into my memory.

"But she's one of us," Milo said.

I had to bite back a retort. My parents had raised Tannith and treated us like sisters. But I'd never been fooled. Not really. Tannith and I were the same age, and Zenobia, New York, was a small world. We went through school together and our circles of friends had overlapped. Hanging out together had been unavoidable, but I'd always known that Tannith saw herself as different. Special. Just like recently. She'd joined in our cousin-cocktail-cupcake coven for grins, but I often got the sense that she saw herself as an alien observer sent to study lesser creatures.

And all this time, unbeknownst to us, she'd been flouting the Edict, sharpening her craft. Getting ready to inflict a final blow to me. It had to be Daniel she was running away with.

We need to talk when I get back, he'd told me. I couldn't bring myself to confide in my cousins. I hoped I was wrong. But if I was wrong, that meant Tannith intended to sink her claws into either Brett or Laird, and for Milo's and Trudy's sakes, I didn't want that, either.

"It's Brett, I know it," Milo lamented.

I frowned. "Brett is gay, though."

"Bi. He had a girlfriend in college. In the picture I saw of her, she even looked a little like Tannith. Dark hair, killer figure . . ." Milo sank down, depressed. "They would make a great-looking couple."

"You and Brett are a great-looking couple," I pointed out.

In no mood to be consoled, Milo was glued to his phone again. "If Tannith has a Cackle profile, I haven't found it yet."

"How do *you* have one?" I asked. Technically speaking, someone from our family should have been blocked from downloading the Cackle app. We were discouraged even from being on Witchbook.

"It's not hard to do if you set your mind to it and do some creative maneuvering."

I looked over his shoulder to see his profile. "Warlock Holmes?"

Alter ego exposed, he smiled sheepishly. "Since I'm doing detective work here."

While I was staring at his Cackle feed, a rabbit hopped into the room. I glanced back at Milo. Peaches was still in his lap. This second rabbit had the same beige fur with gray-tipped ears, although it was slightly plumper. I frowned at Trudy. "You adopted a new bunny?"

Trudy had been exasperated with having to care for the rabbit her daughters, Drew and Molly, left behind when they went to college. I couldn't believe she'd adopted another one on her own.

She swirled her drink in her glass. "He's company for Peaches."

Peaches, still munching Milo's mint sprig, didn't seem at all interested in this new companion.

"What's the new one's name?"

"Herb."

Milo laughed. "Peaches and Herb. Perfect." He lifted Peaches and did a couple of bars of "Shake Your Groove Thing."

"I meant it to stand for Herbert Hoover," Trudy said, "but it works both ways."

Herb hopped closer, gazed straight at me, and thumped his back leg so purposefully that I recoiled. "Don't they do that to signal danger?"

"Do what?" Trudy asked.

"Thump their back leg like that." Not that I was an expert. "Everything I know about rabbits I learned from *Watership Down*."

Milo sent me an amused glance. "You'll be stunned to learn that they don't actually talk."

Trudy downed the end of her cocktail. "Thank God for that."

The rabbit thumped again.

"I might have to put him back in his cage." She glared at the rabbit, which hunched defensively. The standoff over, Trudy fiddled with an internet radio, and soon the room was filled with Rosemary Clooney singing "Come on-a My House." Trudy poured herself another drink, sank into her new chair, kicked off her shoes, and propped her feet up on the ottoman.

I felt the same frisson on the back of my neck that I'd experienced at my house. I tilted my head. "Have either of you had the feeling you're being watched?"

Milo and Trudy aimed curious gazes at me.

"When?" she asked.

"Today, when I was opening that letter. It was like someone was laughing at me. Like Tannith . . ."

Now that the words were out, they made me sound paranoid.

"She's laughing for sure." Trudy swizzled a toothpick around in her drink. "She probably thinks it's hilarious to panic us all."

"You're not panicked," I pointed out.

"Of course she's not. You think Tannith would run off with Laird?" Milo moaned and face planted into his support rabbit. "What am I going to do?"

"It's not Brett," Trudy and I responded together.

I looked around. "Where *is* Laird? Isn't that music going to bug him?"

"He's gone."

Milo and I exchanged glances, which didn't escape Trudy's notice.

"Not run-away-with-Tannith gone," she assured us. "He's off on another research trip."

"For the book that will never get written." Milo took a sip of his purple haze. The words were harsh, but probably true. Laird had been working on his great oeuvre, a biography of Herbert Hoover, for at least a decade. And apparently he was still collecting research.

We all sat ruminating as Rosemary Clooney gave way to Nat King Cole singing "When Your Lover Has Gone."

"Not comforting, Nat," Milo admonished the radio.

The timing of Tannith's letter struck me as particularly diabolical. "Tannith picked a week when all of our partners were out of town to drop her bomb."

My cousins leaned forward. "Daniel's not in town, either?" Trudy asked.

Their alarmed gazes made me self-conscious. And more defensive than I expected to be. "He's checking on a beetle in Vermont."

Milo laughed. "That's what they all say."

"It's true." I took a sip of my purple haze and wished for a splash more vodka. "I think it's true."

"Of course it's true." Trudy smiled at me. "Daniel's not a cheater."

"But if it's not Brett, and it's not Daniel . . ." Milo glanced back at me and explained, "And it's not Daniel, because Tannith would tire of Bug Boy even before the train pulled into Grand Central Station," before returning to Trudy with "You *can't* think Laird has run off with Tannith."

"I know he hasn't," she said.

Milo gasped. "How do you know?"

Trudy opened her mouth to answer, but whatever she was about to say was cut off by the doorbell. She bolted out of her chair and turned down the radio. Then she stared wide-eyed at the door. "Who could that be?"

"You could always answer it and see," I suggested.

Setting her mouth in a determined line, she marched to the door. Milo and I exchanged another puzzled glance. What was up with Trudy?

We couldn't see her face when she opened the door, although I could just glimpse the stranger standing there. The man seemed to be around thirty, had curly brown hair cut short, and bright eyes behind round glasses. "Hi." His voice sounded cheerful, as if he were certain we'd all been expecting him. "Wow, something sure smells delicious."

"Cupcakes." Trudy didn't step aside to let him in.

Stranded on the outside doormat, the visitor shifted feet. "Right! I've heard about the cupcakes. . . ." The guy's face finally registered that he wasn't going to be welcomed with open arms. "This *is* Laird Webster's house? Professor Laird Webster?"

As if there were more than one Laird Webster in Zenobia, New York.

"Yes . . ." A hint of doubt crept into Trudy's voice.

"I'm here to see Professor Webster. Laird, I mean. He told me to call him Laird."

Trudy just stared at the guy.

"He's expecting me. I'm Jeremy, his new graduate assistant?" He poked his head through the door and peered around. "Didn't he tell anyone I was coming over?"

"Laird's on sabbatical," Trudy said.

Jeremy nodded. "I know, but I was in a class of his last year and he said I could work for him while he was drafting the Hoover book. Research and stuff. He suggested I come over tonight. He didn't mention a party, though."

Trudy stood her ground. "He's out of town."

Jeremy's brow creased in confusion. "He is?"

"He went to Iowa. I forget the name of the town."

"West Branch?" Jeremy guessed.

She snapped her fingers. "That's it."

"Hoover's birthplace. That makes sense." He tilted his head. "Funny, he didn't mention it to me when I was talking to him the day before yesterday."

"It was a spur-of-the-moment trip," Trudy explained.

Jeremy darted a glance around her and scanned the room. His gaze landed on me. "Looks like you have company anyway. I don't want to interrupt."

"I'll tell Laird you came by," Trudy said.

"Thanks, but that's not necessary. I'll text him."

"Perfect." Trudy was already swinging the door shut. "Good night, Jamie."

"Jeremy" was all he managed to blurt out before the door closed on him.

For almost twenty years, Trudy had been a faculty wife, hosting parties and putting up grad students who for whatever reason found themselves temporarily homeless. She was the soul of generosity, a natural den mother. I'd never seen her shut the door on someone's nose.

"Laird didn't tell his graduate assistant that he was going to Iowa?" I asked.

Blowing out a breath, Trudy made a beeline for the cocktail shaker. "Laird thinks he's so important, he assumes everyone will somehow know all about his schedule by osmosis."

"Well, at least if he's gone to Iowa, you know he's safe from Tannith," Milo said. "I can't see her following him *there*."

If Laird really was in Iowa. Doubt kindled in my mind. Something was not right here. "Tannith's letter said that the man wasn't going to follow her until the end of the week," I reminded Milo.

"That's right." He looked at Trudy. "Laird might be back by then."

"Doubt it." She poured herself another drink.

Milo brought the Cackle screen up on his phone again. "We can't let Tannith get away with this."

"It takes two," Trudy pointed out. "Whoever's running away with her is also to blame."

Milo shook his head. "Not if he's the object of a hex."

"Do we even know where Tannith is?" I asked. "The letter indicates she's already gone, and when I drove by her house on the way over, there were no lights on. Her car wasn't there, either."

"If she's hexed one of our men," Milo said, "we have to counterhex. Justice demands it."

How could we do that? None of us had honed our powers. In fact, we'd pointedly avoided it. We were babes in the witch woods.

"First we have to find out who her victim is," I said.

"It doesn't matter," Milo said. "The counterhex would be against Tannith."

"How many drinks have you had?" I asked. This was Witchcraft 101, the kind of stuff even we outcasts were allowed to learn at Camp Walpurga. "To counter a hex you have to focus on the subject of the hex. So we *do* need to know who her victim is."

Milo laughed. "All right, Miss Witch Genius, share more of your expertise with us."

"You were the one just telling us we need to counterhex, Warlock Holmes. Besides, it's witchcraft, not rocket science." Just because our families had been forbidden didn't mean we didn't have the gift. "Think of Great-Uncle Onslow. Family lore says he'd never cast a spell in his life and he still managed to turn a barrel of cream into a butter sculpture of a cow overnight."

"And what good did that do?" Milo asked. "He came in third at the county fair."

"I saw a picture. It didn't even look like a cow." Trudy sighed. "I think we should sit tight for a while and see what happens at the end of the week."

The wait-and-see approach didn't appeal to Milo. "Until it's too late, you mean."

"Until we find out whether that letter was even true," she said. "Tannith might be winding us up, playing a big practical joke."

I bit my lip. "That letter didn't sound like a joke to me. It was malicious."

At the memory of it, Milo scowled. "What does she mean, we'll never change? Are we that predictable?"

No one said anything.

Then we laughed.

Later, outside Trudy's, Milo and I lingered on the sidewalk.

"What's going on with Trudy?" I shoved my hands in my jacket pockets against the chilly autumn evening. "I've never seen her acting so manic. Impulse-buying furniture, adopting another bunny? And there was something odd about the way she talked to that graduate student, too. She looked as if she'd tackle him like a linebacker if he tried to set foot in the house."

Milo didn't seem all that curious about what was amiss in the Webster household, though.

"I have a job for Abracadabra," he said, changing the subject. "But I need you to take care of it personally."

I had two perfectly able if slightly sluggish employees, Taj and Kyle, but it wasn't unusual for me to do smaller jobs on my own sometimes. "What do you need done?"

"There's someone I want you to shadow."

Alarm bells sounded in my head. It wasn't hard to see where this was leading. "No."

"How can you refuse? You don't even know who it is yet."

"I'm not going to spy on Brett."

"Who said anything about spying? I'm not asking you to go through his Visa bill."

"Of course not. You've got that covered yourself."

"I just need you to watch him."

"Milo, that's spying."

"Okay, maybe it's a *little bit* like spying, but mostly it's just making observations, right? Just to see what he's up to . . . and if he's getting up to it with Tannith."

"No."

He stepped closer. "Please?"

"Spying on Brett's not going to help matters."

"We have to figure out who Tannith has in her clutches. Trudy doesn't care because she's married to Laird, and we all know Tannith wouldn't gloat about stealing away with Mr. Herbert Hoover. Even if she did, for Trudy it would mean blessed relief."

That wasn't true. "Trudy and Laird have been married for twenty years."

"Exactly. Would *you* want to be staring down year twenty-one with Laird?"

No. I wouldn't have married him in the first place, though. "She's acting so strangely. Subconsciously, she must be nervous that Laird is the one Tannith's targeted."

Milo sighed. "I don't want to be blindsided by this on Friday."

"Will having a few days' notice make it any better?"

"It might." He pinned an imploring gaze on me. Milo had expressive brown eyes. He'd always been a heartbreaker, and he was hard to say no to. Those eyes had gotten me into trouble more than once: from the usual spring-break shenanigans to convincing me it would be perfectly okay to paint a dorm room turquoise, to plant theft from a city park that resulted in a night in jail, a fine, and forty hours of community service.

Those eyes were probably about to get me into another scrape. "I'm not a detective."

"But you could do it. It's an odd job."

I shook my head. "You said Brett's in New York."

"He's coming back late tonight, and being Brett, he'll be at his desk tomorrow morning, daisy fresh. Unless he's already moved to New York. But he wouldn't do that."

"Of course he wouldn't. Not when he's running for mayor here. Not when he has you."

"No, I mean he wouldn't because in her letter Tannith specifically mentions that the person will be joining her at the end of the week. She's not the type to let anyone change her plans." When I didn't answer, he pleaded, "Just watch him for one morning."

"Why morning?"

"Because he has work or campaign events most evenings and afternoons. If he and Tannith are going to have a clandestine meeting, it'll be in the morning."

I did not want to do this. I'd almost prefer cleaning another moldy garage.

"I'll pay you time and a half."

"You won't pay me anything, because you know I wouldn't take it."

He grinned. "Great. I'll pay you triple, then."

I laughed. "I'm worried, too, you know."

"Fine. You watch out for Brett, and if everything seems to be copacetic, I'll trot off to Vermont to return the favor. I just can't spy on Brett personally because he'd consider that a sign of distrust."

"But hiring someone to spy on him isn't a sign of distrust?"

"He'll never find out because you'll be super-sleuthy about it. You read all those books when you were a kid, remember?"

"Nancy Drew and Trixie Belden never faced a foe like Tannith."

"Just consider it a fact-finding mission."

It *would* be good to narrow down whom Tannith planned to run away with. Not that I wished bad fortune on either of my cousins, but if Brett was going to run off with Tannith, then I at least wouldn't have to worry about Daniel.

I let out a long sigh. "I'm a pushover for a cousin in need."

He gave me a quick hug. "He'll be at the bank tomorrow. The one—"

"I know where Brett works. It's my bank."

"Good. Then you'll have a cover story if he catches you."

I had a sinking feeling I was going to need that cover story.

Chapter 4

One good thing about being the head of my own company, even a three-person outfit like Abracadabra Odd Job Service, was that it didn't leave much time for brooding. No sooner had my head hit the pillow than my phone on the bedside table was quaking and chirping me awake again. I silenced it with a sleepy swipe and checked my messages. Nothing from Daniel. So much for calling me after he got to the lodge.

Fine. He was busy. I understood. The fate of the nation's forests was in his hands. Either that or he was having a steamy fling with the cousin I grew up with. Which was worse, playing second fiddle to Tannith or a spruce beetle?

I rolled out of bed and tugged on my fall uniform: jeans, ankle boots, and three layers on top, culminating in my favorite sweater. Milo's snide comment about my wardrobe played through my mind until I checked myself in the full-length mirror. I loved autumn—the nippy mornings, Halloween, and pumpkin spice everything. Most of all, I loved my meticulously curated collection of chunky sweaters that took me from September to Christmas. This was my season.

A frown lined my brow as I remembered that I'd promised to spend part of the day spying on Brett. Maybe a chunky sweater wasn't the best uniform for that, but I wasn't going to rearrange both my workday *and* my wardrobe for Milo. Before I could begin this stakeout nonsense, I needed to get through my morning routine, starting with a swing by Trudy's house.

Her neighborhood was wonderful in the mornings, but especially on fall mornings like this one. Craftsman and Victorian houses painted in a variety of colors sat back from the wide street. Old established maples and oaks created a canopy overhead that stretched from sidewalk to sidewalk. What leaves were left ran the gamut of New England postcard hues, although more leaves were on the ground than in the branches. Additional color was provided by all the campaign signs dotting the yards. More seemed to pop up the closer we came to next week's election. Trudy's neighborhood leaned heavily toward BLAIR FOR MAYOR; I only spied one green-and-yellow sign touting KAREN MORROW, FOR ZENOBIA'S TOMORROW. Milo would be pleased by the ratio.

Carved pumpkins on stoops and autumn wreaths were evidence of how everyone had spent the past weekend. This was the kind of neighborhood suburbanites would drive their kids to for trick-or-treating in a few days, because it was such a picturesque setting for little witches, Spider-Men, and ghosts. Also, the residents were openhanded with candy.

My morning task here was to pick up cupcakes and deliver them to a café called the Buttered Biscuit. I'd started this routine two years ago when Trudy, a teacher, had begun her cupcake sideline. Her school was in the opposite direction of the café, while both her house and the café were on my route to work. Also, it gave me a chance to visit the proprietors of the Buttered Biscuit, who happened to be my parents.

Trudy's house was close enough to Zenobia College so that free spaces on the street filled up quickly. I ended up having to park two blocks away. As I was walking up, a man stood at Trudy's doorstep. It took me a moment to place him as the guy who'd been there the night before. She seemed to say only a few words to him before shutting the door on him as she had last night, leaving him staring at the autumn wreath on her door. Finally, he turned and descended the porch steps, stopping to stare at the house again from the sidewalk.

As I approached, he was walking in my direction, his preoccupied gaze focused on the sidewalk. My curiosity was too intense for me to resist blurting out, "Jeremy, isn't it?"

The question brought him up short right in front of me. He was wearing a grad student's uniform—jeans, T-shirt, and a tweedy jacket. Up close his eyes were green with brown flecks, and those long black eyelashes of his would have made even Liz Taylor envious. I found myself momentarily mesmerized by them despite the befuddled look he had fastened on me. He simultaneously pushed his glasses up the bridge of his nose and hiked the battered leather messenger bag that hung over one shoulder. That, too, was standard-issue grad student gear at Zenobia College.

"Do I know you?" Before I could answer, he added, "Of course I do. I saw you somewhere."

"Last night."

He snapped a finger. "That's it. You were at the lecture."

He'd lost me. "The what?"

"'Methodologies in Economic Equivalences in Historical Research,' at Bellamy Hall."

"No, I wasn't." I wanted to add, *Thank God*. Though it was no wonder he couldn't remember whom he saw there. Probably most of the audience had been half-asleep. "I was at Trudy's house when you came by. I'm her cousin Gwen."

"Oh." It was unclear if he was disappointed or just too distracted to supplement that syllable.

"You were talking to Trudy again just now, weren't you? It's an odd time to be paying a call."

"I was on my way to campus and thought I'd check if she'd heard from Laird."

"Has she?"

"No."

That was curious. Or maybe it wasn't. "Laird doesn't strike me as the overly communicative type."

"He usually answers my texts promptly," Jeremy said.

"Well, you know how it is when you're traveling."

But was it travel, or was it Tannith?

The look on Jeremy's face said he thought something more was going on than a guy too distracted to call on a road trip. No doubt he'd also conveyed that loud and clear to Trudy. Poor Trudy. If she did suspect Laird had run off with Tannith, the last thing she needed was this guy buzzing around the house, rubbing salt in her wound.

"Look, Trudy's having a few problems right now. It might be better to wait till you hear from Laird before knocking on her door again."

Jeremy blinked. "You think Professor Webster's marriage is busting up?"

"I don't know." Granted, I'd just told him to butt out of Trudy's life . . . but maybe he could provide information the rest of us didn't have. "Can you think of a reason why it should?"

"Laird wouldn't confide in me. I'm a graduate assistant, not a marriage counselor."

"Right. But you might have noticed Laird hanging out with certain people more than others."

"Who, for instance?"

Did I have to clunk him over the head with it? "Women. Other women."

"You mean, is he having an affair?" He frowned. "I doubt that very much. Whenever I talk to him, Laird always seems immersed in Hooverania."

I'd never given a lot of thought to how Laird behaved with his grad students, or what he did in his free time. He might have half the student body of Zenobia in love with him for all I knew. He was good-looking—sort of an old, haggard version of Benedict Cumberbatch. And didn't that imply that at some point he'd resembled a young, hot Benedict Cumberbatch? For as long as I could remember, though, he'd looked as faded as the tweedy jackets he wore, the ones with the patches at the elbow.

I found myself staring at Jeremy's elbows. No patches. That was a mercy. I hoped *he* wouldn't fade. It would be a shame to see those eyes of his become less vibrant as his soul was sucked away by Herbert Hoover or whatever he was going to spend his lifetime researching.

"What are you working on?"

He drew back in surprise at the question.

"Your doctoral thesis. What's it about? Give me the elevator pitch."

He took a deep breath. "Well, central to the thesis is the Sherman Silver Purchase Act of 1890, and the effect it had on the political realignments of that decade."

I was fading just hearing him say it.

He squinted. "Are you okay?"

"Just . . . preoccupied." I didn't want to insult the guy's life work. "You know, about Trudy."

He nodded in sympathy. "I wish Laird would answer my texts."

"I'm sure he will. Give it time."

His gaze fastened on me again. "You have a crystal ball or something?"

The words sent a chill through me. "Of course not," I said quickly.

"I didn't think so. You don't strike me as the type."

That last assertion put my guard up. "What type?"

He tilted his head. "Huh?"

"You said I didn't strike you as *the type*. What type?"

He shifted slightly, frowning. "I don't know, really. The crystal ball type?"

Right. I didn't like this. At all.

I took a reflexive step backward and glanced at the watch I wasn't wearing. "I need to get going. I'm already running late."

"Maybe I'll see you again sometime. What did you say your name was?"

I hesitated. "Gwen."

He smiled, and it would have been a nice smile if I hadn't been so unnerved. "Maybe we'll see each other around campus, Gwen."

"I'm not a student. Not anymore."

"What do you do?"

The paranoid in me told me to hold back, but the business owner won. Advertising was everything. I took a card out of my back pocket and handed it to him.

He stared at the little rectangle, which read:

Abracadabra Odd Job Service
"We Make Chores Vanish!"
Gwen Engel, proprietor

A wand and swirl of stars decorated the upper-right corner of the card. Along the bottom was my website address and phone number.

"Abracadabra." He smiled. "Cute name. I've always been interested in magic."

"It doesn't really mean anything," I said quickly. "I just thought it would be something people might remember. And it's at the top of the alphabet. *AAA* and *ABC* were already taken, so if someone's looking in a phone book or a directory—"

He laughed. "Seriously? Don't people just Google now?"

"Not all of them. Older people especially still use phone books. And even Google lists things alphabetically sometimes."

He held up the card. "Mind if I keep this?"

"Please do." I never knew when those business cards would translate into a job. "We even handle small moves."

"Good to know." He slipped it into his pocket. "Well, good-bye." He didn't move to leave, though. We both stood there as if mesmerized. Those eyes of his really were something.

A blush crept into my cheeks. I cleared my throat. "Bye." Taking the initiative, I began walking away, but almost sideways, like a crab. *What's wrong with you?* I forced myself to turn away from him and continued on to Trudy's.

The encounter troubled me. The way he'd looked at me. Something was going on there, some intense undercurrent.

Some trap?

After I knocked, it took Trudy a moment to answer. I was fairly certain I saw a curtain twitch, as if she were peeking out the front window. Even though I came here every morning at the same time.

She opened the door wide, dressed in a long-sleeve knit dress, the kind she wore to teach high school students history every day. Her eyes were bloodshot, though. Had she been crying?

"Are you feeling okay?"

"Just a little tired. I stayed up too late baking."

"Sorry it took me so long to get here. I ran into that Jeremy guy down the street."

She visibly flinched but ushered me into the house. Everything had been cleaned up from last night.

"I told him Laird never calls me every day when he's out of town," she said.

Halfway across the living room, I stopped. The rabbits, one dark and one beige, were in a movable pen she'd set up in a corner near the kitchen. "Wasn't that new rabbit beige?"

She followed my gaze. "He's still beige."

Was she serious? "Trudy, he's black."

"Brown, maybe."

Why would a rabbit change color at all? "Last night—"

"He probably looks different in the morning light."

"Maybe . . ." Except when I looked around, there was no morning light. Trudy had all her curtains closed, which wasn't like her. I glanced back at the rabbits. Peaches was munching on timothy hay. The new one—the newly dark one—Herb, was pressed up against the wire. He thumped loudly.

"I don't think that animal likes me," I said.

"Don't mind him. He's still getting acclimated." Trudy walked

over to the kitchen island where four boxes of cupcakes waited—
two for the café, and a third with extras for me. The bonus box
was my delivery fee. I didn't know what the fourth box was for.

"I went on a baking bonanza yesterday, so I'm sending an
extra box for you. If you don't want to give them away, you can always freeze them."

"I never say no to cupcakes."

"There's a new kind in there today. Strawberry Bliss. They're
pretty awesome, if I do say so myself."

I opened the top box, and the aroma of strawberries and sugar
wafted up at me. "That smells fantastic."

"I'm not sure why I suddenly felt the urge to make that kind.
Just an impulse."

"Like the new furniture. And Herb."

Her expression turned pensive. "You're right. I've been doing
quite a few impulsive things lately."

"You and Laird both, it sounds like. This research trip of his
had to be pretty spur-of-the-moment."

The corners of her lips tugged down.

Maybe I shouldn't have mentioned Laird. "Trudy, if you're
worried about Tannith . . ."

"I'm not," she insisted. "I'm absolutely not."

"Jeremy seems to think Laird's leaving so abruptly was
weird."

She rolled her eyes. "As if that's any of his beeswax."

"It sort of is, if he's helping Laird with his book." In the next
minute, a kind of electric shock went through my brain. "Unless
he really *isn't* working for Laird."

"Why would he lie?"

"I got a weird vibe off of that guy. Have you noticed his eyes?"

"No . . ."

"They're incredible."

She laughed. "Do you have a crush on him? You just moved in
with Daniel three months ago."

"No." I waved a hand. "Never mind. I think Milo's putting

strange ideas into my head. He wants me to spy on Brett, to see if he's the one who's planning on running off with Tannith."

"Oh, no. It's not Brett."

"Well, if it's not Brett and it's not Laird, that just leaves Daniel."

"Tannith could be lying. Just trying to wind us up. You know how she is."

"I know." Since childhood I'd been wound up by her regularly, like a mantel clock. "I guess that's why seeing Jeremy here again today unnerved me. Did he ask you any other questions?"

"No, just wanted to know Laird's whereabouts." Trudy's hands fisted at her sides. "As if I'm my husband's keeper."

I nodded, although after I left her, I felt a little confused. She wasn't Laird's keeper . . . but she was his wife. It wasn't exactly outrageous to expect she'd know where Laird was.

Honestly, looking at Laird and Trudy, I sometimes wondered what the point of being married was. Twenty years together and they barely communicated, bristled with resentments, and were obviously mostly together because of inertia. But now that the two were new empty nesters, what was the point of their union? A better marginal tax bracket?

The sad thing was, Trudy and Laird must have been madly in love at some point. They'd probably been as frisky as puppies together, shared their dreams by candlelight, and couldn't imagine being happy without each other. Now look at them. *I'm not Laird's keeper*. . . . I mean, come on.

And yet . . .

Could I deny that it had been a relief having the house to myself while Daniel had been gone? This was the first trip he'd taken since I'd moved in three months ago, and while the prospect of his running off with Tannith forever shook my foundations, the reality of being able to kick back and do exactly what I wanted to was awfully freeing. Not that I'd done much. The first night after he left I watched a romantic comedy that he would have had zero interest in. I'd scarfed down a half a can of

Pringles—joyful, trashy gluttony he would have arched a brow at. It wasn't so much that I didn't want to be his keeper; I just didn't want to feel that he was mine.

Was that a sign that we were doomed? Or was that me maintaining a healthy sense of separateness?

This was the trouble with waiting until the ripe old age of twenty-nine to get serious about anyone for the first time. I had no clue how these things really worked. Daniel had bowled me over right from the start, when I showed up to repair the gate to his backyard. I'd spoken to him on the phone, but he obviously hadn't expected the handyman we sent over to look like me. I could tell he felt awkward having a woman fixing something for him. He insisted on helping me—so much so that at the end I wrote out a new bill for him. He'd inspected it, shaking his head.

"This is half of what your estimate was," he protested.

"That's because you did half the labor."

"That's not fair."

I'd laughed. He was the first customer I'd ever had who wanted to pay me more than I asked for. While I was fixing the gate, it hadn't escaped my notice that he was incredibly good-looking—an intriguing combination of bookish and outdoorsy—and that he wasn't just lingering because he was interested in gate-hardware installation.

"If you won't take the extra money, you should at least allow me to buy you dinner," he said.

I'd mentally ticked off all the reasons I shouldn't accept that offer. *Taking a dinner date instead of cash is not a good idea. . . . He's too good-looking. . . . Entomology? . . . He's just Tannith's type. . . .*

Just last winter, I'd had a great first date with a guy—or so I'd thought. The very next weekend I heard he and Tannith had gone off on a skiing weekend. I hadn't even known they were acquainted.

I tilted my head. "Do you ski?"

Daniel looked puzzled. "I know how, but it's not something I enjoy that much. Snowshoeing is more my thing."

I couldn't see Tannith strapping on a pair of clunky snow-shoes, not in a million years. "I'd love to have dinner."

He shook his head in wonder. "I'm not sure how we got from dinner to winter sports to a yes, but I'll take it."

That had been in early spring. Three months later I'd moved out of my apartment and into his house, excited that my single-ton days were over. And now, a mere three months after that, I was reveling in being alone.

But only because it was just for a few days, I assured myself. I didn't want to be alone permanently. Maybe this is just how cou-pledom was. You had to take breaks.

Or was I just kidding myself? Maybe Daniel and I were just in the early stages of becoming a permanently dysfunctional couple like Laird and Trudy.

I thought of the way my mother always shook her head over my perpetually single, cranky workaholic Aunt Esme. "She's cursed," Mom would say. But wasn't being stuck in an unhappy marriage ten times worse than being Aunt Esme?

At the other end of the marriage spectrum were my parents, Jane and Tom Engel, the most disgustingly contented couple I knew. They'd met in summer camp as teens, remained pen pals, went together to Zenobia College, and stayed on to make a life together. He had renounced witchcraft forever because my mother wasn't able to practice. They couldn't keep up an argu-ment for five minutes without bursting into laughter. They were like those parrots on nature shows that bonded for life.

The Buttered Biscuit Café, located just off Zenobia's main drag, had been a hangout for students for as long as I could re-member. The two front rooms of the house were the dining areas. Part of the wall separating the front rooms had been re-moved to make way for a long counter that stretched almost the width of the building. Behind the counter was a blackboard that people ordered from. As customers queued up and made their way to the cash register at the counter's far side, a series of trays and cake covers were set out with pastries and other hand food to tempt them. Trudy's Enchanted Cupcakes were always popular and usually sold out by midafternoon.

As I carried the cupcakes in, the place was hopping as usual. Dad was manning the register, while an employee named Darcy took orders. I walked back toward the kitchen, past the coffee post. Students filled the tables, most of them wired up to iPads, notebooks, or phones while they downed coffee and plates of comfort food. Some slackers came in to tank up on the day-olds Mom and Dad left out by the coffee area as "samples."

"It's like leaving cat food out," I'd told my dad once. "You're encouraging freeloading strays."

"It's just day-old stuff," Dad said.

Mom nodded along. "They're doing us a favor, really. Otherwise I'd feel such guilt about all the wasted food."

My parents might be hopelessly naïve, but they're also the two kindest people I know.

I found my mom in the kitchen. She stopped kneading dough long enough to peek into the white boxes. "Don't these look great? The black-and-white ones are always a hit, and those strawberry cupcakes look fantastic."

"Trudy calls them Strawberry Bliss."

My mom let out a rapturous sound. "That's *just* how they smell. I'll make a little card for them."

She hand-lettered label cards for all the baked goods she put out on the counter. Unless I missed my guess, the Strawberry Bliss cupcakes would feature an anthropomorphic strawberry in a state of ecstasy.

Mom looked up at me, her brow puckering. "Is something wrong?"

I hesitated. "Have you heard from Tannith lately?"

"No, but I got a holiday letter from my cousin Lucretia. It's around here somewhere. . . ." She turned in a circle until she found what she was looking for on a counter next to a cutting board. She picked it up with floury fingers and handed it to me. Mom kept up with the witch community, and this was a busy time for communications between families. Regular people tended to send out end-of-the-year one-page summaries of the ups and downs (but mostly ups) of the past 365 days around the Christmas holidays, but some witch families opted to do this at Halloween. Especially, I'd noticed, the ones forbidden to practice witchcraft. Call it overcompensation.

Lucretia's family, though, didn't fall under the Edict. A lot of witches deplored the crass commercialism of Halloween, but Cousin Lucretia was apparently embracing it. The sheet of paper showed a picture-perfect family all wearing black, drugstore-costume-quality witch hats and grinning happily in front of what looked like a giant spider piñata.

"Lucretia's son started peewee baseball last summer," Mom summed up for me, "and her daughter JJ's on the varsity cheerleading squad and is beginning to show real promise in telekinesis."

An embedded picture showed a Smart car on top of a backyard gazebo, evidence of JJ's burgeoning talent. Some parents just couldn't resist bragging.

I put the letter back on the counter. "But nothing at all from Tannith?"

"Not since last week. She brought us the nicest gift—a beautiful mobile for our porch. Tom's going to put it out this afternoon."

My first thought was what a suck-up Tannith was. Which was unfair of me. My parents had been her parents, too, since her birth parents died. Mom and Dad always tried to treat us the same and were scrupulously evenhanded. Growing up, we'd cycled through the predictable sibling conflicts and resentments. After we'd finished college, I thought Tannith had mellowed. She inherited money and was able to live on her own, and I had moved out after I graduated and started Abracadabra. We'd settled into a sort of frenemy truce.

So much for that.

It gave me a perverse pleasure to ask Mom, "Did she tell you she was leaving Zenobia?"

Mom hesitated, but her expression signaled that her answer

was going to be different from what I'd expected. "She did. But she said she didn't want anyone else to know yet."

She'd told Daniel *and* Mom and Dad?

Of course. She'd confided in my loved ones, probably delighting in that they'd all keep me in the dark if she asked them to.

"Thanks for letting me know."

Mom disapproved of sarcasm. "We all knew Tannith wasn't going to be happy staying in Zenobia forever. This is a small city and she's a big personality."

A laugh escaped me. "And what do I have? A small personality?"

Mom didn't approve of peevishness, either. "We were discussing Tannith."

It was all I could do not to roll my eyes. "Did she mention whom she was leaving town with?"

Mom blinked. "No. Who?"

If there was one thing I knew about my mom, it was that she was not a liar. She didn't know whose partner Tannith was planning to steal.

I hitched my purse over my shoulder. "If I find out, I'll let you know."

"I do hope you all will be able to remain close." Mom smiled. "I always envied your little klatch of cousins."

"What, wasn't having a sister enough for you?" I was half joking. Her sister, after all, was Aunt Esme, one of the prickliest, most unpleasant people I'd ever met.

Mom seemed to have genuine feelings for her sister, though. At least she was a *real* sister, and not a Tannith. "Yes, I've been lucky." Mom sighed. "But poor Esme."

"She must have been better when you were growing up."

"Yes." Instead of elaborating, Mom straightened her shoulders and turned back to her dough. "Don't worry about Tannith," she said, eager to change the subject from her less happy sister. "She's got a good head on her shoulders. I'm sure she'll thrive in New York City."

As if I were worried about Tannith! I bit back a laugh and turned to leave.

But I couldn't resist stopping to inform Mom, "Tannith gave me a mobile, too. Probably the exact same one. She gave them to all of us."

I'd stuck mine—a three-tiered mobile of hanging gems and mirrored medallions—in a tree in my front yard. With any luck, some raccoon would steal it.

Mom, being Mom, took my mean little dig and turned it on its head. "That's a nice gesture, isn't it? Spreading a little brightness to everyone."

She had a way of making me feel petty even when I knew she was being over-the-top unrealistic, which she always was when it came to Tannith.

I slunk out of the kitchen, waved to my Dad as I passed the register, intending to hurry out to work. Dad stopped me by gesturing wildly to the coffee station I'd breezed right past. I turned and saw Aunt Esme hunched over a mug of coffee. She was thickset with a bad case of early-onset dowager's hump. Her features looked as if fighting gravity had sapped most of her strength—the corners of her small mouth were pierced with frown lines so deep they almost looked like anger dimples. The most notable thing about her was her once-red hair, now dulled with streaks of gray in it. Frizzy curls of it poked out from beneath an oatmeal-colored toboggan hat.

She loosened the top of the creamer pitcher to pour some into her cup. Even from this distance I could see she'd unscrewed it too much. When she upended the pitcher, the top came off and half-and-half spilled everywhere. I ran over to try to minimize the damage.

"Hi, Aunt Esme," I said brightly. "Let me help you."

She smirked at me. "You going to say, 'Abracadabra,' and make the cream vanish?"

"No, just going to mop it up the old-fashioned way." I yanked a fistful of napkins from the holder.

"There was a time . . ." She sighed, shaking her head.

A time when you weren't so clumsy? Yeah, right. "I'll refill the creamer for you," I said after I'd soaked up most of the spill.

"Never mind. I'll just pour this into a go-cup and take it home. I've got milk there."

"Great idea. Do you need a ride?"

"Why would I need a ride with you?"

Last I heard, she'd been taking the bus. "I thought you've been having car trouble."

She lifted her chin. "The Gremlin's fixed."

Her car was probably one of the last functioning (sometimes) AMC Gremlins on the road. Its once-spring-green paint had weathered to a dull puke color . . . in the places where the body wasn't rusting.

"Amazing they were able to fix it."

"*They?*" She scowled at me. "*I* fixed it. There was nothing amazing about it. I just had to wait for the right part."

With Aunt Esme, I found it useful to assume the serene manner of a therapist with a particularly volatile patient. "That's great. You must be glad to have it working."

"Amazing!" She spat out a laugh at my expense. "Miss Abracadabra doesn't even know how to work on a carburetor!"

I gritted my teeth. Mom always warned me not to take what Esme said personally: *Remember, she's been through a lot.* Just what that meant, no one ever wanted to say. But I hadn't always been as kind as I should have been to her when I was younger, and that weighed on my conscience. When we were kids, Tannith and I would occasionally have fun at Esme's expense if she came over for a family dinner, which she rarely did. At best we treated her with the eye-rolling impatience teenagers reserve for tiresome adults. But we weren't above practical jokes, either, usually instigated by Tannith. Once we mixed together food colorings and put them into Esme's black coffee so that when she drank, her mouth turned purple.

Naturally, we thought this was hilarious. But the joke wasn't just on Esme, it was on me, too. When my mom confronted us,

Tannith disavowed any knowledge of how Aunt Esme ended up with purple lips. In fact, she'd gone Eddie Haskell and turned to me in horror at what I had done. My parents had fallen for this performance. *I* was the one who had to apologize, got my allowance taken away, and was forced to mow Esme's yard for the summer. For free.

What I remember most about that summer of punishment was that during all the afternoons I'd done her yard, Esme had never allowed me into her house. Not even if I had to pee. *There's a McDonald's on your way home,* she would bark at me. *I didn't invite you for a visit.*

Some people never changed.

"Well, maybe I'll see you soon," I told her now.

"Sure! Visitors are always beating a path to my door," she said sarcastically.

With hospitality like hers, who could blame them?

"Bye, Aunt Esme."

"Have a day," she growled, as if having a good one weren't a possibility.

And for her, probably, it wasn't.

Cursed, just as Mom said.

Chapter 5

I rushed over to the tiny office that was Abracadabra's headquarters. I didn't like to be too late in the mornings. Leaving my employees Kyle and Taj together alone could be dangerous—not because they would get into a physical fight, but because Kyle could be so annoying and I didn't want Taj to quit.

Inside, the office coffee maker was gurgling its way to filling up the carafe. It and the ugly plaid couch had been part of a barter I'd arranged with the old shoe repairman who was giving up business in this space. Kyle and Taj lounged on the couch, Kyle looking bored and Taj immersed in a textbook as big as a Gutenberg Bible propped on his knee.

"Hey," they chorused.

"Thanks for starting the coffee."

They both wore red T-shirts with the Abracadabra logo, but Taj managed to make it look sharp. His jeans were clean, his T-shirt tucked in, in an almost-nerdy way, and his hair was buzzed short on the sides. In contrast, Kyle's oversize T-shirt hung off his lanky frame, his shapeless hair flopped in his eyes, and his shoes always seemed to be coming untied. Today he was

sitting on the arm of the couch, his feet propped on the cushions.
I sent a glare his way and he slid off the arm back onto the cushions.

Even if it was a hideous plaid couch, we weren't barbarians.

"Anyway, it's going to have a bat crest," Kyle said, continuing
a conversation he and Taj had been having before I came in, a
one-sided conversation by the looks of things. "Or a dragon. I
can't decide. Which would you rather have?"

Taj kept his eye on the page in front of him. "I don't wear helmets."

"Yeah, but if you did."

"There's no circumstance in the world as we know it that
would require me to put a huge chunk of metal on my head and
parade around like a medieval knight."

"Yeah, okay, but *they* didn't parade around in their armor, either. It was for war. Like, their version of business attire."

"Coffee ready yet?" Taj asked me, even though it was obvious
from the gasping rumble of the coffee maker that it wasn't.

I put two strawberry cupcakes on a plate and carried it over to
them. "Try one of these while we wait."

They grabbed the cupcakes and dug in. This job had few
perks, but Kyle and Taj were used to starting the workday with a
sugar rush courtesy of Enchanted Cupcakes.

"Can you tell the master armorer here that I'm trying to
study?" Taj asked me. "I've got my first astronomy test Friday,
and it's not easy to concentrate with Sir Gabs-a-Lot over here
asking me about sigils."

Kyle's face collapsed in offense. "Crests, not sigils," he said
through a mouthful of cupcake. "I was just asking your opinion.
Jeez."

"And I was obviously trying to read."

"Can you help me unload my car?" I asked Kyle.

He hopped up and followed me to the door. "The deal is, I'm
designing a helmet, and I can't decide whether to use a bat or a
dragon."

"Bat. Dragons are overdone."

His eyes popped open in astonishment at my strong opinion. "You really think so?"

I had no idea, but I winged it. "All that *Game of Thrones* stuff is so over, isn't it? You don't want people to think you're hopping on a trend just as it's becoming stale."

His jaw dropped. "Dragons aren't a trend. They're eternal."

I undid the latch on the back of my Kia. "To people in the know, like yourself, maybe."

He preened modestly. "That's why I feel it's important to ask questions. To find out how average people think."

One thing having my business had taught me was that when dealing with employees, sometimes it was useful to pretend that my soul had already left my body. Anything that kept me from wanting to clunk them over the head. Kyle had been the employee who'd stuck with me the longest. He'd dropped out of Zenobia College early last spring to "take a semester off" and earn some money to continue being a C philosophy student. Since then, he'd gotten it in his head to become an armor designer. He was saving so he could open his own metalworking studio, where he would build his designs for LARPers, historical exhibits, and Hollywood.

I figured he'd be with me a while yet.

I loaded him down with boxes filled with office supplies I'd bought yesterday, grabbed the last box myself, and slammed the back of the Kia closed. Back inside, Taj had put his astronomy book away and was pouring coffee into our individual to-go cups. When Kyle and I were done stowing the supplies in the storage closet, Taj handed us each a steaming mug.

Kyle took a tentative sip. "Hey, you even remembered my four sugars."

"Of course." Taj didn't add his usual dig about Kyle drinking caffeinated sugar water.

"I have some news about today," I announced. "I know we were all supposed to return to Mrs. Caputo's this morning to clean her attic, but I've had something come up."

"Isn't this a Cranky Carl errand day?" Kyle asked.

I groaned. I always tried to put Cranky Carl day out of my mind, but this time I'd really forgotten. That would cut into my stakeout time. "That, too. So I'll have to send you over on your own. You guys okay with that?"

I expected a mutiny. Mrs. Caputo was the one with the garage that had taken us a full day to make a dent in. Now we had to tackle her attic, and it looked like I was abandoning them. Like a lot of our older clients, Mrs. Caputo could be a challenge. She tended to follow us around and give us the history of everything that needed to be pitched out. She both fretted about the time the work took and pressed us to take breaks and eat whatever she wanted to get rid of from the refrigerator. Yesterday it had been curried chickpea salad, which had turned out okay, but a few weeks ago Kyle had eaten some bad deviled eggs offered by one of our other clients, and I'd had to pay him for the days he'd been out sick.

I expected anything from a minor mutiny to the usual whining from the guys, but they didn't raise objections at having to deal with Mrs. Caputo alone. They just sipped their coffees. Very chill.

Very odd.

"Taj and I can handle it," Kyle assured me.

Taj nodded. "Yeah, nothing we haven't managed before."

I watched their faces warily. "If you run into any problems, you know how to reach me."

"Sure." Kyle eyed the cupcake box. "Would it be okay if we took those with us and shared with Mrs. C? She's been awfully nice about giving us snacks and stuff."

"Okay." I still had the spare box Trudy had given me.

"That's a great idea, Kyle." Taj gave him a playful slap of approval on the back.

I needed to get moving, yet I still hesitated. "All right, so . . . you guys are good? You can take Kyle's car?"

"Yup."

I shook off whatever was bugging me and grabbed my keys. "I'll see you this afternoon."

They collected their stuff and walked out with me.

"I'd go for a dragon," Taj said. "As a whatsit."

"Crest," Kyle said. "Really?"

"Yeah. Bats are cool, but dragons are awesome, know what I'm saying?"

"Totally."

I climbed into the Soul, disturbed by so much agreement.

The day threatened rain, but it was still gorgeous—brilliant autumnal leaves on all the trees against a cloudy sky on the verge of rain. Downtown Zenobia always charmed me. The city center had preserved most of its nineteenth- and early twentieth-century buildings—two- and three-story brick and brownstone business buildings, some in their original brown and rust shades, others painted in blues, yellows, and reds. The marquee of the one-screen movie theater, the Astoria, dominated the block where the bank was. The town had more coffee shops, cafés, and bookstores per block than anywhere else I'd ever been. But we still had more mundane goods for sale in our downtown—clothes, shoes, hardware—as well as professional services, from opticians, lawyers, real estate agents.

I arrived early enough to claim a parking spot down the street from the bank. Close enough to see the entrance, far enough away that I wouldn't be too conspicuous. I hoped.

I picked up my to-go mug and sipped at my coffee. After what seemed like hours, I checked the time on my phone. Only forty-five minutes had crawled by. I shifted, noticing for the first time how butt-hostile the seats were.

There was no sign of Brett, but why would there be? He was working. What did Milo expect me to see, Tannith and Brett skipping down the street holding hands? Now that I was here doing it, a stakeout seemed a pretty goofy way to check up on somebody. Did cops even do these anymore, or was that just on television?

A quick rap on the passenger-side window was all the warning I had before the door opened. Milo jumped into the passenger seat and shook himself off like a wet Labrador.

I recoiled from the splatter. "How did you get so wet?"

His disbelieving glance was pointedly restrained. "You haven't noticed it's raining?"

So it was. Amazing. I hadn't taken my eyes off the bank's doors, but I'd been zoned out.

"I'm beginning to have second thoughts about your detecting abilities," he said.

"I told you a stakeout was silly. I hadn't thought about how boring it would be, though."

He sank down in the seat. "I hadn't thought about how soggy it would be."

"You're in the landscaping business. You should appreciate rain."

"I appreciate it. I just wish I could control it."

Milo is an amazing landscape architect. That's how he met Brett. As a city council member, Brett had to approve funding for the plans Milo had presented for the redesign of the Zenobia town center's commons.

Milo glanced at his phone. "I've been searching social media for a witch flashing Tiffany's new bling. So far nothing's come up."

"Did you ask Brett about the jewelry store when he came in last night?"

"Of course not—and naturally *he* said nothing."

"You should just ask him."

"How? I'd have to admit I spied on him. Mr. Ethics would hit the roof." Milo sniffed the air like a hound catching a scent. "Do I smell cupcakes?"

I twisted, reached for the box in the back seat, and passed it to him. "There's Strawberry Bliss, and I think at least one Ebony and Ivory."

Milo sang his choice—chocolate with vanilla frosting. "Second breakfast." He took a bite. "It's always better than the first."

"Trudy's side hustle is going to turn us all into lumpy sugar fiends."

He nodded and swallowed happily. "Were things back to normal in Websterland this morning?"

"When I walked up, that Jeremy guy was at her door again, and she wasn't any more welcoming to him this morning than she was last night. After he gave up and retreated, I stopped him and talked for a bit. He told me Laird still hadn't checked in."

"Hm."

"Trudy hadn't heard from Laird, either. She looked as if she'd been up all night. And here's the weirdest thing: Herb the rabbit was almost black."

"The new one? He's brown. Light brown."

I repressed the urge to pump my fist. "Thank you! She made up some malarkey about the lighting being different."

"So . . . you think Trudy dyed her rabbit?"

"It seems unlikely." I tapped my fingers on my go-cup. "She obviously doesn't want to talk to Jeremy. It's almost like she's afraid of him. Why?"

"If I'd been stuck with Laird all my life, I'd be shooing history geeks away from my doorstep, too."

"You've got to get over your thing about Laird."

"He tossed a lead pipe at me!"

"A game token."

"It could have put an eye out."

After Milo swallowed the last of his cupcake and licked a stray bit of icing off his knuckle, he got out his phone again. "I've also been searching to see if Tannith has put up a profile to lure Brett or Daniel."

"Or Laird."

"Um, sure." He scrolled. "I can't find anyone like her even on eCharmed."

"What's that?"

"Online witch dating. It's quite an eye-opener. You think the profiles on Tinder are fantastic . . ."

It gave me an idea. "I don't guess you've run across anyone like Jeremy on eCharmed, have you? Green eyes, dark hair, obsessed with hunting down missing professors?" That little quiver I'd felt when looking into Jeremy's eyes came back to me. I drummed my fingers. "There's more to him than mere history geek."

"Sounds like he put a spell on you."

I've always been interested in magic, he'd said. Could he be one of us?

I shook my head. *No.* It didn't seem possible. Mom would have told me if new witches were in town, wouldn't she? We had to be careful not to be seen even fraternizing with people who practiced spellcraft.

"He just has nice eyes," I said.

"So what do you think is so suspicious about him? Besides his asking after Laird."

"He was asking at seven in the morning."

Milo thought for a moment, then shrugged. "If he works with Laird, he probably knows that Trudy's a teacher. When can you track down a teacher if they're not at school? Before work at oh-crap o'clock, or in the evening. Last night didn't work for Jeremy, so . . ."

Put that way, Jeremy's being there didn't seem so suspicious. Just normal curiosity about a colleague. Maybe my instinct about him was all wrong.

While Milo stared at his phone, I returned to thinking about the new rabbit. "The odd thing is, Trudy didn't even like getting stuck with Peaches. Why did she adopt another bunny?"

He didn't look up. "She explained that. She wanted Peaches to have company."

A weird, color-shifting rabbit, though? My gaze narrowed on the dashboard. "And another odd thing. When we were talking, it seemed almost that Herb was paying attention to what we were saying."

Milo shook his head sadly. "Oh, God. You're imagining Trudy as Snow White communing with the bunnies and birds."

"I never mentioned birds. And need I remind you that there *are* people who communicate with animals? Or at least specific animals." Animal familiars were common among practicing witches.

"And do I need to remind you that if Trudy had a familiar, the Council would probably find out about it and confiscate it?"

"That's what worries me," I said. "What if this is all about witchcraft? You know how Laird hates any talk of spells or magic. He even hates us calling our get-togethers the cocktail coven."

"Right. Laird's a pill. What else is new?"

"What if Trudy's started dabbling in witchcraft? Maybe Laird found out and stomped off in a huff."

"That's—" Milo finally looked up from his phone. His mouth stopped moving mid-dismissal, and his face twisted into a frown. "Not an impossibility."

"It would be just like Laird to go off in a huff, wouldn't it? For that matter, I wouldn't put it past Daniel, either. The one time I mentioned our family thing to him, he acted like I was nuts."

"It's a lot to take in."

"Daniel acted almost offended. *Ludicrous* was the word he used. And when I laid out the facts for him and explained about the Dust Bowl, he went all Mr. Science on me and lectured about weather patterns and soil erosion—all the usual cover stories. Like I was an idiot."

"Some people won't accept the simplest explanation, even when you hand it to them on a silver platter."

"I know, right?" I took a few deep breaths, willing myself to calm down. Thinking about that argument with Daniel months ago raised my blood pressure all over again. "What does Brett think about our family?"

"Brett's a politician. He likes everybody."

"But what does he think about the history of our family?"

"Oh, you know."

Milo's shrug said it all. "You haven't told him," I guessed.

"*Of course* I haven't told him. Brett is—well, he's Brett. Bretts don't believe in magic. They work in banks, attend city council meetings, and run for mayor. If you want a good interest rate on your mortgage, you contact Brett. If you want to hex your annoying neighbor, you certainly wouldn't go to Brett Blair, the Wonder Breadiest man in western New York."

"You're not asking him to practice witchcraft, just to believe in it."

"And to believe that there's a council that can forbid a whole family from practicing for generations? If you think sane, sensible Brett is going to swallow that—"

The last part of Milo's sentence was cut off when cold air hit us and we realized the back door had opened. Brett slid into the back seat, leaned forward, and gave Milo a kiss on his temple. "He can hear you," he whispered, smiling. "What am I not supposed to swallow? And don't be disgusting."

Brett might be the most Wonder Bread man in western New York, but he was also the best looking. Think Robert Redford in his *Barefoot in the Park* stage. Brett had the same sandy good looks and a dazzling smile. It was puzzling why he wasn't out in Hollywood making millions instead of running for mayor of Zenobia, New York.

Milo and I avoided each other's gaze. Brett was Milo's boyfriend, so the onus was on him to come up with some fib. But when the awkward silence stretched a half second beyond my comfort zone, I blurted out, "Cupcakes. Milo didn't think you'd eat the cupcake I brought you—I mean, the one I brought *just in case* I ran into you at the bank this morning. I guess I had a premonition that I would."

"Not a *real* premonition," Milo piped up. "Just a hunch. You know, like a usual sort of . . . hunch."

Brett laughed. "I think you'd better let me be the judge of my junk food intake." He opened the lid and peeked in. "What are they?"

"Strawberry Bliss."

He wasted no time pulling one out and biting into it. "Mm, perfect." He leaned forward. "So . . . why are you two sitting here?"

"I was just going to the bank," I said as Milo blurted out, "Just passing through."

We both shot the other an accusatory look. We should have gotten our stories straight.

"Well, as long as you're here"—Brett seemed not to care that we sounded like babbling idiots—"how about both of you coming to the library with me? I have to meet with some city workers. I could use a little moral support."

"I can't," I answered truthfully. "I've got a job I need to get to. In fact I might be late if I don't leave soon."

"How about you?" Brett asked Milo. "I know you said you were busy this morning, but you don't look busy now."

"Uh . . ." Milo nodded. "Sure. I guess I've got time. I just need to meet a client at her house at one o'clock."

"Great." Brett pressed his hand on my shoulder. "Thanks, Gwen. That was the best cupcake I've ever eaten. I was anxious about this talk I have to give, but now I feel calmed by Strawberry Bliss."

"Maybe having Milo for moral support has something to do with that," I suggested.

Brett smiled that thousand-watt smile that would probably land him in the Senate someday. "You could be a politician."

Milo got out of the car but kept the door open a moment and sent me a meaningful look. "I'll talk to you later, Trixie."

I nodded. My first stab at detecting hadn't been an amazing success.

Carl Franklin—aka Cranky Carl, who always insisted I call him Mr. Franklin—had contacted me months ago when he'd lost his driver's license after hitting both a mailbox and a parked mobility vehicle in one week. He was a widower, a retired insurance salesman, and the crabbiest man in Zenobia. My standing appointment to drive him on errands every week always seemed to remind him of all that had gone wrong in his life.

He was waiting at the end of his driveway when I pulled up. "Been out here ten minutes," he grumbled as soon as he thumped into the passenger seat.

I was right on time, but I knew better than to argue. Early exposure to Aunt Esme had taught me that much. "Where to?"

"Better go to the drugstore first. You know how long they take over there. Back in the day, it seemed like druggists were at least adults. Now you never talk to anybody but teenagers, and they're poky about everything. If we got the groceries first, the milk would curdle in the time it took for the pharmacist to count out thirty pills."

Good grief. Ask a simple question . . . "Drugstore it is, then."

We drove in silence for a while, until I pointed out the beautiful fall colors. Big mistake.

"I can see that," he snapped back. "With my new glasses, I can make out every point on each individual maple leaf. I don't see how it's fair that I can't get my license back for another three months. I'm old. I could be dead in another three months."

"You're seventy-eight and in good health. Plenty of people are worse off than you."

He looked over at me in disgust. "Thank you, Pollyanna."

I did tend to chirp and spout platitudes when I was around Mr. Franklin. Maybe it was annoying, but the urge to compensate for all the negative energy he was releasing into the world was hard to resist.

"Would you like me to go in with you?" I asked when we arrived at the pharmacy.

"What am I, six years old?" He shook his head. "I can at least *walk* on my own."

He got out, took two tries to close the door properly, then stumped through the drugstore's sliding doors. It was a relief to let him be some poor clerk's problem for ten minutes.

I took the opportunity to call Kyle and Taj.

Kyle answered, "Hey, boss lady!"

I drew back. His cheery tone was such a switch from Mr. Franklin's crabbiness. For that matter, it was a switch from Kyle's usual laments. I would have thought I'd reached a wrong number, but I could hear the piercing yap of Mrs. Caputo's dog, Binky, in the background.

"How's the job going?"

"Great! Sondra is treating us to lunch and telling us how bad the hippies at Woodstock smelled."

Sondra?

"Well . . . good. How's Taj doing?"

"Fine. He's helped me come up with some good ideas for breastplates to go with my helmets."

"Uh-huh." Everything was fine. So why did I feel so uneasy? "Do you think the attic will be finished today?"

"Sure, no worries."

When I hung up, I shifted in my seat. *No worries?* It felt as if I were being punked.

The passenger door opened and Mr. Franklin was back, landing on the seat with a huff. "The toddlers running that place are hopeless. They've stopped stocking Bugles!"

"Did you get your prescription?"

"Yes, but when I went looking for a little sack of Bugles, they weren't there. There wasn't even an empty rack where they usually are. When I complained to the clerk, he just shrugged me off. 'We can't stock everything,' he said." The old man's face was crimson at the memory. "Is that what customer service has come to?"

I started the engine. "We'll get you some Bugles at the grocery store."

"By the time I get to the grocery store I'll be passing out. Haven't you heard of hypoglycemia?"

I remembered the last cupcake. "That box in the back seat has a cupcake with your name on it."

He sent me a doubtful look. I expected an argument. Instead, he asked, "What kind?"

"Strawberry."

He opened the box and sniffed tentatively. "Smells okay," he admitted.

The rest of the drive was quiet except for his chewing and smacking sounds as he licked icing off his fingers. After I parked at the supermarket, I grabbed a moist towelette from a cubby in the dashboard and handed it to him.

He accepted it with a gracious "Thank you for the cupcake. It was delicious."

Right then I should have known something in my world was very wrong.

We both got out of the car this time. I accompanied Carl grocery shopping to speed things up a little. Once when I'd let him go in on his own, he stalled out in front of the canned hams and then threw a tantrum when I charged him for an extra quarter hour.

When I grabbed a cart and pushed it through the automated doors, he asked, "Do you know what they call a grocery cart in France?"

"No . . ."

"*Le chariot.*" He chuckled. "A chariot. I always thought that was kind of funny. Imagine Charlton Heston zooming through the Food Lion in one of these."

"When were you in France?"

"Never in my life, but twenty years ago Millie and I took French at a night course at the college. I still remember some of it."

Millie was his wife, who'd been gone ten years. He'd mentioned her the first time I'd driven him but never again till now. "Maybe you should take a trip there sometime."

"Maybe I will." He tossed Grape-Nuts in his cart. Then he took them out and replaced them with Frosted Flakes.

The whole shopping expedition was one curveball after another.

"I'm tired of regular spaghetti sauce," he said. "Why not try Alfredo?"

In the next aisle, he eschewed his beloved split-pea soup for butternut squash—I pointed out that it wasn't his usual brand, and it was in a carton, not a can. "I'm not fossilized yet!" he answered with cheerful abandon. Then he picked out some mango-ginger Greek yogurt that cost twice as much as his normal blueberry. Finally, he insisted on buying enough Halloween candy to hand out treats to every single kid in Zenobia.

"How many trick-or-treaters do you usually get?" I asked.

"Who knows? I always turn my lights out. This year I suddenly feel like handing out candy."

As we loaded the things into the car's trunk, anxiety overtook me. Had I said anything that would have caused him to go nuts like this? I worried he'd get home and have buyer's remorse. "You know, Mr. Franklin, if you ever need to go to the grocery store in the middle of the week, or even on the weekend, just call me. I've usually got time to squeeze in a quick errand."

"That's very kind of you, Gwen. But I wish you'd call me Carl."

Seriously? What was going on?

We drove all the way to his house in silence, although he stared out through the windshield, sighing. After we'd parked and I'd deposited the last bag on his kitchen counter, he asked, "Would you like to stay a while? I could make fettuccine Alfredo."

"Uh . . . I don't really have time. It's a workday, you know."

His face drooped in genuine disappointment, and he reached out and took my hand. "I really appreciate you helping me out."

"Of course." I backed away and fled to the Kia, spooked by so much niceness from the crankiest man in town. The cupcake box was open on the passenger-side floor mat. I could still smell the strawberry.

I gnawed on my lower lip. Taj and Kyle getting along . . . Brett's fears lifting . . . Mr. Franklin's crankiness disappearing. What was the common denominator? They'd all eaten Strawberry Bliss cupcakes.

Trudy's business was called Enchanted Cupcakes, but those cupcakes were no more enchanted than my business was magical for being called Abracadabra. It was just us having a little fun, kicking at the powers we couldn't claim as our own. But apparently now those cupcakes were imbued with real enchantment.

And Trudy also seemed to have a familiar—a rabbit that changed color.

And a strange man was watching her house.

This could be trouble. I needed to talk to someone who knew just how much trouble.

I pulled out of Mr. Franklin's drive and headed back to the Buttered Biscuit.

Chapter 6

It was just going on two o'clock, and the café was winding down after the lunch rush. Fewer than half the tables were filled, and those mostly with campers, customers who were finished eating but were going to remain at their table nursing the same coffee until the dinner crowd pushed them out. Old country music on the loudspeakers added to the laid-back mood. Employees frazzled from the lunch-hour rush took their time cleaning up during the afternoon lull.

I glanced at the counter, which only had a few platters of cookies on display, plus a carrot cake and a quarter of a pie. "No more cupcakes?" I asked Darcy, who was sweeping up crumbs around one particularly messy table.

"Those went early. A few got eaten, and then somebody came back and bought a whole box of them."

Didn't take long to create cupcake junkies around this place.

"Are my folks here?"

She nodded toward the kitchen.

"Thanks." I headed back through the swinging door to the

kitchen area. If my rushing pulse felt out of sync with lingering diners and Hank Williams twanging on about lonesome whip-poor-wills, my parents' being completely absorbed in something over the stove didn't help matters. They were arguing, but my parents didn't argue like normal people. Even when they were in full-throated disagreement, they sounded as polite as those cartoon gophers.

"Excuse me, but I think you're wrong, honey," my mom was saying.

"I sensed that, but I'm sorry, seitan has protein."

"Does that—" Mom glanced over Dad's shoulder and saw me. My face must have been a study in panic, because she immediately came over and took hold of my arm as though I were a shock victim. "So glad you're here, Gwendle-bug," she said, using my name from when I was two.

"There's a problem," I said.

"And you're going to tell us all about it. First, though, you need to help us settle a dispute." She tugged me over to the stove. "Taste these two gravies and tell us which you'd prefer."

"But—"

Her hand squeezed my arm. "Breathe, taste, and concentrate on this for two minutes."

Dad nodded along with her.

This is how they operated. Their gravy-tasting ploy was meant to take me out of myself and make me focus on something that *wasn't* my problem, thus calming me. It had been an irritating tactic when I was a kid, and nothing had changed.

"Maybe a big problem," I warned them.

My father handed me a spoon. "Just dip it in the saucepan and give it a taste."

I huffed in frustration but took the proffered spoon and tasted the gravy. It had an earthy, salty flavor. The mushroom taste was strong but not overpowering. "Nice" was my verdict.

Dad then handed me a glass of water and a new spoon. Grumbling, I took a swig of water to clear my palate, then tested the stuff in the other pan. I frowned. "This tastes like salty glue with chunks of rubber in it."

Dad raised his hands in surrender. "Mushroom it is, then."

"We'll save the other for our World Vegan Day menu," Mom said, magnanimous in victory.

"Glue-rubber gravy?" Dad asked.

"Gwen didn't really mean that."

"Yes, I did."

"It's really not so bad," Mom consoled him. "I liked them almost equally."

"It wasn't even close," I told Dad. "The mushroom was better."

Strangely enough, the gravy experiment *had* calmed me down a little, mostly because I was so distracted by what annoying people my parents were. I couldn't believe these two goofballs had raised me and Tannith. It had been a guarantee of maladjustment.

"Now what's this problem of yours?" Mom asked.

I took another slug of water, swished, and swallowed to rid my mouth of seitan residue. "I have good reason to believe that Trudy's practicing."

"Practicing what?" Mom asked, before Dad pulled her to him in a protective embrace.

"*Practicing,*" I repeated. "She might even have a familiar."

As understanding dawned, my mom's face morphed from serenity to five-alarm panic.

"Upstairs," Dad commanded. "Now."

Mother crossed the kitchen to the window between the kitchen and the serving area. "Darcy, Tom and I will be upstairs for a little while."

They barely waited for their employee's "m'kay" before hustling me up the back staircase.

The Buttered Biscuit had been located in this downtown Victorian house for thirty years, and my parents had owned the building for almost that long. When I was growing up, though, they'd rented a house a few neighborhoods away in a more sub-urban area. With two kids, the two-bedroom apartment above the restaurant would have felt claustrophobic, so they'd rented it to students until Tannith and I left to be on our own. Then they'd moved back in. To be honest, it felt claustrophobic with just the two of them, because they used the spare bedroom as a storage room for restaurant supplies and an extra fridge.

The apartment was full of the furniture from our old house. They'd never been big interior decorators. The couch, which had a multicolored, blotchy print from the nineties, was flanked by two Pier 1 rattan moon chairs with lavender cushions. An ancient, wall-devouring entertainment center hovered over this mess. Usually we just went into the kitchen to sit, but today they stopped in the living room. Dad locked the door, while Mom closed the wood-slat blinds. One lamp was turned on.

"What is going on?" Mom asked.

I was wondering the same thing. I suspected what Trudy was doing could mean trouble, but from their reaction, I didn't know the half of it. One thing made me feel better: I wasn't overreact-ing. I'd done right in coming here.

I filled them in on everything happening at Trudy's, except the parts that involved Tannith's letter. I couldn't see how it was related, and the sibling in me still abhorred a snitch. I summed up, "Laird is gone, I think Trudy has a rabbit familiar, and her cupcakes really are enchanted now."

Mom and Dad exchanged a meaningful look. "The cup-cakes," they chorused.

"They were gone in a flash this morning," Mom explained.

"That's what Darcy told me. She said some guy came back for a whole box." A disturbing possibility occurred to me. "Do you remember what this guy looked like?"

Mom frowned in thought. "He looked like a frat boy. He was wearing one of those shirts with the little polo men. I remember thinking that it seemed odd that fraternities were going in for cupcakes, but you never know what college kids will get up to."

"Why are you asking about him?" Dad asked.

"There's been a guy hanging around Trudy's for the past day. He *says* he's a grad student helping out Laird, but I'm not sure I believe that. He has green eyes, dark brown hair, short but kind of curly, and wire-rimmed glasses. His name's Jeremy."

"That rings a bell. . . ." Dad frowned, then shrugged. "But there are probably a few customers who fit that description."

"This person might be a Watcher, Tom." Mom actually trembled. "Oh, God. And Trudy has those lovely daughters."

I'd heard the term *Watcher* all my life, but I wasn't sure what exactly it was they could do to us. I thought they would just give out a warning or maybe extend the Edict by a few years. I'd certainly never thought they were something that would put Trudy's family in danger, or who would cause my centered, sensible mother to quake in her Naots. "So these Watchers are serious business?"

My mother paced to the fireplace, then turned sharply. "Sit down, Gwen."

I sank into a moon chair. My parents, by silent agreement, settled on the couch.

Mom clasped her hands together over her knees. "You know our branch of the family—every living descendant of Lucian Zimmer—is forbidden to practice."

Was she kidding? "The one-hundred-fifty-year Edict because of the Dust Bowl." We'd all heard about that.

"That's right. I mean, you can hardly blame them for being worried. If the truth had gotten out, they would have been burning witches from one end of the country to the other. We were lucky the Council of Witches didn't cast us out forever. Instead, they said we should remember who we were, even though we couldn't practice. We were allowed to remain nominally part of the witch world, although we've been forced to make our way like normal people. Your father and I have never had any trouble complying with the Edict."

Dad put his hand over hers. "We've always had our creative outlet here, at the Buttered Biscuit."

Mom nodded. "That's right. From the very beginning, your dad and I knew we would be okay as long as we were together. We even met at witch camp—the same one you went to."

"That never seemed fair to me."

I'd spent a summer at Camp Walpurga, too. It was hard doing mundane camp craft and riding old plugs when the other witch kids were learning spells and charms, and mixing potions. While everyone else did night flights and owl handling, we Edict campers were relegated to shell art and advanced lanyards.

"It wasn't fair, but your father and I found each other, and to us, that was more powerful than any magic."

God, they were sweet. Sickening, but sweet. "So I'm guessing from what you're telling me that there were relatives who *didn't* follow the Edict?"

Mom and Dad exchanged an anxious look.

"Lots of people have defied the Edict in big and small ways," he said.

Mom swallowed. "But I had one cousin in particular, Odin, who was naturally adept. Brilliant, in fact. If he'd been born into a different family, he would have earned a place on the Grand Council."

"Cousin Odin? I've never heard of him."

My mom's face looked pinched and troubled again.

"We don't talk about him," Dad said. "It's a painful subject."

"Especially for certain of us," Mom added.

Had Odin been an old beau? I didn't see how that was possible. Mom and Dad met when they were adolescents.

"You know how when you're a kid and adults tell you not to cross your eyes because they might get stuck that way?" Dad asked. "Well, that's kind of what happened to Odin."

"What?"

Mom explained, "Odin had a talent for making himself disappear. One day while Odin was invisible, the Watchers caught up with him. No one's seen him since."

"How do you know it was the Council's doing and not Odin's screwup?" I mean, if he was part of our family, a screwup wasn't unlikely.

"We were informed by the Council that Odin no longer existed."

I blinked in shock. "You mean they just obliterated him?"

Mom nodded sadly. "Evidently."

"But how? I mean, couldn't Odin still be floating out in the ether somewhere?"

"It would take a more adept witch than any of us are to know the answer to that." Mom's eyes filled with tears. "Odin was such a fun guy. He was several years older than me when he disappeared forever. He'd just turned twenty-one and he was the handsomest specimen you ever saw. Your aunt Esme loved him."

My lips curled into a frown. Aunt Esme's being crazy about this guy made me wonder how brilliant and fun he could have been. "What about Odin? Did he love Esme?"

Mom nodded. "Oh, yes—they were nuts about each other. I'm sure they would have wound up together, probably married as happily as your dad and me, if only . . ."

If only he hadn't been vaporized by the Council of Witches. "Although maybe given that there seems to be a crazy streak in the family already," I said, thinking of Aunt Esme, "it's just as well that we didn't get two cousins intermarrying."

Mom clucked at me in disapproval. "They were second cousins—they only shared a great-grandfather. Nothing wrong with that."

"Uh-huh." Nothing wrong except that the common ancestor was one of the most notoriously incompetent witches of all time. Rattan squeaked as I struggled to sit up straight. "Okay, you said people have defied the Edict in big and small ways. I'm assuming Odin's disappearing act was big. Who defied the Edict in small ways?"

"Who hasn't?" Mom asked. "I cast a spell to get out of going to the principal's office once. I made my teacher lose her voice as she was escorting me to the office. The poor woman was so distressed by it that she ran off to her GP and forgot all about me."

"Wow! If I'd had a success like that, I don't think I could have stopped."

"I might not have, either, if it weren't for . . ." Mom swallowed.

I tilted my head. "Cousin Odin?"

Mom and Dad exchanged looks again.

"Your Aunt Esme," she said.

Finally, understanding dawned. *She's cursed.*

I'd heard those words for so long, they'd stopped having real meaning. "I thought that was a figure of speech. You know—that she was unlucky."

They shook their heads. "Esme got caught," Mom said. "Oh, she started small—a little incantation, a potion cooked up in a saucepan . . . that kind of thing. Kid's stuff. But then, after what happened with Odin, she turned wild. She was in her late teen years then and had a rebellious streak anyway. But Odin was the love of her life. After what the Council did to him, she turned Dad's toolshed into a sorcery studio."

"Burned the place down once," Dad said, "and when he replaced it with a new shed, she blew that one up."

"I think she was trying to find some way to avenge Odin. People felt sorry for her—put it down to hormones and puppy-love tragedy—and for a while the Council turned a blind eye. But then Esme cast a spell on a local coven leader, who said everything he ate for six months tasted like Limburger cheese. The poor man dwindled down to a skeleton." Mom sighed. "That was just a hex too far."

"They cursed her," I said.

Mom nodded. "A life without joy, they said. She could never fall in love again, never have anything else that brought her happiness."

I leaned forward. "Did Esme *ever* have something that brought her happiness?"

"Odin." Mom sighed. "If you could have seen the two of them together . . ."

Dad nodded wistfully. "Esmerelda was something."

It was hard to imagine my raspy-voiced, frizzle-haired aunt as something, except something to avoid.

"You have no idea what your aunt lost," Mom said. "She gave up so much—more than the rest of us."

She must have been some witch.

"And you know how she lives now," Mom continued. "She just does the taxes for everyone in the family. She was never even good at math in school. They gave her that power when they cursed her."

"Hexed with mathematic competency and a thorough knowledge of the tax code," Dad said sadly.

Mom dashed a tear from her eye. "It's been terrible to watch my sister suffer so. That's why I always encouraged you girls to find other outlets."

I felt incensed. "Don't you think it would have been useful for us to have this information?" I never fully comprehended the danger I was flirting with.

"We told you about the Edict," Mom said.

"But not what was at stake if we defied it. I always thought Watchers were almost like negative Santas—all-seeing beings who draw up naughty-and-nice lists. I didn't think they would kill us or torture us."

"But you and Tannith were such good girls," Mom said. "And you have to remember that your position is different than ours. Your children, if you have them, might conceivably live to practice witchcraft and be full members of the community. Certainly your grandchildren will. We didn't want to instill a prejudice against your witch heritage or turn you against the system."

"But what about Trudy? She could be in real danger."

Mom bit her lower lip. "I didn't expect this. Trudy's what—ten years older than you?"

"Yes."

Mom considered this. "Well, perimenopause can wreak all sorts of havoc."

"Empty-nest syndrome, too," Dad said. "That's a big adjustment."

"I think it might have something to do with"—I almost said *Tannith*, but caught myself—"with a marital difficulty."

Mom clasped Dad's hand again. "Mixed marriages are always a concern."

Marriage between witches and nonwitches, she meant.

"It takes an understanding partner," Dad said.

Mom looked pointedly at me. "How's Daniel?"

"Fine. He's in Vermont tending to a beetle." I couldn't think about Daniel right now. "What should I do about Trudy?"

"Tell her just what we've told you," Mom said.

"Or, if you want, we can talk to her," Dad offered.

I blew out a breath. "Let me try first." For the past day, Trudy hadn't seemed inclined to confide in me. She'd been cagey and evasive, but she probably didn't understand what was at stake, either.

"That would probably be for the best," Mom agreed. "A defiant witch is more likely to bow to pressure from contemporaries than an authority figure."

They saw themselves as authority figures? My poor parents.

I stood. "I'll do my best."

"We know you will," Mom said. "But you must be *very* careful who else you talk about this to, and how you act. If *you've* found Trudy out, the powers that be will no doubt have eyes on her, too."

Yikes. I'd come here worried, now I was leaving raging with fear and paranoia.

I drove directly to Trudy's house from the Buttered Biscuit. It wasn't far, and when I got there, she wasn't home yet. I was going to wait in the car, but then I remembered she kept her spare key duct-taped to the bottom of a metal statue of a frog pushing a wheelbarrow that sat on her porch. I untaped the key and let myself in.

The first thing I noticed was that Herb the rabbit was back to a tan color. What was Trudy up to?

Then again, if switching her rabbit's color and enchanting a few cupcakes was the worst Trudy had done, maybe the Watchers wouldn't bother with her.

But then what about Laird? He hadn't left her over an extra rabbit, surely. Or cupcakes.

I poked around the house, checking for signs of a sorcery studio, but I didn't see anything. The girls' rooms were just as my nieces had left them. And the basement, as Trudy had said, was now the repository of all the old furniture, plus boxes of clothes. I peeked into a box. Laird's clothes. What could that mean? I headed back upstairs, my worry growing.

Still, nothing but the bunny switching colors screamed witchcraft. And a few cupcakes. Maybe I was overreacting. Trudy was just doing some small-time sorcery spitballing.

A movement caught my eye, and I looked over at the cage in the corner. Herb was staring right at me. When he realized he had my attention, he rose on his hind legs and stuck his twitching nose through the chicken wire. Odd.

I got up and inspected him more closely. How could you tell a familiar from a regular old rabbit? I'd heard of familiars all my life, but I'd never encountered one.

"Can you hear me?" I asked, as if he were deaf.

The rabbit thumped his back leg, which seemed so much like a reply that I recoiled in shock.

"Crap, Herb. What's Trudy up to?"

Without giving myself a chance to think twice, I fetched an animal carrier from the basement. Then I scooped up Herb and stuffed him in the box. Trudy had been lying to me—lying by avoiding telling me the truth. There was just one person in town who might be able to help me untangle what was going on. *If* she would agree to help me. That was a big if.

I snapped the cage closed and left the house, replacing the

key where I'd found it. When I straightened up from retaping the key to the frog, I nearly slammed into someone. Jeremy.

"What are you doing here?" Fear quavered in my voice. My heart was probably beating as fast as Herb's.

He looked as alarmed as I was. "Are you okay?"

"Yes, just wigged-out to find you prowling around."

"I wasn't prowling. I wanted to tell Trudy I received an email from Laird."

"Okay." *Be careful who you tell what's going on*, Mom had warned. What if Jeremy really was a Watcher?

In the carrier, Herb thumped against the plastic. Was that a warning?

Jeremy shifted feet. "The email was from a different address than he normally uses, though. I'm not sure it was really him."

"You think someone is impersonating Laird?"

Thump, thump.

"Do you know when Trudy will be home?" he asked.

"I haven't spoken to Trudy since this morning."

Thump.

Jeremy looked down at the cage. "Is that your rabbit?"

Busted. I shifted uncomfortably. "Why do you want to know?"

He laughed. "Don't take this the wrong way, but you look sort of guilty. Like you've been caught bunny-napping."

"Ha! Right." I made myself laugh along, but it came out as a sickly wheeze. "Very funny."

His head tilted. "So . . . what are you doing?"

"Well"—I gulped—"Herb's been acting strangely, so I offered to check him out. Have the vet check him out, I mean."

I felt like the Grinch explaining to Cindy Lou Who why he was stealing a Christmas tree.

"That sounds . . . reasonable," Jeremy said.

"Of course it does." I brushed past him, pressed the unlock button on the Kia, and loaded Herb into the passenger seat. "I'm a reasonable person. Rational, reasonable, and cautious." *Not a practicing witch, Mr. Watcher.* "I certainly don't kidnap innocent animals."

"I didn't mean to offend you." He pushed his glasses up. "In fact, would you—"

I cut him off. "Sorry, I can't talk now. I'm late." I got in the car and slammed the door shut. I backed out and pulled away so fast that the wheels skidded on the day's accumulation of wet, fallen leaves on the street. Sucking in a breath, I forced myself to slow down and drive carefully. I couldn't help glancing in the rearview mirror and seeing that Jeremy was staring after me.

Watching me.

Chapter 7

Aunt Esme lived in a run-down two-story stone farmhouse on the other side of the river that ran alongside downtown. The house had stood alone for a hundred years, but sometime in the past decade, developers had created Maple View, encroaching on my aunt's home with cookie-cutter houses. It was now the sort of neighborhood Esme would have avoided at all costs.

Aside from my summer of lawn-mowing punishment, I'd only been to Esme's a few times. When we were little, Mom had driven Tannith and me over here to trick-or-treat, so Esme would have at least one knock at her door. Not that she'd ever seemed happy to see us as she'd pitched a measly one or two pieces of candy into our plastic pumpkin pails. She always had the worst candy—cheap bulk caramels with the white swirls, or saltwater taffy that had probably been sitting in a drawer since her last vacation in 1972. The kind of candy that remained uneaten in mid-November.

Other than that, Aunt Esme was barely present in our lives. Mom would visit her, but we rarely went along. Occasionally I would see her by chance. Once when I was at the mall with Tannith and a group of our teenaged friends, we'd spotted Esme going into Victoria's Secret. Everyone had made fun of the frumpy, frizzle-haired woman in her gray crone clothes.

Sorry, ma'am, we don't sell crotchless cotton granny panties, Tannith had snarked, and all the other girls had roared with laughter. I'd laughed, too, red-faced with shame at how terrible it felt, but too immature to say anything. If the universe sent out Watchers to look for mean girls, we all would have been floating in the ether with Cousin Odin from that moment on.

She was something, Dad had said today. Now I understood her grouchiness a little more.

Understanding didn't mean I relished this interview, though. Only the direst necessity landed me on her doorstep with a rabbit carrier held at my side like a suitcase. I rang the old farmhouse bell and looked around. Ivy climbed over the brick, and a few tendrils snaked through the slats of the rotting wood shutters. Trees in full fall splendor surrounded the property. Though most of the lots in the neighborhood were small, my aunt's parcel was three times as large as the others. It set hers apart from the other houses, creating the impression that the rest of the neighborhood was socially distancing itself from my aunt. Which perhaps was the case.

On the other side of the door, a lock unlatched. I straightened expectantly, then waited as more tumblers turned, chains unhooked, and bolts slid back. After an eternity, the thick door creaked open, and my aunt stood before me in all her wizened glory.

She scowled in greeting. "Twice in one day? How did I get so lucky."

"From what I've heard, you went one hex too far."

A reddish eyebrow quirked upward. "You know about me." She jutted her chin toward the beige animal carrier. "What'd you bring me, a sympathy rabbit?"

How the heck had she known it was a rabbit without looking? On any other day that might have freaked me out. Today, it made me more certain than ever that I'd come to the right place.

"The rabbit's what I've come to talk to you about. Can I come in?"

She squinted at me. "What's the magic word?"

Seriously? I was supposed to guess the magic word to gain entrance to a cursed witch's house? "I'm not sure. . . ." I shifted the rabbit cage to the other hand and took a shot in the dark. "Open sesame?"

She rolled her eyes. "*Please!* The magic word is *please.*"

"Oh, right." She'd been looking for manners, not magic. "Could I please come in?"

"At least I know you're not a Watcher." She stepped back to allow me to pass through. "Even the Grand Council of Witches wouldn't have sent a nincompoop like you."

I stepped across the threshold into a drab old house that probably hadn't been updated since 1942. The dark wood moldings stood in stark contrast with the faded wallpaper—a different pattern in every room. Heavy velvet curtains the color of Grey Poupon mustard, with contrasting braiding and tassels in faded blue, were pulled closed across all the windows. Light came from a standing lamp in the corner and the bare bulb hanging from an elaborate medallion in the center of the ceiling. The stiff parlor furniture was in the Queen Anne style, with cushions that were stained and lumpy with age. It was grim, with no sign of modern comforts, not even a television or a modern paperback on a shelf. Whatever the family paid her to do taxes, Esme wasn't wasting it on her interior decoration.

"Don't just stand there gawping," my aunt said when she'd finished relocking everything. The cursed couldn't be too paranoid, I supposed. "Sit down and tell me why you've decided to pay me a visit after all these years. Not that I've been pining for your company, mind you."

"For the record, I think it's very unfair what they did to you."

Her mouth dropped open. For a moment I thought she might cry, but instead she slapped her hands together. The clap made me jump. "*Unfair*, she says! Ha!" She did a crazy clog dance. "Ha ha!"

Was that a laugh? The raspy sound didn't have a drop of humor in it. I shrank back, a little frightened.

She stopped hopping and wagged a finger at me. "Let me tell you, that curse was the best thing that ever happened to me."

Sure, Jan.

As if answering the thought, she said, "Well, at least I'm not wasting my life like you are, trying to be *happy*. Ha! Good luck with that."

Maybe it was preferable to skip references to what had happened to her. The past seemed to be—understandably—a sensitive subject. "Anyway, Mom and Dad told me what had happened, and that's why I'm here."

She looked astonished. "*They* sent you?"

"Oh, no. I came here on my own. They don't know anything about it, and I'd prefer it if you didn't tell them. You see, I have a problem. All my cousins here in town do, actually—although it's Trudy I'm most worried about. Do you know who Trudy is, and Milo?"

"More or less." Esme folded her arms and hunched down onto her sofa. "Relations."

Vermin, she might have said.

"Trudy's in some sort of mess, but she won't tell me what it is. My guess is that it has something to do with this rabbit. I think she's tried to make him into her familiar."

Esme eyed the cage again. The rabbit wasn't thumping anymore. In fact, he'd gone silent and had retreated into the farthest recess of his carrier, where he huddled in a defensive crouch. "Not sure if I'm following exactly what the problem is here," she said, "except of course Trudy is in for a crap ton of trouble if the Council finds out what she's doing."

"Right. That's what I thought. But the difficulty might go deeper. You know Tannith, of course."

Esme's frazzled brows drew together and her gaze darkened into a glower. I took that for a yes.

For five uncomfortable minutes, I laid out all the odd things that had happened since Tannith's poisoned letter had arrived at all our doors. Esme listened with her eyes closed and was so unresponsive that, by the time I finished, I wondered if she'd fallen asleep. After my words petered out, silence stretched uncomfortably.

Was I supposed to say something to wake her up? Or maybe she wanted me to leave. Clearly, I'd been wrong to think crazy Aunt Esme could help me.

Her eyes popped open. "Crazy, am I?"

My jaw went slack.

She blasted another windy, mirthless laugh my way.

"Yes, I heard you. Oh, I have nitwits' thoughts running through my consciousness like tired Top Forty hits from the eighties playing at the CVS. Believe me, hon, your little insults go in one ear and out the other like Air Supply or Kajagoogoo."

"I'm sorry—"

"Don't apologize. The various insults random pea-brained-animated stumps like yourself toss my way amuse me no end, when I bother to think about them at all." She stood and paced. "But what you were saying before . . . Now *this* interests me. It's a puzzle. A very dangerous puzzle, I think."

"Yes, dangerous. That's what's worrying me."

She nodded. "And it involves the Queen of the Animated Stumps."

"Pardon?"

"Tannith! You think I don't have eyes, that I can't see across a shopping-mall corridor?"

I felt the bottom drop out of my stomach. "We were horrible."

"Yes, you were! And Tannith was the ringleader, I could see that." Esme bobbed on the balls of her feet. "Oh, yes! I'm most interested in your little problem." She left the room and then stomped back, glaring at me with impatience. "Well, are you coming, or are you going to sit there gaping at my Grey Poupon drapes?"

I *really* needed to watch myself. "Now?"

She rolled her eyes. "Yes, *now*, you nitwit. Bring the rabbit."

I stood, but an attack of nerves stopped me from taking a step forward. "Where are we going?"

For the first time in all the years I'd known her, my aunt smiled. I almost wished she hadn't. The sight of white teeth slashing across that normally scowling, wrinkled countenance terrified me.

"We're going to my laboratory."

Chapter 8

On shaky legs I followed my aunt down a flight of rickety wood steps to the basement, a damp, claustrophobic hole with a dirt floor. There was just enough room down there for a washer and dryer. The rest of the space under the house was apparently solid rock. *Some laboratory.*

The moment the sarcastic thought entered my head, Esme pivoted. "Ya think?"

Oops. I clutched Herb's carrier in a white-knuckle grip. He was thumping again, and no wonder. "It smells like something died down here."

"Of course it does. Eau de Dead Rat, I call it. Watcher repellent. Took me months to get it just right." She stopped next to the rock wall and looked up at where I was still standing on the last staircase step. "What's the matter? Nervous you're going to be my next victim?"

I froze.

She blasted out another unsettling laugh. "C'mon, say, 'Open sesame.' That was a riot."

"That's okay. I've said enough stupid things for one day."

"Have a daily limit, do you?" She howled with laughter at the thought. "C'mon, do it for Crazy Aunt Esme. I'll even say the magic word. *Please* say, 'Open sesame.'"

Sighing, I muttered, "Open sesame."

The moment the words left my lips, a sound like the grinding of stone against stone was accompanied by a chunk of the rock wall moving, opening up a world beyond of light and color.

I gasped. Had my words done that? "How did you open that door—was it magic?"

Her grating cackle blasted me again. "Sure, the magic of a lever hidden behind a rock that I pushed. The magic of engineering they probably had all figured out in ancient Mesopotamia!" She beckoned me with an impatient gesture. "Come on. I don't like to leave the portal open too long."

I hurried through the dirt-floor basement and crossed the threshold in the granite wall, which required going down a few steps. As soon as I reached the bottom of them, the door ground closed behind me.

I'd been wrong. It wasn't a new world, it was just a room—but what a room. It had been carved out of the rock and soil beneath her house, but it must have extended beyond the house structure overhead and into the backyard. The space was a windowless cave, but it didn't feel at all claustrophobic.

Unlike the dirt-floored, stinky laundry area just outside, this long chamber had ten-foot ceilings and a white-painted floor polished to a blinding gloss. The walls had been done in a pale pink, but the lights around the room were in all sorts of colors—red, blue, white, and yellow—so that color blended into different hues wherever I looked. Against one wall stood a massive, antique apothecary's cabinet, whose many tiny drawers held who knows what. Another wall was floor-to-ceiling bookcases filled with hardbound volumes. Several worktables jutted like islands across the width of the room, most with projects underway on them: covered bowls, terrariums of frogs and newts, cauldrons steaming on hot plates, and beakers of bubbling, foaming liquids.

Those last items made me nervous, especially when I remembered Dad telling me about those toolsheds being blown sky-high.

"Only one blew up," Esme corrected from behind me. "The other one just went up in flames because I'd left a lit cigarette." She shrugged. "I quit smoking after that. Bad habit anyway."

I knew I was being rude, but I couldn't stop gaping. I was looking at my aunt, but the Aunt Esme I knew was no longer there. She'd been replaced by an entirely different person—the hump was gone, her face was no longer creased with wrinkles, and her hair, unleashed from its confines of beanies and buns, cascaded down to the middle of her back. Gone were the frumpy clothes, too. A slinky, long-sleeved dress of shimmering jade fitted her curvy figure like a second skin.

I gulped in a breath. "You really are a witch."

"Thank you!" She laughed. "That's the nicest thing anyone's said to me in decades."

"But you *can't* be a witch. The Edict. The curse. They took away your powers."

"How do you think they could manage that? All they can do is frighten us, so that we become obedient little mice."

I couldn't force myself to bring up Odin. "But the Council cursed you—no more happiness, no more love, no more witchcraft."

"That's right—no *more*." She tossed her head back. "What did I want with *more*? I already had what I wanted. They couldn't take away the witchcraft skills I'd already developed. No one has that power."

"Aren't you afraid you'll be found out?"

"Screw that. Are *you* going to spend your whole life letting other people decide what you can be?"

I opened my mouth to respond, then shut it. I wanted to be

brave, but I wasn't nuts. Being cursed was not high on the list of my aspirations.

"Suppress your powers and you become a danger to everyone, most of all yourself." She wagged a finger at me. "You might not believe that now, but you will."

"I'm not looking for witch mentoring," I protested. "I just need a little help."

She shook her head in disgust. "Fine. But if you want me to help you find a way to convince Trudy not to practice witchcraft, you can take that rabbit, walk out the door, and never come back."

"I just want to make sure that we—that *she* doesn't get caught."

"Then you've come to the right place. Of course, I did get caught once, but so far the geniuses the Council's sent to spy on me haven't winkled out any of this." She gestured around the room and ended by tapping on the table next to her. "Now bring that bunny over here."

"His name's Herb."

I unlatched the carrier, but it took effort to extract Herb. He was one terrified rabbit. As I pulled him out, he bit me. I felt as if his teeth had pierced all the way down to the bone of my thumb. I groaned and held it as I hopped around in pain. "I'm probably going to get rabies now."

Esme regarded me with disgust. "No, you won't." She opened a drawer and pulled out a small vial. "Rub some of this on the bite."

"Magic ointment?" I stared at the liquid skeptically.

She raised a brow. "Would you rather go to a doctor and get a rabies shot?"

I opened the vial and shook a couple of drops of something brown and viscous onto the toothmark-shaped puncture. In the next second, I was howling in agony.

My aunt chuckled. "Stings, doesn't it?"

"What's in that stuff?"

She shot me a look. "Sometimes it's best not to ask."

What was I doing trusting this person? "How long have you been mixing potions?"

"How long have I been cursed?"

"Thirty years?" I guessed.

"About that. Since I was seventeen. See, the good part of being cursed to be a CPA at seventeen is that you can afford a house. And when you have a house, you can lock the doors. You can create your own world. It's like being a prisoner. They can control you, but they can't control your dreams."

That was beautiful. That was . . .

Wait. "That's from *The Shawshank Redemption*."

She clutched her chest. "*Such* a good movie! That ending—I ugly cry every time." She grinned. "And such a good playbook about how to create a secret spot to escape into in times of hardship. Don't ever let anyone tell you art isn't instructive."

Her confiding in me gave me courage. "Maybe a film inspired your laboratory scheme, but it's Odin who motivates you, isn't it?"

Her smile disappeared, and for a moment the old Aunt Esme flashed in her eyes. "Mind your own business."

"You're going to make him reappear, aren't you?"

"Who wants to know?" she asked sharply.

"Me, I guess. It's a sad story."

"You want me to spill the sob story of my life so you can get feels from it? Odin was a real person, dammit. Vibrant, fun, intelligent. And handsome? You've never seen such a man! Tall, muscles like a Greek statue, and blue eyes like Paul Newman's. But most of all, he was talented. He was performing feats nobody else could. He had more talent in his fingers than the entire Grand Council of Witches possessed. He was working on something that would have—"

Her mouth snapped closed.

"Would have what?"

"Never mind. One day he was yanked away from the world— from *me*. And why?"

"The Edict." The Edict that we were at this moment defying. I wondered if *I* would disappear some fine day.

"An Edict that had nothing to do with us," Esme said angrily.

"But Lucian Zimmer—"

"That was over sixty years before you were born. How responsible should you be for blunders your great-great-grandfather made? Odin never caused a natural disaster, and neither did I."

Not yet, anyway.

"I heard that," she grumbled.

"Sorry." I sighed. "Life isn't fair."

She snorted. "Very original thinking you're engaging in there. *Of course* life isn't fair when a Grand Council hands down capricious decisions that are designed to make it unfair. People like my sister and her husband can muddle along obeying and abstaining, but I'm not going to. I don't think you will, either."

"Wait a minute." I took a step back. "I don't practice witchcraft."

"Never?"

"Well . . ." Heat crept up my neck. "A few times when I was a teenager, maybe. I could move things sometimes."

"Oh—move things," she echoed sarcastically. "Impressive!"

In an instant, she'd vanished.

How had she done that? My mouth felt too dry to speak, but my pulse rushed. Part of me longed to ask, *Can I learn to do that?*

"Look at yourself!" her voice taunted from the void. "Too afraid to say what you want. Haven't you dreamed of this for years—or at least thought of little transgressions, like how much easier it would be if you could make dirty dishes clean themselves when you were too pooped after dinner to face doing them yourself? You never wanted to conjure an emergency gift for someone whose birthday you forgot? Never attempted to give yourself a little supernatural push when you were bicycling up a steep hill?"

Was she a good guesser or were these little desires universal among people with witch blood?

Esme laughed and reappeared. "That fat-headed Council asked you to do the impossible—to be a witch and not be a witch at the same time. They set us all up for failure. And those of us who get caught are made examples of to scare the others. Well, screw that. They caught me once, but they haven't beaten me, and I'm not going to let them catch you, or Trudy."

"Do you think they will?" The idea filled me with horror. I wasn't Esme—I wasn't brave. Life was difficult enough. I didn't want to be cursed.

"Oh, I think there's a very good chance they'll catch you if you harebrained children continue on as you have. They've put a Watcher on you."

I froze. "How do you know?"

"From what you've told me. From your own fear. I can smell a Watcher in all this somewhere."

She chucked a finger under Herb's chin, and he jumped back so quickly that he almost fell off the table.

I grabbed his rump at the last minute, saving him from the fall. "Herb must be Trudy's familiar. That's why I'm worried. If he is, she's further gone than I ever would have dreamed, and she has no idea what kind of danger she's putting herself in."

Esme's eyes narrowed on the animal. "I'm not sure what his relationship is to her, but I do know he's not a normal rabbit."

"How can you tell?"

"Look at those eyes. He reacts to everything, but not in an ordinary animal way. There's a flicker of intelligence going on in that pea-sized brain."

Herb kicked out a particularly reverberant series of thumps.

"Do you think that's some sort of code?" I asked.

She lowered herself and went almost eye to eye with him. Her nose wrinkled. "He stinks of magic."

Even though her pronouncement vindicated my hunch, anxiety overcame any satisfaction I might have felt. It would have been better to be wrong. My fear for Trudy, for all of us, spiked. To think, I'd considered Tannith stealing one of our partners the worst thing we had to worry about. Now Trudy was dabbling in spells and enchantments, practically inviting the Grand Council to curse her. To curse us all.

Esme straightened. "The Watchers are going to be on you like white on rice."

Why? Why did this have to be happening now? "Everything was going so well." I knew I sounded whiny, but I couldn't help it. "I've built up a good business, Daniel and I just moved in together and have been getting along, and we'd even saved up a little for a long vacation together next summer."

My aunt's face brightened with interest. "Oooooh, where to?"

"Daniel wants to take a deep dive into predatory arachnids, so we're planning a two-week trip to Death Valley to study scorpions."

She blinked. "Well, you know what they say—there's no place for romance like Death Valley."

"Who says that?"

"No one!" She shook her head. "Are you an idiot?"

A natural defensiveness kicked in, and I parroted the same words Daniel had used to sell the idea to me. "Do you know how many movies have been filmed in Death Valley?"

"Sure. Any film that needs to show someone being terrorized or dying in a hot, bone-dry hellscape."

"There are also rock formations—" Her incredulous stare cut me off. I lifted my chin. "I don't need to justify my vacation choices to you. All I was saying was that everything was going well. I really don't want to be vaporized because my cousin got it into her head to start talking to rabbits."

"If that's what's happening."

"What else could it be? You said Herb is enchanted."

"Right." She lowered her voice. "But hasn't it occurred to you that Trudy might have picked up this rabbit in all innocence because the Council planted him as a trap?"

No, that hadn't occurred to me. My blood chilled. "A Watcher can be an animal?"

"Sometimes. That's why I've never gone in for familiars. I did have a bird once, decades ago, but it got so that I didn't trust him. All that fluttering around, and he talked too much. Birds are big networkers."

There was a lot I didn't know.

"So you think Herb's a Watcher?" Panic shot up my spine. "If he is, it's too late. Herb knows everything. He knows about *you*, and all this." I gestured around the laboratory. "What are we going to do?"

"If it's true, we're going to kill the rabbit."

Herb's back leg started thumping like a jackhammer.

"Listen to that." Esme clucked in disgust, then bent toward him. "It's called incriminating yourself, mister!"

As much as I feared the Council finding out Trudy had been dabbling in magic—if not positively soaking in it—the ethics of killing a sentient being didn't sit well. "Herb is Trudy's pet, though. And you said yourself that there was some kind of intelligence in him."

Esme rounded on me, looking as if she wanted to tear her hair out. Or maybe tear mine out. "Haven't you been listening? If this rabbit is a snitch, Tannith's petty shenanigans with letters will seem like fun and games. The Council doesn't stick with just one punishment, you know. Invisibility is cruel, but how would you like to be turned into a tree, or a rock? I haven't relished a life without joy, but how would Trudy stand up to a life without another living soul?"

Without even her daughters. Molly and Drew meant everything to Trudy.

"Point taken." *Sorry, Herb.* "What are you going to do with him? I mean, you're going to be sure he's a Watcher before you . . ." I turned away from the rabbit's field of vision and made a slashing motion across my neck. "I mean, what if *he's* been cursed? That could happen, couldn't it? Maybe Watchers like Herb are coerced into doing the Council's bidding."

Esme looked like she was going to argue, but thought better of it. "All right, Little Miss Bleeding Heart. I'll put him through his paces before I make the final call."

The final call sounded so . . . final. "What are the paces?"

She sighed. "You should just run along. This is advanced witchcraft, and having you breathing down my neck isn't going to help matters. Animal spells require steady nerves. Things can go wrong in an ugly way."

I bit my lip. I needed to check on Kyle and Taj anyway. They might be close to finishing with the attic by now. "All right." I threw a last look at poor, doomed Herb. His nose twitched double-time in supplication.

"I'll see you to the door," Esme said, hustling me out.

I headed toward the portal we'd come through, trying to close my ears to the plaintive thumps behind me. By the time I tossed a look back, Esme distracted me. She'd transformed into Aunt Esme the crone again. Once in the stinking laundry room, I hurried ahead of her up the stairs. I hoped I'd done the right thing in coming here. At least now I knew a lot more than I did before I'd knocked at the farmhouse door. This entire day had been an eye-opener.

Esme unlocked all the dead bolts and chains on the door but gave me a sharp stare before turning the knob. "Don't be a nitwit," she said in her gravelly voice. "Be careful what you say, and to whom you say it. Capisce?"

I nodded.

She opened the door and I started to rush out, but she grabbed my sleeve to stop me.

I turned and looked down at her. The anger dimples were back. It was hard to believe this was the same woman from the basement. Everything that had happened down there was beginning to seem like a fever dream.

"What is it?"

"If you *do* go to Death Valley, could you bring me back some scorpions?"

"Sure, Aunt Esme." She let go and I rushed to the Kia.

"And maybe a few toads!" she called after me.

I waved and collapsed onto the Kia's driver seat. *Jesus take the wheel. My family.*

I started the engine of my car, then remembered to check my phone. Esme's basement was apparently a Wi-Fi dead zone. I had a squillion messages and my phone hadn't rung, chirped, or vibrated once during the past hour.

I opened the messages.

KYLE: *We didn't finish yet but we're stopping for the day. Going to dinner with Mrs. C.*

Dinner with Mrs. Caputo? That was weird.

DANIEL: *Did you get my phone message?*

No, I hadn't.

MOM: *Gwendle-bug, I hope you're okay after our talk today. We're here if you need us. XOXO, Mom.*

DANIEL: *Where the H are you?*

I needed to call him back. I was about to swipe over to the phone app when my gaze fell on the next message in texts.

TRUDY: *OMG, I need help! Herb's missing!*

TRUDY: *I can't find him anywhere! I think he might be stolen!*

TRUDY: *WTF, Gwen! Why did you steal Herb??? Don't deny it—Jeremy saw you w/ him!!!*

TRUDY: *BRING HIM BACK!*

Oh, crud. Not only did Trudy know Herb was missing, she'd been talking with Jeremy of all people. Jeremy, who'd been watching us like a hawk. Grad student, baloney. He was a Watcher. He had to be.

I tapped out a fast message to Trudy: *On my way. Do not say another word to Jeremy. Get rid of him! Will explain all when I get there.*

I gunned the Kia back to Trudy's house. She was standing on the porch and flew down the steps as I pulled up to the curb. I'd never seen anyone so distraught.

"Did you bring him back?" She planted her forehead against the back passenger window and made visors of her hands to peer inside. "Where is he?"

I looked around. The only person I spotted was a man three houses down raking leaves, but you never knew. "Let's go inside."

She didn't budge. "Just tell me where he is."

"This is serious, Trudy."

She laughed hysterically. "Yes, it damn well is."

"That rabbit could be putting us all at risk. Especially you."

Her face screwed up. *"Laird?"*

What was she talking about? "Herb."

Her face went red. "That's what I'm saying, Gwen. Herb *is* Laird."

Chapter 9

"Where are we going?" Trudy asked after I'd peeled off down the street.

"Aunt Esme's." I'd tried calling but had gotten no answer at the number I had for her. Of course not. No messages penetrated that subterranean laboratory of hers.

Trudy turned to me as if I'd lost my last marble. "Why there?"

"Because that's where Herb is."

"You gave Laird to that old crone?"

"I didn't know he was Laird. I thought . . ." Remembering Esme saying she was going to kill Herb, I swallowed back terror. My hands were already shaking so hard the steering wheel was vibrating. I took deep, even breaths and tried to stop my brain from contemplating the peril I'd left Laird in. "Why didn't you tell me about Laird right away?"

"I hoped I could fix things."

"What happened?"

"I don't know! It started with the letter from Tannith—actually, the day before that. Laird and I had a fight. He said he was going to move to the basement."

The basement. Not New York City, then. "Why?"

"Because . . ." She gulped. "He said he didn't love me any-more. That he'd just stayed with me because of Molly and Drew. And now that they're gone . . ."

"What a jackass." Maybe not a needs-to-be-killed-by-a-crazy-witch jackass, but still.

Trudy crossed her arms. "He had a lot of crust to say that, don't you think? I mean, *he* stayed for the girls? For years I prac-tically felt like a single parent! He never even helped them with their homework."

"Why would he want to move to the basement? I mean, why not get his own apartment?"

"He said he didn't want to leave the house, and that if anyone should go, it was me because—get this—I don't have as much stuff!"

"That's not even true. You've got all that kitchenware, for one thing. And that beautiful stove."

"That's what I told him. 'If you think I'm going to leave two years after I lived through a kitchen remodel, you've got another think coming,' I said. I wasn't going to budge. He said fine, he'd just live in the basement. It has its own entrance, and he already had his office down there. He even asked me to help him drag the couch down so he could sleep on it. I did help him take both it and the awful old leather chairs down, but it nearly threw my back out, so I told him I was finished helping him at all."

She lifted a fist to her lips. "And then yesterday morning that horrid letter from Tannith arrived. I read it and stomped right down to the basement and confronted Laird. Of course he de-nied being involved with her. But he'd already told me he didn't love me, and it seemed just like him to weasel out of telling me the whole truth right away. I figured he was going to confess in stages, so I didn't freak out.

"But of course I freaked out. My blood was boiling! I felt like I was going to go ballistic—literally, like there was a rocket launcher firing inside me. You know how in Pilates class they say you have a core? Well, I finally found mine, and it was full of rocket fuel. Tannith's letter blasted me off. I opened my mouth to tell Laird exactly what I thought of his unholy union with Tannith and—well, that's not what came out of my mouth. I'm not sure *what* I said. I was spewing fiery gobbledygook at him. It was so painful that I think I passed out. And when I finally opened my eyes, there was Laird, twitching at me."

"What did you do when you realized you'd turned him into a rabbit?"

"Well, I was still so PO'ed that at first I decided to redo the house how I wanted. I mean, served him right if he was a rabbit. My back still ached from moving the couch, so I went to the furniture store and bought all new things in colors he'd hate. I even shelled out for same-day delivery and Scotchgard treatment."

"But you must have been doing something with spellcraft. The cupcakes you gave me this morning really were enchanted."

She blinked in surprise. "Which ones?"

"The Strawberry Bliss ones, for sure. They've affected everyone who's eaten them like a hit of magic mushrooms."

"Interesting." She tilted her head, mulling over this information. "I made them yesterday when I'd just got the furniture and was feeling good about being single again. But then, after you all left last night, I realized I couldn't let Laird spend the rest of his life as a rabbit. I mean—it was a little bit of a strain trying to hide his identity from you. How on earth would I explain what had happened to the girls? So I did what Milo was talking about—I went online and read about spells and spell reversals. Then I watched a few BrewTube videos." She blew out a breath. "It's a lot harder than I thought it would be."

"I believe you."

"I managed to change his color. You noticed that. But that's it. Then I became terrified, especially with that Jeremy character sniffing around this morning, and I tried again. But I only succeeded in changing his color back."

"We have to be extremely careful around Jeremy," I warned. "He could be a Watcher."

Trudy eyed me, puzzled. "You still haven't explained why you stole Herb, or why we're headed to Esme's."

A vehicle logjam at the bridge gave me time to explain everything that had happened that day. Well, almost everything. I still couldn't confess to her that Esme thought we should do away with Herb/Laird. I prayed we'd arrived in time.

Without knowing the worst, Trudy seemed almost optimistic when I told her about the awesome powers Esme had honed in secret all these years. "Maybe she'll be able to change him back. You really think she's a good witch? I mean, an accomplished one?"

I had my doubts. Wouldn't an accomplished witch have been able to tell that rabbit was Laird right away?

I didn't want to scare Trudy, though. "She knows a lot more than we do."

Trudy shook her head. "That's a low bar."

"You were good at infusing enchantment into those cupcakes."

"That was accidental. I think Laird's betrayal has made my latent witch powers go haywire. I just seem to be throwing spells subconsciously." Trudy frowned. "I have to be careful. If I get too worked up at school and accidentally hex a student, that would be the end of my teaching career." She worried her thumbnail. "No telling what that would do to my retirement."

I pulled into Esme's driveway again and parked behind her Gremlin. Before we got out, I turned to Trudy. "The important thing is to stay calm. We're going to get this situation under control." I reached out, took Trudy's hand in mine, and squeezed. "Edict or not, we're a witch family. We've got this."

Tears filled her eyes. "I just don't want to have to tell the girls that their father's going to spend the rest of his life eating alfalfa pellets."

"You won't. Think positive thoughts." We got out of the car, and I added across the hood, "And don't freak out about the smell. It's just a dead-rat concoction Esme sprays around."

Trudy's steps faltered, but she followed me. I rang the bell— twice—but several worrisome minutes crawled by before sounds of the great unlocking began from the other side of the door. I sent Trudy a reassuring look. "Esme has security concerns, because of the Edict."

The door opened and Esme—crone Esme—glared up at us. "I didn't expect you back so soon."

"Is Laird still alive?" Trudy asked.

Esme shot a look at me. "You said his name was Herb."

"It turns out there was a little more to the story. You see—"

"Shh . . ." Esme peeked past us as if the porch columns had eyes. "We'll talk inside."

We hurried in and she shut the door. Trudy's panic was back, manifesting itself in a strange unconscious whine, but the methodical locking process could not be rushed. Only when the last night chain was secured did my aunt turn back to us. "Stop your keening. He's fine."

"Oh, thank God!" Trudy collapsed against the flocked wallpaper.

"Herb is Laird," I told Esme. "Trudy's husband. She put some sort of spell on him by mistake."

For the first time, Esme looked startled. Then she turned a disbelieving gaze on Trudy. "*You* did that?"

"I didn't mean to. We were arguing, and something came over me."

Esme's brows arched. "Must've been a hell of an argument."

Trudy fanned herself. "I'm just so relieved he's here."

"He's here, all right."

"Do you think he'll have to be a rabbit forever?" Trudy asked worriedly.

"Definitely not. You'd better come with me." Esme led the way down the hall.

Trudy let out a disgusted sound when we got to the basement

stairs and the smell intensified. Despite my having done all this just hours ago, the same trepidation filled me as before. I couldn't help noticing that my aunt was quieter than she'd been earlier this afternoon. She wasn't insulting us nonstop. In fact, she wasn't looking at either of us.

When Trudy got her first glimpse of the magic laboratory, she exclaimed in surprise—and Esme's subsequent transformation shocked her even more. "My goodness!" Trudy clasped her hands like a mother watching her jeans-wearing daughter try on a prom dress. "You're so beautiful. You should try to look like this all the time."

"Yeah, right," Esme grumbled.

"She's cursed," I explained to Trudy. "Really cursed. It's a long story."

Trudy's lips formed a discreet *Oh* and she cast an expectant, impatient look around the room. "Where's Laird? Could you please change him back now?"

"He's already changed."

Trudy's gaze continued searching the tables and nooks. Nowhere was there a forty-two-year-old history professor in evidence.

"Your husband is no longer a rabbit," Esme informed Trudy. Esme went to a counter and pointed to a terrarium with a mesh lid. "He's a toad."

We gaped in shock. This was not a practical joke. The toad she pointed out puffed up and let out a croak. He even looked a little like Laird.

Horrified, Trudy raised her hands to her face. "You changed him from a rabbit . . . to a toad? Why?"

"Well, it's like this," Esme explained matter-of-factly. "Gwen had just been telling me about her proposed trip to Death Valley. I looked up the toads there—like the red-spotted toad. So that was probably it. I had red-spotted toads on the brain."

Crimson rose in Trudy's cheeks. "Why did you change him at all?"

"Because we were trying to figure out if he was a creature of magic. I wanted to see how easy it would be to manipulate him."

"So you turned him into a toad?" Trudy asked, her anger rising.

"Toad spells are some of the easiest." Esme shook her head. "Even so, it took me three tries."

Trudy's breaths were coming more rapidly. "Great! Three tries to screw it up. This is even worse than his being a rabbit."

"I don't see that," Esme said. "He's more compact and easy to take care of now."

Trudy's hands fisted at her sides. "He's. A. Toad."

"A good-looking specimen, if I do say so myself—and I was only going on a picture on the internet. Anyways"—Esme shrugged—"toad, rabbit . . . what does it matter?"

"It matters!" Trudy's voice looped up in anger. "At least before, he was a mammal. Now he's a damned amphibian!"

"Don't get ugly with me." Esme took a step toward Trudy. "Do you have any idea how difficult animals spells are? No, of course you don't. They require practice, knowledge, and skill."

I tugged on Trudy's sleeve, trying to indicate that getting into a screaming match with a much more advanced witch with nothing to lose was probably not the best idea. But did Trudy heed my warning? No.

"Poppycock! I turned him from human to rabbit practically without thinking."

"Because you're an *amateur*," Esme sneered. "You mutter a few enchantments willy-nilly and create a big mess, and then you come crying to me to fix it for you."

"*I* came—?" Trudy was so angry she couldn't finish the thought. "*Fix it?* You made it worse!"

My mother's daughter, I lifted my hands, attempting to play peacemaker. "Maybe we should all calm down and work together to find a solution."

Trudy rounded on me. "This is *your* fault. If you hadn't stolen Laird in the first place, none of this would have happened."

"I didn't know it was Laird," I said in my defense. "You didn't tell me. You were lying and being evasive."

"I didn't think you'd break into my house, kidnap my rabbit, and bring him to this old crone!"

"Old crone?"

The imperious, righteous anger in Esme's voice echoed around the walls, terrifying me. Trudy, on the other hand, looked like she might just spin into a Tasmanian devil tornado of rage. Was she trying to get us killed?

I waved my hands. "I'm sure Trudy didn't mean—"

"Obrosheha vey!" Trudy shouted.

Esme's eyes widened in shock. "Stop that!" she yelled back. "Don't you dare do that here!"

My heart fluttered. *Do what?* What the hell was happening?

"Ammim zee lapinus spectorus!" Trudy spat back at her.

I turned to stare at my cousin, who seemed to be in some sort of trance. Then her eyes closed, and she collapsed to the floor.

I let out a shout and dropped down next to her. "Trudy!" I sprang right back up and ran to the sink in the corner. Pouring some water on a cloth, I hurried back and placed it on her forehead. Esme had gone. I wondered if she'd made herself invisible again. *That's one way to win an argument.*

I kept my attention on Trudy. "Trudes, wake up."

Her eyelids fluttered and then opened. Dazed eyes looked around the pink, blue, and yellow room in confusion. "Are we . . . ?"

"In Esme's laboratory. Esme's made herself invisible. I think you scared her. You both scared me."

Trudy pulled up to sitting, rubbing her head. "I'm going to have to take an anger-management class."

I tried to laugh. "It's okay, Aunt Esme," I called out to the room. "You can come back now."

She didn't reappear, but a bunny hopped across the white tiles toward us. It was a light brown bunny with gray-tipped ears. Trudy and I stared at it.

"It looks like Peaches," I said. Or the first Herb. "You must have changed Laird back into Herb the rabbit."

"That's a step in the right direction, at least."

I sighed as we got to our feet. Trudy was really hung up on the toad-rabbit distinction. "The goal is to make him human again, though," I reminded her.

When we were standing, we both noticed the terrarium. Laird the toad was still inside. He croaked.

In unison, we looked down at the rabbit. The bunny sat up on its hind legs. Understanding dawned.

On *her* hind legs.

Trudy let out a long, ragged breath. "Houston, we have a problem."

Chapter 10

Milo, wearing a tuxedo, arrived twenty minutes after we put out our SOS, which was minutes after we realized that not only was Laird still a toad, but, thanks to this new tic of Trudy's, Aunt Esme, the person we'd hoped would untangle this mess, was a rabbit.

When I opened the door, he stood with his hands in his pockets, frowning at Esme's distant neighbors. "Look at all those Karen Morrow signs. This is a disaster."

I took his arm. "There's a disaster inside that'll take your mind off the election."

"You know I've never actually been inside this place?" When the air from the basement wafted out to him, he jumped back a step and shook off my grasp. His expression changed from curiosity to horror. "What is that smell?"

I'd left the door to the basement ajar. "Eau de Dead Rat. Aunt Esme's specialty."

I stood aside, but Milo stayed firmly on the non-stinky side of the threshold. "You said this was an emergency. You didn't mention stench. I'm wearing a rented tux."

"This *is* an emergency, and the stink is only in certain parts of the house." My lips twisted. "Usually."

"I had to duck out of a reception at the Zenobia Country Club for local business bigwigs," he complained.

I couldn't focus on local politics now. "I'm sorry, Milo. Trudy and I didn't know who else to call. We're in trouble."

"What kind of trouble?"

There was no way to sugarcoat it. "Laird is a toad."

Milo rolled his eyes. "He's always been a toad. If he's left Trudy, she's better off—"

"I'm not speaking metaphorically. I mean he's an amphibian. He hops and croaks."

Curiosity piqued, Milo stepped inside. I shut the door and began the onerous task of locking up. Esme had good reason for being paranoid, and I figured I'd better follow her example.

"What *is* this place?" He looked around. "The House Time Forgot?"

"Aunt Esme doesn't waste much effort on interior design. At least, not up here."

"Where's Trudy?"

"In the basement."

As I led him downstairs, I filled him in as quickly as I could on all that had happened to Esme, and why she needed to hide any evidence of joy in her life, and especially any kind of witchcraft, from the powers that be.

As we descended, Milo wrapped the white silk scarf he'd been wearing outside over his nose. "You should have warned me to bring a gas mask."

"The smell's meant to scare Watchers away from this." I pressed the stone that opened the door to the laboratory and its jumble of colored lights, stainless steel, and polished wood.

"Holy . . ." Milo's jaw dropped. "*Trudy?*"

While I'd been gone, she'd climbed up on one of the work-tables and was curled up in a fetal ball. She lifted her head feebly. "Hi, Milo."

He hurried over to her side. "It's going to be okay," he said. "We'll find someone to reverse the spell on Laird. We're from a family of witches. *Somebody* must know how to do it." He pivoted. "Where's Esme?"

"There." Trudy and I pointed down at the rabbit busily cleaning her long, lop ears.

"So much for my first suggestion," Milo said. "Who did that?"

Trudy raised her hand. "It's a new thing. I get very angry and turn people into rabbits. And now I'm going to end up cursed, or in jail. My girls will never forgive me."

Milo rounded on me in confusion. "You said Laird was a frog."

"Toad," Trudy and I corrected.

"Esme changed him from a rabbit to a toad," I explained. "Trudy got mad—"

"Not unreasonably," she interjected, sitting up and dabbing her eyes with a soggy handkerchief.

I gestured toward Esme, who was scratching herself with her big hind foot. "There's the result."

"You should have heard her," Trudy said in her own defense. "She was acting like Laird's spending the rest of his life in a terrarium was *no big deal*." Trudy sighed. "Unfortunately, she was also our best shot at reversing the spell. I Thumper-ized my best hope of getting Laird back to normal."

Milo bit his lip, taking a moment to absorb everything. "Okay . . . things look grim, obviously. But I can post a call for help on Cackle. Surely someone out in the social-media sphere will be able to point us in the right direction." He whipped out his phone.

I put my hand over his before he could bring up the app. "Think. Even if we could find some witch willing to help, we'd have to admit that we'd been dealing in spellcraft. The Council could punish us all in any number of gruesome ways."

"But what about Laird?" Trudy said. "We have to think of him." She cast an afterthought glance at the rabbit. "And Esme, too, I suppose."

That's what worried me. "Esme was already cursed. If the Council finds out about this"—I gestured to the laboratory around us—"what will they do to her next? Mom was just describing horrible punishments they can mete out."

"Worse than being a rabbit for the rest of her life?" Milo asked.

"Or a toad?" Trudy glanced at Laird.

"Yes. They can inflict perpetual, unremitting suffering or obliterate you from the world." I explained about Cousin Odin. "Would you rather be obliterated or be a rabbit?"

As my words sank in, Trudy did something I'd rarely seen her do. She slumped.

"Don't give up," I urged her. "We just need to try everything we can to solve this on our own before we give up and get help." *Or go terrarium shopping at PetSmart.* "We're witches, and there's so much in this laboratory for us to learn from. And we know you have powers, Trudy." I took her hands in mine. "If you can put a spell on someone, it stands to reason that you have the ability to reverse it."

"You heard Esme, though. She told us this type of work takes practice and skill."

"It didn't take you practice to turn Laird or Esme into rabbits. You did it on instinct. We just need to find the right words to make your instinct work in reverse."

"You can't control instinct."

"Of course you can. We all taught ourselves tricks when we were kids, on the sly." I turned to Milo. My voice looped up with energy, like I was in an old Mickey Rooney–Judy Garland movie, trying to convince the kids we could put on a show ourselves. "Remember when you said you made the chalk slip out of your teacher's hand?"

"Chalk isn't alive," he pointed out.

"And you're not ten years old now, either. Look at all these books we have to work with." I gestured toward the floor-to-ceiling bookcases. "In all these volumes of spellcraft, we're bound to find what we need. We can at least give it a try."

Milo wandered over to the book area. "And if we're caught?"

That put a damper on my gee-whiz energy. "Esme has spent her entire adult life constructing this place to hide from the Council. We should be safe as long as we do our research and experimenting here."

Trudy straightened again and squared her shoulders. "You're right, we have to do something. Drew and Molly will be coming home for their first vacation from college in a few weeks. Seeing their dad like this would ruin Thanksgiving."

"It'll be sorted out by then," I assured her.

I was all talk. I had no idea if we would be able to pull this off without professional help. To be honest, the chances seemed slim. But after hearing about Odin being vaporized, I wasn't yet desperate enough to throw myself on the mercy of the Council of Witches.

"What about Jane and Tom?" Trudy asked. "Do you think your parents could help us?"

I shook my head. I didn't want to put them at risk, and I truly doubted they would be able to tap their powers for something like this. "Mom was just telling me that she hasn't done any witchcraft since she was a teenager."

"Neither have I," Trudy said.

Milo and I couldn't help tossing pointed looks at our lop-eared relation.

"I mean until recently. Laird said that if I ever dabbled in witchcraft, it would be the end of us. He was right, but not in the way he meant." Trudy frowned at the toad. "I should have hexed him after he cheated on me."

Milo turned from his study of Esme's books' spines. "Laird cheated on you?"

I'd never heard this, either. "When?"

"Years ago, when the girls were still little. With an adjunct professor in radio-TV-film, of all things. God knows what they found to talk about. Laird hates television."

"They probably weren't doing a lot of talking," Milo said under his breath as he flipped through an encyclopedia-size book.

Angered by the memory, Trudy's face turned red and she twisted the handkerchief in her hands, which suddenly went up in a tiny explosion of smoke and flame.

She jumped back with a startled cry, flapping her hands and blowing on them. "Did you see that?"

As if we could have missed it.

"What did you do?" I asked.

"Nothing." Her eyes looked at mine imploring me to believe her. "I swear."

Milo and I exchanged looks. It hadn't been weirder than changing things into rabbits, but still. That handkerchief was *gone.* "Do you remember what you were thinking?" he asked.

Trudy shrugged. "Just about that adjunct professor. But I didn't even blame her or any of the others as much as I blamed Laird."

"There were others?" I asked, shocked.

"Well, none that I could prove. But I had my suspicions."

Milo was right. Laird had always been a toad, long before Esme turned him into one.

"I'm a menace." Hysteria rose in Trudy's voice. "I'm going to have to call in sick to the school until I get whatever this is under control."

"Instead of standing around getting keyed up, come over here and research," Milo said. "Just be careful not to focus any anger on the books. We can't risk a possible solution going up in smoke."

He was right. We joined him by the books, and he handed each of us a musty old tome. The first book I looked at, *Enchanting Enchantments* by Octavia Braithwait, had been written in the 1950s and was subtitled *Bewitching Tips for the Modern-Day Sorceress.* Where had Esme found this? After I'd skimmed a few pages, it seemed doubtful I'd find a solution there. I put it aside and pulled the next book off the top of Milo's pile. This was a dusty leather-bound tome entitled *Moribundus Veritudus*. That sounded more like it.

The three of us settled on the floor reading until our backs ached, the only sound the turning of brittle old pages.

Once, Milo let out a whoop, which caused Trudy and I to glance up hopefully.

He shook his head. "Sorry, it's just the witch who wrote this was *obsessed* with bat intestines. He writes about them like they have more uses than baking soda."

Another time, though, he looked up more thoughtfully. "Imagine what I could do with a truth spell right now." His eyes glinted with mad scientist fervor. "What if, during the mayoral debate tomorrow night, Karen Morrow could only tell the truth. What could sink a political candidate's chances faster than not being able to lie?"

Trudy's jaw dropped. "That's cheating."

"Not if it just makes her say what she really thinks," Milo said.

"You can't use witchcraft that way," Trudy said. "Just for your own ends. It's evil."

He drew back. "You turned your husband into a rabbit!"

"That was an accident," she retorted, growing prickly as she did when the subject came up.

I lifted my hands to calm them. "Brett's going to win that debate—and the election—on his own. He doesn't need witchcraft. He's got charisma."

Milo conceded, but grumbled, "A little spell or hex wouldn't hurt his chances, though."

I'd long suspected Milo had dabbled more than he'd ever admit even to me, especially when we were younger. A few misfortunes of rivals had miraculously worked in his favor in key moments—like when his opponent in a citywide debate championship in high school had come down with food poisoning after a lunch break. Or when, in college, the guy who was trying out against him for the role of Mordred in *Camelot* had developed laryngitis the morning of the audition. Maybe those had just been coincidences, and no doubt Milo had plenty of talent on his own, but . . .

Maybe Esme wasn't wrong. Trained or not, we were all witches. Stifle a talent too long, and it was bound to exhibit itself one way or another.

"What's wrong?" Milo asked, his voice anxious. "You're staring at me like I was suggesting tossing out ballot boxes or something. I was just wondering about a little honest spellcasting. . . ."

I shook my head. "We need to concentrate on rabbits and toads."

We read for a while longer before Trudy stopped us. "What exactly did I say during my trance, Gwen?"

I tried to remember, but her exact words eluded me. "I remember hearing the word *lapinus*, but that's it. It sounded strange—like no language I'd ever heard. A combination of Latin and German, maybe."

"Great," Milo muttered. "Trudy's invented Wiccan Esperanto."

Around eleven, I began to nod off over a musty page. Milo and Trudy weren't holding up any better. The rustle of page turns came slower and slower.

Milo looked at his watch and groaned. "The reception's long over now. Brett's not going to be pleased. I missed Karen Morrow's speech."

"You know what she said. All that woman ever does is yammer about fence heights." Five years earlier, Karen Morrow's neighbor had built a privacy fence that obstructed the view from Karen's side porch of a park catty-corner to her house. Karen hadn't missed a city council meeting since.

Milo's eyes narrowed. "This was my last chance to glean what her plan of attack will be before the debate tomorrow."

"I can tell you that right now, without a crystal ball," I said. "She'll talk about all the times Brett voted for fence-ordinance variances, the audience will nod off every time she speaks, and Brett will win by a landslide."

Milo yawned and stretched. "Just the same, if you come across any vote spells, let me know."

"Aren't you going to come back and do more searching tomorrow?" Trudy asked us, her expression panicked.

The next day Kyle, Taj, and I were supposed to finish the attic. I hoped they could manage on their own. At least they seemed to be getting along well with Mrs. Caputo. "Look, I'll try to take as much time off tomorrow as I can and come over here and keep reading."

"I can do that, too," Milo said. "I've got a crew planting shrubs at a new condo development. I would love to miss it."

Trudy looked like she was going to cry. "Thank you. I'm going to tell the school I need to take a leave of absence."

Given her penchant for transforming things on an emotional whim, taking leave wasn't a bad idea.

"We'll find the answer," I assured her, hoping I conveyed more certainty than I felt.

As we were preparing to go home, though, the problem of what to do with the two charmed creatures reared its head. "I better take Laird home with me," Trudy said.

She didn't volunteer to take Esme, so I did.

We needed to find Esme's keys. This was going to take longer than any of us had the patience for, so I simply put Esme on the ground in the living room and asked her to take us to the spare key. She led me to the kitchen, but being a rabbit, it was hard for her to point directly to where it was. I finally found it on a hook on the wall, next to the measuring spoons. When I came outside with Esme hopping after me, Milo was arguing on the phone with Brett.

Trudy explained, "He's angry at Milo for not coming back to the reception."

I locked up the house. All of our relationships seemed to be unraveling, even without help from Tannith. I hadn't responded to any of Daniel's messages. There hadn't seemed to be any time. Besides, anything I could tell him about this day would just ruffle his skeptical feathers.

Milo shoved his phone into his coat pocket. "The way Brett reacted, you'd think I'd walked out of the Met Gala. He even accused me of lying just so I could duck out early. Like I'm untrustworthy or something." He stomped toward his car, then turned back to us. "By the way, if either of you see Brett, the story is that Aunt Esme's in the hospital."

We nodded and watched him get into his car and drive off. "Trouble in paradise," I said, but Trudy wasn't listening to me. She was holding the terrarium, lost in thought. "I used to worry sometimes about my marriage breaking up, but I never imagined it ending like this."

I looped my arm in hers. "I'll drive you back now. We could all use some sleep."

"I still have baking to do."

I'd forgotten the cupcakes. "I'll help you."

"That's okay. It won't take me long, and I could use some me time. I don't think I'll be able to sleep anyway."

When we got to her place, though, she suggested I come in and borrow some rabbit supplies. As I followed her, she rattled off a list of do's and don'ts of rabbit care. I listened as closely as I could. I was exhausted, and I'd barely eaten all day.

"I'd offer to have Esme stay here," Trudy said, "but I don't think that's such a good idea."

"No." Esme and Trudy together were not a good combination. I couldn't forget the handkerchief that went up in a puff of smoke.

Trudy's brow wrinkled with worry, and she opened the fridge. "You look a little peaky. Would you like a cupcake? I've got some day-olds."

I glanced at the Tupperware tub she pulled out.

"I better not." No telling what kind of spells were in them.

Trudy loaded me down with hay, food, a litter box, and a small paperback book called *Bunny Love—Living in Harmony with Our Long-Eared Companions.*

A midnight snack, a shower, and bed. That's what I envisioned on the quick drive to my house. Then maybe tomorrow I would wake up refreshed and see what I could find about hexes on the internet. A lot of misinformation was online, but you never knew when you'd hit on something useful. In my driveway I got out, spooked by a sound until I realized it was just the wind hitting Tannith's mobile and making the charms hanging on it clink together like chimes. Evidently the raccoons didn't want the thing any more than I did.

I had Esme in my arms and was trying to unlock the door when the sound of my name coming from the dark sent me rocketing into the air. I spun around, my arm protectively around Esme and my keys positioned in my fist like they taught in self-defense class.

"It's just me," a male voice said in a loud whisper.

When my eyes adjusted, "me" turned out to be Jeremy, approaching with his hands up. The gesture did nothing to calm my raging nerves. Why would he be here? How did he even know where I lived?

Either he was about to perpetrate a home invasion, or he was a Watcher.

"I don't know why you're here, but it's late. I've been working all evening."

"No, you haven't."

Crap. How did he know that?

How do you think?

He pushed his glasses up his nose, his gaze moving from the rabbit up to my face. "Don't you read your email? I wrote you several times today. Then I went by your office. Nobody was there."

"We rarely are. We're usually working off-site." At least he didn't say he'd been following me around town, or that he'd been at Esme's house.

His gaze focused on Esme. "Do you always carry your rabbit with you when you work?"

"No," I said quickly. "I'm just . . ." *What was he doing here?* My head ached from reading witchcraft books. I didn't have the mental agility to deal with this right now. "Trudy wanted me to keep this rabbit for her."

"So you've seen Trudy this evening?" he asked eagerly. "Has she heard from Laird?"

"Not—" I almost said *not exactly*, which would have raised more questions from Mr. Inquisitive. "No."

He exhaled in disappointment. "Can I talk to you for a moment? It's kind of important."

"It can't wait till tomorrow?"

"This is a life-or-death matter."

What *hadn't* been a life-or-death matter today?

"All right. What is it?"

He shifted. "Can't we go inside? You look kind of uncomfortable standing there." When I hesitated, he said, "You can text a friend."

I shook my head, not following. "Why?"

"To tell them I'm here. I'll give you my name and all my information. That way you'll know that I'm not a murderer or something."

"No, that would just mean that it would be likelier that you'd be caught in the event that you did murder me. Assuming all the information you gave me wasn't a lie to begin with."

He drew back. "Wow. That's some next-level paranoia."

I was beginning to think I wasn't paranoid enough. "How did you find out where I lived?"

"Your name was on your business card. I did an internet search. You're listed under one other address besides this one, but you weren't at the other place." He cleared his throat. "Obviously."

"You went to my old apartment?" I didn't like the sound of that.

"I know it sounds odd, but it's important that I talk to you. I could make you some tea. You look like you could use some."

Tea had sounded good fifteen minutes ago. Now I felt like I was going to need something stronger. "Couldn't you just tell me what it is you think is so urgent that you have to come over here in the middle of the night?"

"Okay." He let out a long breath. "I think Trudy's killed Laird. I'm considering going to the police."

I glanced around at my neighbor's houses, and around the yard. "You'd better come in."

Chapter 11

Jeremy was as good as his word—I showed him into the kitchen and he made herbal tea while I went back and forth to the Kia to retrieve the rabbit supplies. I didn't have a pen for Esme, but I thought it would probably be okay to let her go free range in the house. Neatnik Daniel would be appalled, but Daniel wasn't here.

I couldn't help noting how calm Esme was in the presence of Jeremy. When she and I were alone in the living room, I asked her what she thought. She merely looked at me.

"You talk to your rabbit?" Jeremy was standing in the doorway, regarding us with a puzzled expression.

"Doesn't everyone?" I straightened from my rabbit-communicating crouch. "Anyway, she's not mine. I'm just taking care of her. She and Trudy's other bun aren't getting along, so . . ."

He nodded toward Esme. "She seems pretty mellow."

Maybe I was wrong about Jeremy. Surely if he was a Watcher, Esme would be freaking out. Or at least thumping a warning at me. But she seemed okay with his being in the house.

I, on the other hand, was a nervous wreck. How was I going to convince him not to go to the police? Not that Trudy had killed anyone, but under the circumstances it might be hard to convince the police of that. If she was behaving erratically with family, I could just imagine how she'd stand up to a police interrogation. What if she ended up hexing a cop?

I followed Jeremy into the kitchen, where he handed me a mug of honey chamomile tea, my favorite.

"When I saw Trudy earlier today, she was completely coming unglued over the rabbit." Jeremy picked up his own mug. "I'm surprised she let you have him overnight."

"Her. This is Esmerelda."

"She said she thought someone had stolen him." His brows knit. "I'm sure she called that one a him."

I sat down at Daniel's chrome dinette. "Different rabbit."

"Right. But Trudy was, like, berserk almost."

"I left her a note, but I guess she didn't see it."

He took the chair opposite mine. One of his legs was fidgeting. I worried he wasn't buying my story.

"Look. I have to be honest with you. I seriously doubt that email I got today was from Laird."

Don't react. I blew on my tea and took a careful sip. "Why?"

"It just doesn't sound like him." Jeremy took out his phone, brought up his email, and showed it to me. "Read that."

> Jeremy: I'm in Iowa doing research. Had to leave on short notice, but I had an awesome opportunity to look at some interesting papers here. The information will be great for the book. Will tell you all about it upon my return. Regards, Laird

"Looks legit to me," I said.

Jeremy took his phone back and read the message to himself again. "It's so nonspecific. He doesn't even tell me what the opportunity is. And that word—*awesome*? That's not a Laird Webster word."

No, it was a Trudy Webster word.

"It's odd that he doesn't say why he's changed email accounts. He also fails to give me any instruction on what to do while he's gone. I could be organizing notes, or researching something here. It just seems strange for him to leave me hanging this way."

I cleared my throat. "Well, I did tell you I suspected that he and Trudy were going through a rough patch. She confirmed that for me today. Laird's probably not quite himself." Understatement of the century.

Jeremy scooted his chair closer to mine. "I'm worried that something very bad has happened to Laird."

I jerked my mug to my lips, trying to cover that my heart had stopped. The quick movement made me splosh tea on the table. "Like what?"

"Like he's dead," Jeremy said flatly.

I got up to retrieve a cloth from the sink to wipe up the spilled tea—and to avoid those green eyes seeing right through me. "If you think Trudy killed Laird, you need to think again. She wouldn't do anything like that."

"But she's so on edge. She acts guilty."

"She told me they had an argument. She probably feels bad about driving him away."

Jeremy leaned back again, drumming his fingers on the table.

"What you're suggesting is ridiculous," I insisted. "You don't know Trudy like I do. She wouldn't harm a fly." She might transform that fly into a rabbit, but that was another story.

"But what if it was accidental? During an argument, say, he might have fallen down the basement steps."

"Then he'd be in the hospital."

Jeremy's brows drew together. "He's not. I called all the ones in the area."

"You did?" Holy cats. This guy was nursing hard-core suspicions. Strangely, that gave me a little optimism. If he was wasting time calling hospitals, he clearly had no idea what had really happened—and certainly didn't suspect witchcraft. He wasn't trying to tease something he already knew out of me, as I assumed a Watcher would. Jeremy was still stumbling in the dark.

"No hospital or morgue in the area had Laird listed . . . but don't murderers usually hide the bodies of their victims?" Jeremy's mouth twisted. "How big is their backyard?"

"Stop! This is crazy talk. Just think. If she'd just murdered Laird and buried him under the begonias, why would she be so preoccupied with my taking her rabbit?"

"I suppose you're right. If she'd been trying to hide Laird's death, she wouldn't be obsessing over her pet."

It was ironic that Trudy's panic over rabbit-Laird was making Jeremy doubt she had killed person-Laird. "She especially wouldn't be involving you of all people in her problems."

"Why me *of all people*?"

"Because—sorry if this sounds harsh—we were thinking that it's odd that you've been stalking the house and obsessing over a guy who's just gone out of town for a few days."

"*Stalking?*" He straightened, feet flat on the floor. "I'm just worried."

I sipped my tea. If he wasn't telling the truth, he was the best liar in Zenobia. But even if he was simply worried about Laird, I needed to figure out a way to throw him off our scent.

Time to turn the tables on him. "I never cared what happened to any of my professors the way you're panicking about Laird's work trip."

"It just seems odd to me. The way Trudy acts toward me seems odd, too."

"They've been going through so much upheaval with the kids leaving and Laird going on sabbatical and being home all the time now. You know how that is."

"I don't. I've never been married."

"Right, and you don't have a significant other."

He looked almost offended. "How did you know that?"

"Because you're sitting here in the middle of the night, fixated on Laird Webster."

"Not fixated, not obsessed. Worried. *Somebody* ought to be. I don't mean to sound callous, but your cousin hardly seems to care about her husband's whereabouts at all."

"And you're a good judge of how people feel?"

"Well . . ." He shifted. "I notice things."

"What about me?"

His eyes widened. "You mean, have I noticed you? Of course."

"But you haven't sensed that I'm on edge, too, because my boyfriend's also on a business trip now. He texted me several times today and I haven't had a moment to myself to get back to him."

"Oh." Jeremy looked like he might launch out of his chair. "Sorry—I mean, I didn't know you were—that I might be intruding."

"That's what I mean. You aren't all-seeing." For a moment, I sipped tea and enjoyed his discomfort. "It's okay. Daniel's not about to walk through the door."

"Daniel." He said it as if he was discovering the name for the first time.

"Zenobia College research fellow. Entomology."

"Oh."

"I just wanted to point out that you might not be as observant as you think."

Jeremy's head bobbed. "Right."

Someone this goofy definitely couldn't be a Watcher. But that didn't mean he still couldn't be dangerous to us. "Where did you come from?"

"Missouri."

"You're a long way from there."

"Zenobia offered me a free ride. Did you attend Zenobia?"

"I did, but I grew up here, too."

"Were your parents professors at the college?"

"No, they own a restaurant here in town. The Buttered Biscuit."

His face lit up as if he were meeting a celebrity. "Are you kidding me? I go there all the time."

So did a lot of people. It was almost as much an institution in the town as the college itself.

"The owners—those are your parents?"

I nodded. "Yup."

He scrutinized me anew. "They're so nice. I forgot my wallet once and they just gave me a meal."

"That doesn't surprise me."

"I paid them back the same day," he assured me.

I laughed. "I believe you."

"So are you ever there?"

"Every morning." I glanced at the Kit-Kat Klock, whose stomach told me it was almost one in the morning. "In fact, I'll be swinging by there at around eight, so . . ."

"You eat breakfast there?"

"No, I drop off cupcakes there. Trudy makes them, I deliver them."

He sucked in a breath. "I've eaten those cupcakes."

I'd never felt so close to being a rock star. "All I do is deliver them, but I do have to get up early, so . . ."

He shot out of his chair. "I should go. Sorry if I kept you up too late."

"That's okay." I herded him toward the front door as efficiently as I could. "I'll probably see you around. Maybe at the Buttered Biscuit."

He stepped onto the porch. "Or maybe at Trudy's, after Laird gets back."

"Right."

The porch light hit his face as doubts resurfaced across it. He looked into my eyes, and then his gaze drifted lower. *Go home*, I thought.

"Well, I'll go home now."

His words made me flinch. Had my thoughts gotten through to him? "Good night."

"Good night, Gwen."

He buried his hands in his pockets, turned, and walked away.

Hopefully I'd seen the last of him for a while. A light breeze hit Tannith's mobile, causing the crystals on it to tinkle. I glared at it, annoyed. One of these days I needed to remember to get my stepladder out and take that thing down.

Chapter 12

Griz

The images inside the lava lamp fade away, leaving only blobs of color floating up and down in clear ooze.

"Who *is* this person?"

I've never seen my mistress so agitated. She paces restlessly, like I do when I spot another cat outside the patio door and I can't get out. In what Tannith calls our undisclosed location, there is no patio. But if she were a cat, she'd be seconds away from clawing glass.

As it is, I worry she will hurl the lava lamp at the wall, or at me. I slip a glance at the couch, ready to dive under it if her temper flares. The situation has grown uncomfortable. I miss home.

"Laird never mentioned a business trip to me." She stops, steepling her fingers in front of her in thought. "The man said Trudy was acting funny, though. He thinks she's a murderer!" Tannith laughs in delight at the thought. "That plodding school-teacher, a devious criminal? What a dolt that guy must be. A perfect companion for Gwen. Maybe I should call in a missing person report to the police, if he won't."

"Yes!" I chime, although I'm not entirely certain what she's talking about. Her suggestion simply seems to make her happy, which is a relief to see. Things have been tense these past few days. Tannith's plan hasn't worked out as she intended.

Her smile doesn't last. "I don't know where Laird is, though. I wish that idiot had been able to get Gwen to be more specific."

"I don't understand why he didn't. That's why he was there."

Tannith rolls her eyes. "I realize your brain is the size of a walnut, but surely even you picked up on the way those green eyes were looking at Gwen. Laird was a pretext." She shakes her head. "It's shocking what men can find attractive if they're desperate enough. And the moony way he was looking at her when he left? Pathetic. Why would Gwen encourage this guy? She must know she's not going to keep her claws in Daniel for long."

"She doesn't have claws."

"Don't be literal." Tannith resumes her pacing. "Stupid Trudy! Not knowing what's going on over there is so annoying. If she can't be bothered to put out the stuff I give her, I'm done giving her presents." She crosses her arms. "My so-called family are all such ingrates."

I twitch my tail in sympathy. That sympathy comes with a touch of irony. Tannith is all I have, and sometimes lately I also get the feeling she doesn't appreciate me. How can that be? She was my rescuer. I had a life before we met, of course—I have a few pleasant memories of my early days, of cuddling in a furry pile of siblings, of a maternal sandpaper tongue giving me a bath. Perhaps I didn't appreciate my family enough. I always set myself slightly apart from the litter, believing I was special, and dreamed of a wider world. One day I saw a hole in the fence and I took my chance.

The chaos of the world overwhelmed me at once. Machines threatened to flatten me. Dogs with fierce jowls strained at leashes to get at me. I crawled up a tree and got stuck. Humiliatingly, a fireman rescued me and I was delivered to a house of incarceration. I was still a kitten—a fact in my favor—but I was also a short-haired black cat, which apparently meant I was less desirable.

Except to very special people, it turned out.

When Tannith peered into my cage, I sensed at once I'd found my soul mate, my destiny. We could even communicate! I felt that I'd discovered a being who saw the specialness in me.

Since Tannith found me, I've tried to be everything she wanted me to be. Perhaps I've fallen short. I don't think I've ever delivered on the black-cat magic she expected me to have. But I have never given Tannith anything less than my full devotion.

Now I'm beginning to wonder if she feels anything for me. Can one-sided devotion sustain our relationship?

In exasperation, she throws herself down into an easy chair and steeples her fingertips in thought. "The thing I really don't get is Gwen having that rabbit. And calling her Esmerelda—is that a joke on Aunt Esme?"

"None of them have your cleverness."

She shrugs. "Milo can be amusing, but hanging around with Gwen and Trudy too much has dulled his wits, too."

Earlier we'd been watching her male cousin.

"Why is Aunt Esme in the hospital?" she wonders aloud.

Brett had mentioned that twice. He'd wanted to know which hospital their aunt was in, so he could send flowers. *Why would you send flowers to one of my distant relatives you've never even met?* Milo had asked him.

Why would you abandon an important fundraiser for a distant relation you apparently don't even want flowers sent to? Brett had shot back.

They were at a stalemate and went to bed thirty minutes apart.

Tannith growls in frustration. "They're all up to something. It's driving me crazy."

"You expected them to react badly."

"But not like this! I intended that letter to send them spinning like skittles. This secretiveness isn't like them. It's as if they're coordinating something." She frowns. "What if they're planning revenge on me?"

I blink. If they're that foolish, they'll get what they deserve. Tannith is cleverer than they are. She will always win.

At least, that's what Tannith tells me.

"It's as if they've figured out that I've been spying on them. But they couldn't have—Milo and Gwen wouldn't have left out my gifts if that were the case."

"Unless they're trying to mislead you."

She laughs. "You think they're chess players? They can barely think one move ahead, never mind two or three. No, the key is Trudy's house. I need to know what's going on in there. Unfortunately, I can't waltz up to the door now that I've sent out that letter."

Is she admitting to making a mistake? A tactical error? I look away, uncomfortable.

"I need a way to make them let me in without their knowing what I'm up to."

While she plots, I swish my tail and eye a wadded piece of paper I batted under a chair earlier in the day. It's still there, acting as if it's found a safe haven. That's what I was letting it think. *Stay smug, Mr. Paper Wad.*

Tannith claps her hands, and I hop in surprise. She smiles at me in a way I don't like.

"I've got it!" She stands, grinning like summer has come nine months early. "They're such animal lovers. They would *never* abandon an animal in distress."

"What animal?" I ask, but her crafty smile as she stares at me tells the tale. A hair ball churns in my gut.

"Pack your bags, Griz. You're going visiting."

Chapter 13

Gwen

As I went through the zombie motions of getting up and dressed, it was like any normal day. Humming, I washed my face, dragged a brush through my hair, then pulled on jeans, shirt, cardigan, and boots. Everything was hunky-dory until I walked into the living room and the sight of Esme sitting up on the couch brought me up short.

"Good morning," I said, not wanting to be rude.

She hopped down, followed me into the kitchen, and hunched by her bowl.

Normal days don't begin with filling a plastic bowl with green pellets for your aunt.

What would I have done if Daniel had been here? He didn't like cats, so I could just imagine what he'd say to having a rabbit in the house. At least in her current incarnation, Esme was a vegetarian. They had that in common.

I downed a cup of coffee, though I doubted one cup would do it this morning. It all came back to me now. Last night after Jeremy had left, I'd stayed up too late worrying. Then I'd started worrying about not getting enough sleep before my alarm went off. I tried counting sheep, but the critters hurtling through my head morphed into rabbits and toads.

My phone vibrated on the counter and I picked it up before the ringer went off. It was Daniel.

"I expected you to call me back last night," he said by way of greeting.

"I'm sorry. Things have been busy. I didn't get back from Trudy's till late."

"Didn't you see my texts?"

"Um . . ." I bit my lip. How many had there been? I remembered a few, but then I'd tuned out. It was hard to concentrate on anything but the craziness going on. "Sorry. I collapsed last night. Is something wrong? I'm running a little late, so—"

"There's something I needed to ask you, but never mind."

"If it's about what you wanted to discuss, I think I know what it is."

"No, you don't," he said quickly. "I probably shouldn't be talking to you about it anyway. I'll call Jane."

"*Mom?*"

He laughed. "Moms know us better than anyone, right?"

"Um, no." I frowned, confused. Would he be calling my mom if he was about to run away with Tannith? "Maybe you should just tell me what this is about."

"Nope, it's a surprise."

"Yeah, but—"

"Just go to work. I'll call you later. You're always fuzzy in the morning."

That was news to me. "Need I remind you that surprises can be too . . . surprising?"

"Not this one. It'll knock you off your feet."

After he hung up, I stood in the kitchen, ill at ease. He didn't talk like a guy about to dump me. That should have been comforting . . . except for that business about calling Mom. Why would he do that?

Esme thumped to draw my attention to her bowl, which was empty again.

"Sorry." I dropped another handful of pellets in. "That was Daniel."

The rabbit sent me a look that told me she cared as little about my personal life now as she had when she was a human.

While she was having seconds, I texted Kyle to let him know I was running late and that he and Taj should meet me over at Mrs. Caputo's.

After Esme was done eating, I loaded her up and headed over to Trudy's for the cupcake handoff. Trudy could have delivered the cupcakes herself, since she wasn't going to school, but I wanted to keep the routine as normal as possible so my parents wouldn't suspect anything was amiss. The fewer people who knew about the mess we were in, the better.

As I climbed the steps to Trudy's porch, a pet carrier on the welcome mat caused me to freeze. It was similar to the one in my car that Esme was sitting in. I approached it slowly, leaned down, and nearly fell back on my butt when Griz meowed at me.

I dropped to my knees. "Hello, Grizzlefellow," I cooed through the carrier's grill. "What are you doing here?"

And how long had he been sitting out here?

He hissed, and I laughed. Griz and I were old friends. Tannith had dropped him off with me the year before while she'd been on vacation. He acted aloof and temperamental sometimes, but I could tell he was just a big softy underneath. I love cats. Even cranky ones. My parents hadn't let me have one growing up; I think they considered any cat to be too witchy for comfort. The official reason had been that Tannith was allergic, but who'd ended up adopting a cat out on her own and *not* reacting with so much as a sniffle?

I cast a worried glance at the door. Was Tannith inside talking to Trudy?

The morning breeze brought my attention to a taped note fluttering on the top of Griz's carrier. A familiar cursive *T* graced the flap of the envelope.

I stood and knocked on the door. Trudy didn't even get a greeting out before I thrust a finger at the carrier. "Will you look at this? She's dumping her cat on you. The nerve of that woman."

Trudy was still blinking in confusion when I handed her the note. She obviously hadn't gotten much sleep, either. "Why would she do that?"

"Because she's a monster. Although I'm sure she's got some flimsy, self-serving rationalization." It would have to be a doozy after that letter she sent us all.

Trudy glanced around the porch and at the neighboring yards. "You'd better come inside."

Good thing one of us was thinking. I was so distracted by Griz that I'd forgotten to be paranoid about Watchers. I picked up the carrier and lugged him in. "I've got Esme in the Kia. I thought she'd enjoy coming with us better than staying at our place."

"Of course," Trudy said. "And we might need her."

I set Griz's carrier down and made little kisses through the bars as Trudy opened Tannith's envelope. Griz growled. "You're such a little crankster," I said.

Tannith did not deserve him.

When she was done reading the note, Trudy handed it to me.

> *Dearest Ermintrude,*
> *I know you love animals almost as much as I do, so I'm entrusting Griz to your loving care for a few days. The place I'm staying—temporarily—doesn't allow pets.*
> *I hope you're not too worried about Friday, but even if you are, I know you won't take your anxiety out on little Grizzle.*
> *See you soon!*
> *Regards,*
> *T*

That was it?

"She's a horror." I bestowed a sympathetic look on Griz. "Poor little guy."

Trudy was distressed. "What's her plan? She gets my husband, I get her cat?"

"From what you've been saying about Laird, you'd come out ahead in that deal."

Trudy folded her arms. "She's pushing me, knowing I'll take care of her cat even though I'm boiling with anger at her."

"*Are* you boiling with anger over Laird? After all . . ." I cast a quick glance at the pathetic creature in the terrarium.

"It's the principle of the thing. He's Drew and Molly's father. For all Tannith knows, she's hitting my house like a human home-wrecking ball."

"I wish *I* could keep Griz." I unlatched the metal grate and reached deep into the carrier to pull him out. That was a feat in itself, since he did the usual cat thing of resisting being tugged out. I had to brace the carrier with my feet to extract him. Once he was free, I smothered him in a hug and gave him a noisy kiss on the top of his head while he did his best to eviscerate me with his back claws.

"Ooh, look at your fancy new collar." It was black leather with stainless steel studs. I inspected the tag dangling from it, checking to see if Tannith had inadvertently tipped us off about her new location. But the disk was just a round, two-sided mirror medallion.

"His tag's blank," I told Trudy. "Does she just not have her next address to etch on it, or do you think it's a fancy readable chip?"

Trudy took a sip of coffee and shrugged. "Might be a reflective device to alert birds."

I lifted Griz by his armpits so that we were eye to eye. "You wouldn't attack a bird, would you? Not my sweet Grizzle-belly."

He fidgeted until I finally let him go, whereupon he fled back into his box. Tannith had traumatized the poor guy.

"It takes him a little while to warm up to a new place," I told Trudy. "When he stayed with me at my old apartment, I coaxed him out by shaking a bag of dry food at him."

Trudy sipped her coffee. "What am I going to do with him?

I've already got Peaches, and now there's . . ." She frowned. "I'm sure it's not safe to leave toads around cats."

I'd forgotten. "But we'll be taking the terrarium with us, so you just have to worry about Peaches. I'm sure they'll be fine. Griz is a little sweetheart."

"Molly and Drew would kill me if anything happened to Peaches."

"Shut Peaches in their room, then."

I helped her move the rabbit pen to the twins' room. When we came out, Griz had crawled out of the carrier again and was watching us, his tail swishing fitfully. He looked so small and forlorn. So alone.

"Maybe we should have left Peaches out after all," I said. "Griz'll be lonely."

Trudy released a breath. "Better he's lonely than Peaches ends up as cat chow." I must have looked as doleful as Griz because Trudy lifted her arms with a sigh. "Don't worry—I'll leave the television on for company while we're gone. Cats like television."

"They do?"

She blinked. "They do on YouTube."

Neither of us had ever had a cat. I was going to google it, but when I opened my phone, the time startled me. "I'd better get going." I grabbed the boxes of cupcakes. Trudy was a whiz. There were the same two and a half dozen as always.

"I'll just run these by the Biscuit and then meet you at the house," I told her. "Do you need the key?"

"I still have a couple of things to do here. You'll probably get there before I do."

"Okay." I bent down to Griz, who arched and hissed. I laughed. "Have a good day, sweetie pie."

The Buttered Biscuit was hopping when I arrived, which was just as well. The less I chatted with my folks, the better.

Unfortunately, Dad spotted me as I was handing off the boxes to one of the employees and hurried over before I could make my getaway. "Your friend is here." He pointed to a corner table. Jeremy waved at me.

I groaned. Just when I'd convinced myself he couldn't be a Watcher . . .

Dad looked puzzled by my reaction but was sidetracked when a nearby customer asked him if the biscuits could be made gluten-free. *It was on the menu.* Four high school summers spent working for my parents was enough for me to know I would never have the patience to own a restaurant.

I went over to Jeremy's table. "Is this a coincidence?"

"Not exactly. You put the idea in my head. I have a nine o'clock class, so I thought a little fortification might be a good idea."

I let out a breath. *If that's all this is . . .*

"And I hoped I'd get to see you." Noting my distress, he continued, "I mean, I know there's Daniel, so I wasn't thinking— well, you know. I just enjoyed talking to you last night."

He had? "I thought it was more like a question-and-answer session than an actual conversation."

"I learn a lot about people through asking questions."

If he was a Watcher, he was so cagey. "What's your class this morning?"

"American History overview. We're reviewing the first section, the dry stuff the students snooze through." He laughed. "Until the Salem witch trials. Everybody loves that unit."

"Are you kidding?"

"Well, it's dramatic."

I scowled. "They weren't even witches."

He blinked at me. "I'm sorry?"

"They weren't witches. That was the whole point. The entire episode should be called the Fatal Misogyny Tragedy. Well, maybe *one* of them might have been a witch. But the rest were just women people didn't like for one reason or another. Not witches."

"Yeah, obviously." He looked as if he was about to laugh again, but then he read my expression and sobered. "I mean, it was tragic, yes. That's why it grabs the students' interest."

Would a Watcher be able to bring himself to dismiss witches like that? No. But even if Jeremy wasn't a Watcher, what did it matter? This was not a friendship I should be pursuing. I was a witch by birth, my cousin had turned Jeremy's mentor into a toad, and anyway, I had Daniel. Or maybe I didn't have Daniel. But even if I was actually single and didn't yet know, did I want to get involved with another academic, another witch skeptic?

It just wouldn't work, Daniel or no Daniel. Green eyes or no green eyes.

"Do you like cats?" I asked him.

He put down his fork. "My cat Herman died last summer. I had to put him down. Stomach cancer."

I sank down in the empty chair opposite him. "I'm sorry."

"It's okay. He was eighteen."

"That's old bones. You must have been a good owner."

"Why did you ask me about cats?"

I frowned. The question had just popped out. "I'm thinking I might have a future as a cat lady. But I've never adopted one. Or any animal. Just been a petsitter a few times."

"That's right. Esmerelda isn't yours."

"No, I'll only have her for a few days, I hope."

"You hope?"

That made me sound callous. On the other hand, why did I care what Jeremy thought about me?

He leaned forward. "Don't worry. It's different when they're your own."

I braced myself against his disarming smile by flipping my phone open to check the time. "I really need to get going if I'm going to swing by and check on my crew."

"Don't you work with them?"

"Most days, I do. Today I have another job to tend to." I stood up.

"Anything fun?"

I backed away, which seemed the safest response to his nosiness. "Definitely not fun. Just, you know, work. Nothing you'd be interested in."

"Well, maybe I'll see you around sometime."

"I wouldn't wonder. I seem to bump into you several times per day now."

I waved goodbye to my dad, who was pretending he hadn't been watching me talking to Jeremy. He gave me a thumbs-up. God only knows what he meant by that. My parents always swore that they liked Daniel well enough, but in my experience when something is qualified with *well enough*, it means it'll do until something better comes along. I'm sure that's what they were hoping now—that Jeremy was that something better that would save them from having to interact with an uptight entomologist for the rest of their lives.

It was saying something about these last days that the biggest preoccupation of my life for the past six months—Daniel, and our future together—had taken a back seat to a rabbit, a toad, and a mysterious history student who kept popping up when I least expected it.

Chapter 14

Mrs. Caputo wasn't looking her best. She greeted me in a saggy yellow robe, her wig slightly askew. I debated whether to say anything about her crooked hair, but decided she needed understanding more than correction.

"Is everything okay?" I tried to keep my head from listing to the side as if to compensate for her wig imbalance.

"I'm not at my perkiest this morning, that's for sure." She and a barking Binky led me back to her kitchen, which was dominated by a round breakfast table covered with a retro vinyl cloth. "I should never try to keep up with those boys."

I drew back. "Kyle and Taj aren't letting you do any of their work, are they? I told them that you said you shouldn't carry heavy things. Especially on stairs."

"Oh, no—they wouldn't let me lift a finger. They're perfect gentlemen." She sank down into a plastic-cushioned chair that expelled a sigh. "It's just that I'm not used to their music."

My antennae were up. I had strict rules about playing music in other people's houses or work spaces while we did our jobs. "What music?"

She frowned in thought. "I'm not sure what they call it. Techo-something? It was that repetitive backbeat stuff with singers who talk and gesticulate. It's not bad, but it's so much *louder* in person than when you see little bits of it on the television when you're flipping through channels."

I'd have to have a talk with the guys. "Would you like some coffee?" I asked, even though this was her home.

"That's kind of you. I have a pot of half caf already made in the Mr. Coffee."

I hurried over to the counter and poured coffee into a mug that declared GRANDMA IS MY NAME, BRIDGE IS MY GAME. "Sugar?"

"I've got the bowl over here." After I gave the cup to her, she heaped two spoonfuls into it and stirred. "I'm no prude, God knows. The first live concert I ever saw was Cream at the Eastman Theatre in Rochester. Now *that* was music. And Clapton . . ." She smiled in dreamy memory as she sipped her brew. "I was a wild girl before I settled down with Henry, but I couldn't even figure out how to dance to that stuff last night. Though I seemed to manage well enough to feel it in my sacroiliac this morning."

"Wait—you, Kyle, and Taj *went out* to listen to music?" I was trying not to get distracted by the image of Bridge Grandma doing hip-hop moves. "Last night, after dinner?"

"Well, we stopped at a few bars first. But there wasn't really anything doing at any of them. It was all pretty chill."

What the heck was going on here? Leave these three on their own for a few days, throw in some Strawberry Bliss cupcakes, and it turns into a weird intergenerational debauch.

"We'll be out of your hair soon." Then I wished I hadn't mentioned hair.

"No hurry." She smiled. "I'm fond of both of them."

I needed these guys to finish up the attic before this turned into some kind of Harold and Maude and Harold scenario.

I went up to the attic and found Kyle and Taj among the stacks of boxes that needed to be moved to the nearly cleared garage, and bags full of garbage destined for either the garbage pod out front or various recycling centers and charitable-donation sites. They'd barely made a dent.

Since I'd inadvertently drugged them with cupcakes and then bugged out on them, I could hardly complain.

"Hey, Gwen," Kyle said. The two of them looked like they were moving in slow motion. "How's it going?"

"I can't stay long this morning. But you two have it under control, right?"

"Sure," Taj said.

"Good." I held out the box of hopefully non-intoxicating cupcakes. "Here you go. Bittersweet chocolate and butterscotch." I was taking Trudy's word that only the strawberry ones had been enchanted.

My employees were on that box like zombies scenting brains. This was not good. Never mind the weirdness going on with Mrs. Caputo, I'd created two cupcake fiends. Bittersweet chocolate and plain butterscotch. Nothing bewitching about those, I hoped. Milo had eaten an Ebony and Ivory yesterday and seemed fine all day.

"It might be a little hard to reach me today," I warned them. "The place I'm working is sort of isolated."

"'Kay," Kyle said through half a cupcake. They both looked completely unconcerned about where I would be, or if I ever came back.

Next week I would wean them off cupcakes and start them on energy bars.

"Try to be kind to Mrs. Caputo today. She's not used to twentysomething hours."

"That woman?" Taj laughed. "She's got more sauce in her than most of the girls I know."

"We've barely had any sleep," Kyle complained.

I wasn't sure I wanted to hear any more details. "Just get the attic done. I'll call this evening."

You should be here, helping. Then again, I also needed to help turn my cousin's husband back into a human again. Not to mention my aunt. *Family first*, I told myself.

*   *   *

Milo and Trudy were waiting for me when I arrived, sitting on the porch next to a large ice chest. My heart lifted. "Did you already find ingredients for spells?"

"No, this is lunch," Trudy explained, "plus some sodas. I'm not eating or drinking anything from inside that house."

Probably not a bad idea. We hauled Esme, Laird, and the ice chest down to Esme's lab. Once we'd unloaded, we popped open drinks and faced the task at hand. The wall of books, which had seemed to hold so much promise the previous evening, looked more daunting now that I knew how dense and impenetrable most of the tomes on those shelves were.

"This is ridiculous," Milo said. "If we knew the spell Esme used to change Laird into a toad, we would probably have better luck finding what we would need to reverse it."

I agreed, but one big obstacle remained. "Unless you can interpret nose twitches and thumps, I don't know how you'll find out what spell Esme used."

"Warlock Holmes was up early this morning on Cackle," he replied. "I learned that every witch worth their salt keeps a Book of Shadows."

My expression was probably as blank as Trudy's.

"It's a log a witch keeps to detail everything they've learned about the craft," he explained. "My guess is Esme would have made a notation of the Laird spell somewhere, unless the spell was one she'd already used so often that she didn't feel the need to write it down."

Hope bloomed inside me. "That's great!"

Another sensation also shivered through me as he mentioned the Book of Shadows, as if some force had hit a tuning fork inside me and it was vibrating all through my bones. It wasn't that I wanted to be a real, practicing witch, but at the thought of accumulating all this knowledge and personalizing it, something primal tugged at me. What had Esme learned—and what powers had she taught herself to wield?

I looked around at the laboratory. Had she chiseled this cave herself, or had that been magic, too? Then my gaze fell on the terrariums of toads, frogs, and newts. And Esme herself, munching on timothy hay.

The idea of possessing so much power was awesome, yet horrible. I needed to get my work done here and get out of this place or I would become as compromised as Esme, not to mention as prone to being cursed by the powers that be.

Suppress your powers and you become a danger to everyone, most of all yourself, Esme had warned. I didn't view her as a fount of wisdom, but was she right about this? If I continued on like Mom and Dad, obeying the rules of the Edict, was I going to be like Trudy someday and just start spitting out spells and hexes helter-skelter?

Focus. Getting Laird and Esme back to normal came first. After that I could concentrate on witch self-care.

"We need to consult Esme," I said. My cousins looked at me blankly. "She helped us find the key last night. Why shouldn't she lead us to her Book of Shadows?"

We crossed over to speak to her. She stopped munching mid-blade and crooked an ear.

"You'll show us where you've hidden your Book of Shadows, won't you?" I asked.

Esme thumped, startling us. No matter how many times it happened, I just didn't expect animals to be able to understand me.

"Does a thump mean yes?" Milo asked. "Thump once for yes." She thumped.

"Is it in this room?"

Thump thump.

"So it's somewhere else in the house?"

Thump.

Milo crossed his arms. "Twenty questions with a rodent. This should be fun."

"Okay," I said. "So while Trudy and I continue reading through the library for spells, maybe you should hunt through the house for Esme's Book of Shadows."

Milo liked that idea. He was a born snoop. "Not the stinky parts, though."

"Especially the stinky parts," I said. "Remember, she'd be hiding the book from a potential Watcher. She obviously thought dead-rat smell would repel them."

"It certainly repels me."

After Milo and Esme left, Trudy and I seated ourselves at the base of the bookcase. I'd picked up a promising book called *Maledictions, Conjure Bags, and Philactery: A Neophyte's Grimoire*. So much of this information was new to me that I often fell down research rabbit holes to be able to parse the meaning of sentences. All this knowledge to absorb. I kept getting sidetracked by topics that interested me. *Disappearing spells*. I wouldn't mind trying one of those. I started taking notes—then remembered unfortunate Cousin Odin. I didn't want to end up like him, disappearing forever. Also, this wasn't about me.

Still, with each new page, I regretted my ignorance. How different my life would have been if I'd been allowed to learn with my peers. I didn't want to turn people into toads, and I certainly didn't want to cause another Dust Bowl. The world had enough problems. But surely witches could also harness all this craft for the greater good. Or maybe just my greater good.

Trudy let out a huff and dropped the book she was looking through, which sent up a cloud of dust when it hit the floor. "This all sounds like gobbledygook to me. What if we can't reverse the spell? Molly and Drew will have to be told." She sniffed and said wistfully, "I was just beginning to look forward to them striking out on their own, maybe getting married. I love weddings. How can I tell my daughters that their father will have to hop them down the aisle?"

"We'll figure this out."

"If only I hadn't hexed him." She shook her head. "I don't know why I lost control. His leaving me shouldn't have hurt. I don't love *him* anymore either, if it comes to that. My pride was hurt because he was announcing a separation. I immediately worried about having to tell people and explain to the girls, and of course I knew Laird would find someone else."

"You don't know that."

She shot me a you've-got-to-be-kidding look. "Men always find someone else. Even Charles Manson found someone else."

"Well, if Laird wanted to move to the basement, he certainly hadn't found anyone else yet."

"If that's the case, then what he's essentially saying is that he prefers solitude to being with me." She laughed. "But that's how I've felt for years! You know why those cupcakes were Strawberry Bliss?"

I shook my head.

"Because aside from my panic at getting caught for having Thumper-ized my husband, I was *happy*. I loved playing my own music loudly again, and my new furniture. I loved the idea of not living on pins and needles because Laird needs conditions to be just so in order to concentrate on Herbert Flippin' Hoover. When I made those cupcakes that afternoon, I really felt blissful, and sanguine about my life. I mean, thirty-nine is really nothing these days. And I've already raised a family. I can coast. Everything will be good."

This talk of Laird made me remember Jeremy. "Did you happen to write Jeremy an email as Laird?"

"Yes—did he get it?"

"He got it, but I'm not sure he bought it."

"Why not?"

"You didn't use Laird's usual email address, for one thing."

"Of course not. I don't know Laird's password."

"Jeremy's suspicious."

She started pacing. "It's so unfair. Why couldn't Laird have just behaved like a normal jerk husband and moved in with another woman or gone to a hotel. If he'd left, he wouldn't have been there for me to hex him."

"Not that I want to defend Laird, but maybe he was trying to let you down easy or thought it would be more economical."

"I don't care. He should have had the decency to get out of my sight."

When she started pacing toward the terrarium, I said, "Trudy, come back here. Stay away from Laird."

It was bad enough he was a toad. Toads, according to the references I'd come across, were fundamental animal spells. I was fairly certain we could find a reversal solution somewhere in Esme's library. So far, though, I'd seen no mention of rabbits. Rabbits seemed to be a specific quirk of Trudy's. If she turned Laird into a rabbit again, he would be thrice changed, which, from what I'd been reading, was not a good thing. According to the literature, flesh could only trans-speciate so many times before it started wearing out like an old sock.

"We need to be careful," I told her. "We have to learn to witch responsibly."

She sank down on the floor next to me. "It's so hard to believe that I have this . . . tic."

"Just try not to look at anyone when you're feeling angry."

As surreptitiously as I could manage, I scooted a little farther away from her. Why take chances?

She sighed. I wasn't too enthusiastic about hitting the books again myself. My eyes were beginning to itch from staring at tiny print, as well as from the spores of mold or dust or whatever all those aged tomes were emitting when we opened them for the first time in who knows how many eons. Esme's lab seemed clean enough, but the books could have stood a good going over with a Dustbuster.

"Where did she get all of these books?" I wondered aloud as I got back to the grimoire I'd been looking at this morning.

"Probably ordered them from somewhere."

Like Milo, Aunt Esme must have been cultivating a fake witch persona all these years. She'd probably been buying these books online wherever she could find them. Unlike Milo, however, she hadn't been getting her jollies merely spying on her witch brethren. She'd dedicated every bit of her free time to educating herself. Now we were trying to absorb knowledge in mere hours that had taken Esme decades to acquire. We were staking our future—not to mention Laird's and Esme's lives—on our shaky abilities.

I'd been daydreaming over the same musty page for ten minutes when Milo burst through the door. Esme hopped in after him before the lab portal closed.

In his hands, he carried a coffee-table-size book with a gorgeous red leather cover. "Esme's Book of Shadows. She hid it under the clothes dryer. Unfortunately, it was in the smelliest part of the house. I desperately need a shower."

I jumped to my feet. "First we desperately need to read that book."

"It's so big," Trudy said.

"I worried about that, too." Milo started flipping through the pages. "But then I realized that if Esme could lead us to the book, she could also lead us to the correct passage in the book."

With a flourish, he pointed to a carefully handwritten page reading *For Spellcasting Humans to Reptile, Amphibian, or Insect Form.*

"He's already a toad," I reminded him.

"Patience, patience." Milo flipped forward a few pages. As the pages moved the air, I got a good whiff of the funk coming off him. The dead-rat smell was so pungent, it was all I could do not to pull the collar of my shirt up over my nose. Judging from the thinning of Trudy's lips, she was dealing with the same struggle.

"Here." He stopped again. The book was as beautifully written as one of those ancient texts copied out and illustrated in bright colors by medieval monks. On this particular page, there were fanciful illustrations of frogs hopping up and down the margins of the page in brilliant greens, red, and gold.

I glanced over at the rabbit, who was nibbling hay nearby. "I never knew Esme was such a brilliant artist."

"Maybe she did that with witchcraft, too," Trudy said.

Why not? Ink on paper had to be easier to manipulate than flesh and blood. If she could learn to cast spells like a wizard, who was to say she couldn't figure out how to illuminate her manuscript like a fourteenth-century monk?

"It's written down here in black and white," Milo said. "How to reverse a toad spell."

Despite the odor, Trudy and I leaned in. "But it's not a spell." She frowned. "It's a potion."

"Even better," Milo said. "Presumably if we cook this up properly, we won't even have to worry about our powers. Right?"

"I've only ever done a hex." Trudy's tone was doubtful.

"Your uncontrollable hexing is what got us into this mess," he said with exasperation. "The beauty of this is that I or even Gwen should be able to handle getting Laird back to normal."

I rounded on him. "What do you mean, *even Gwen?*"

"I know, I know. You achieved amazing feats with Barbie dolls."

"Oh, and has Warlock Holmes done any better?"

"You think I was just hanging out on Cackle all the time for no reason at all?" He ducked his head modestly. "I've done a little spellcasting."

I thought so! "Like what?"

He shrugged. "Just . . . dabbling."

"What kind of spells?"

He cleared his throat and blurted out, "Okay, okay. I put a spell on Brett after I first met him. Just one teeny spell."

My mouth dropped open. "That's completely unethical!"

"Oh, come on. Everybody does it. Every witch, that is. Looking from the outside in, it sure seems that there's a lot more hocus-pocus hanky-panky going on than the witch world wants to fess up to."

"That could just be people bragging on Cackle and eCharmed."

"Maybe, but the truth is, *I* did it." Milo frowned. "Or I think I did."

Now I could understand why he was so paranoid about Tannith. "You're worried that if you put a spell on Brett, Tannith would be able to put one on him or even reverse yours that easily."

While we were talking, Trudy had commandeered Esme's Book of Shadows.

"This is crazy, guys," she said, her nose buried in the book. "We're supposed to gather all this weird stuff together and boil it down for *three hours*. Then we have to make Laird drink it."

"How do you make a toad drink?" I asked.

Trudy was so deep in study that she barely seemed to hear me. "Eight leaves of rue and bay and lavender." Her face scrunched. "That doesn't sound like a very good recipe to me."

"It's not for cupcakes," Milo said. "I doubt it's supposed to taste good."

"Definitely not. The next ingredient is a personal item of the toad victim, followed by a bear's tooth, oak bark, and the thirteen snails."

My lip curled. "I wouldn't want to drink it."

"Getting Laird to drink isn't the issue," Trudy said. "Where are we going to find a bear's tooth?"

"My house," Milo said simply.

"You have a bear sitting at home?" Trudy asked, astonished.

And then I remembered. "The rug!"

Around the time our ignominious ancestor Lucian Zimmer was busy turning the entire Midwest into a desiccated wasteland, Brett's great-great-grandfather was an arctic explorer. It wasn't clear if he'd actually discovered anything, but he had used up quite a bit of his family's fortune, lost an earlobe to frostbite, and destroyed whatever wildlife crossed his path. Various gruesome souvenirs of his arctic exploits had been parceled out to his family: walrus tusks, etched whale teeth, and furs of all types. A polar-bear rug had been passed on to Brett when an uncle died.

"If it's a single tooth we need, I'm sure I could pull one without Brett noticing," Milo said.

I wished there was a way to be certain this could work. "We need to make sure it's safe to give this potion to Laird. What if his matter's been transformed too often?"

I was assuming that merely changing color didn't count.

"You said three times was the beginning of the danger limit," Milo said.

I looked down at Esme, whose nose seemed to be twitching at me with interest. "You didn't turn Laird into anything else before he became a toad, did you?"

She thumped twice.

An idea occurred to me. "Wouldn't this all be easier if we simply brought Esme back first?" I nodded toward the book. "Is there anything in there about reversing rabbit spells?"

Milo lowered his voice and turned slightly away from Esme. "I asked her about that already. She doesn't seem to know anything about rabbit spells. I think that's why she turned Laird into a toad. It's what she's most familiar with."

This news made us all shift uncomfortably. Even if we were successful transforming Laird, it appeared we would have our work cut out for us trying to get Esme back. And if we *couldn't* get her back, it would only be a matter of time until the Council found out about all of this and came after us.

Chapter 15

Griz

I am alone. As alone as I have ever felt in my life.

Tannith left me here. Just dumped me on the porch. In the cold. That's what I'm still trying to absorb. At least I'm inside now, but everything's unfamiliar. Some kind of animal is locked in a room nearby, the sickeningly sweet smell of sugar permeates everything, and a large television has been left on with the volume up at levels that drive me to distraction. Of course the images flickering there draw my attention. But instead of being entertained, I'm disoriented. This is a nightmare.

She also gave me an ultimatum: *Find out what's going on there, or else.*

Or else what? She'll abandon me here permanently? Take me back to the shelter? Hex me? There's no telling what she'll do when she's angry. It's the not knowing that's terrifying—that and the sinking feeling that I'm being set up to fail.

How can I function under this kind of pressure?

Nostalgia for our old life consumes me. Just a week ago, we were so happy. It was just Tannith and me in our cozy little house, with a yard I was free to meander into at will. That was part of my black-cat magic power—I could walk through doors to the outside world. Well, at least through the door that had a flap on it. Both at our temporary location and here, the doors don't allow me to walk through them. I feel trapped and a little foolish. I have one less power than I believed. Which means I have no power at all, except that of communicating with Tannith. But she doesn't seem to listen to me anyway. Is one-way communication real communication?

I glance up at the television. The people on it have changed. Now it's a large crowd listening to a plump man in a suit. Dr. Tim, he's called. He's talking about marriage, and faithfulness, and weathering times of trouble as a couple. People join him, weeping in sorrow at what messes they've made of their lives. They're living examples of situations that can test a marriage—money problems, differences concerning the raising of children, drug dependency.

My tail is twitching. Those poor fools think *they* have problems. No one knows what it's like to be dumped on a porch, in the cold, and to be simultaneously told to spy on people *and* be left entirely alone in an empty house. To be tasked with watching people who aren't even around.

The man on the screen puts his arms around a frumpy woman. "I know your pain," he says. "Your suffering is real."

I blink. The timbre of his voice is so warm, so kind, it's like he's speaking to *me*. I would do anything to have Tannith put her arms around me like that right now.

"What are you doing!"

I shoot up several feet in the air and come down, arched and bristling. I hop about for a moment, wondering where Tannith's voice came from. When she speaks again, I realize the voice is coming from the disk on my collar. This freaks me out even more, and it's a moment before I manage to regain my composure. I hope she's not seeing this in the lava lamp.

"What's going on, Griz?"

"Nothing," I answer quickly.

"What? I can't hear you. Why is the television playing so loud?"

"I don't know. She turned it on before she left."

"Hm." The suspicion in her voice ramps up a notch. "Wonder what *that's* covering up."

"There's some kind of animal in a closed room nearby."

"What is it?"

"I don't know. I only got a glimpse, and I can't smell anything but sugar."

She sputters. "I don't need to smell it. Just describe it."

"It's about my size—only bunchier, with far-bigger ears than necessary."

"For God's sake, don't you know what a rabbit is?"

"Oh." I've heard the word, but I've never seen one. I feel foolish, but I cover it with defensiveness. "How should I know anything about rabbits? Except for my forays into our yard, I'm a civilized, indoor cat."

"Give me a break. You were found mewling up a tree."

"Years ago! Is it fair to fling my past at me like that?"

"Listen, hair ball. I'm not interested in bunnies, or sparing your feelings. You need to find out what's going on in that house. Where is Laird?"

"He's not here. No one's here."

"Where did they all go?"

"I don't know." Does she expect them to tell me these things?

A long sigh issues from my neck—having her voice there is disturbing. "All right. Let's take a tour of the place. Walk slowly so your collar doesn't jiggle."

As carefully as I can, I pad around the entire house—except for the rooms that are shut off from me. Aside from some different furniture, Tannith detects nothing amiss.

"Can I come home now?"

Her reply is immediate and sharp. "No. The fact that I can't tell what's wrong just means that Trudy and Gwen are doing a good job of concealment. You have to stay there and keep your eyes open."

"But—"

"I'm going to do something to stir those idiots up. I need you there to view the results. So stop mewling, or you'll wind up back at the shelter."

That quickly, she is gone. Or is she?

How can I tell?

The only thing worse than being left entirely alone is being entirely alone *with someone watching*. Warily, I hop onto the sofa. Dr. Tim is facing the camera and earnestly explaining how relationships are never smooth sailing all the time. Every couple hits high winds and rough seas every once in a while.

Is that what's happening to Tannith and me? Just a bit of choppy water?

If there's one thing that terrifies me, it's water.

Chapter 16

Gwen

The apothecary drawers in Esme's laboratory yielded some of what we needed for the spell. The rest we were going to have to round up on our own.

To speed things along, we divided up the remaining items. Then Milo confessed that he didn't have anything to pull a bear's tooth with.

"You don't have a pair of pliers in your toolbox?" I asked.

"*I* don't run a handyman business. I'm a creative."

You would think that pliers would come in handy for a landscape architect. Or just in getting through life, period. "You don't have any tools at all?"

"Brett and I have a hammer, a pair of scissors, and one of those little sewing kits I pinched from the Marriott Marquis last time I was in the city."

We decided that I would go with Milo, and that we would swing by my house to scrape oak bark off one of Daniel's trees. Also, I could grab a pair of pliers. Trudy would concentrate on the personal item and the snails. Once the bear dental extraction was done, Milo and I would hunt down plants. Hopefully this could be accomplished by evening.

That was the plan, anyway.

The first snag we ran into was the bear tooth. After a hundred years, you'd think the bear's teeth would drop out of its gums as easily as snapping a twig off a dry branch. Live and learn. Those teeth had petrified into the dead animal's jaws as if they'd been set in cement.

The size of the bear's head, not to mention its claws, always stunned me. It was hard to contemplate the thing without feeling in awe of how frightening the animal must have seemed when men were facing it down across the icy landscape of its native habitat. Here in the living room of a house in western New York, the animal was finally getting its revenge as Milo and I took turns grunting and cursing as we tried to extract an inconspicuous molar. Finally, I moved to one of the teeth farther forward in the mouth.

"Not an incisor!"

I frowned at Milo. "Why not?"

"Brett will notice."

"Brett sits around counting his rug's teeth?"

"No, but he might notice if his polar bear suddenly develops a hillbilly gap in his smile."

"So just say he lost a tooth."

"How would I explain where the tooth went?"

"Tell him you vacuumed it up by mistake."

"Then it would be in the vacuum cleaner."

"Not if you emptied it before you realized the tooth was gone." I couldn't believe we were arguing over this. "Our real problem is that we might not get any tooth at all."

"Let me try again." He took the pliers from me. "Hold on to its head to brace it."

I did as instructed, straddling its neck to keep it still. It was a little like our old days of playing Twister, except contortions were a lot more difficult now. Plus the stakes were higher.

Milo yanked with all his might. "Hey—" He fell backward just as the door opened and a cool breeze came into the room, followed by Brett.

Milo and I bounded to our feet with the agility of a pair of Cirque du Soleil gymnasts.

"Brett!" we chimed, as if there were something unusual about a man walking into his own house.

"You're home early," Milo observed.

"I have to study my notes for tonight."

"Oh! The debate!" I'd almost forgotten that this was the big night, when he would face off with Karen Morrow in front of reporters and an auditorium full of mildly interested citizens. "Good luck—I'm sure you'll do great."

Despite our best efforts to distract him, he was staring straight at the bear. My breathing stopped, but before he could investigate, he got a whiff of Milo. "What's that smell?"

Milo shifted uncomfortably. "I . . . had to climb into someone's smelly garden shed today. That's why I'm home early."

"For a minute I worried it was Cuddles," Brett said.

Milo interpreted for me: "That's what we call the rug."

I might have gone for something more like Mangey or Anthraxy.

Brett glanced again at Cuddles. It would probably have helped us look less guilty if beads of sweat hadn't been visible on Milo's forehead. He was also holding my pliers behind his back.

"So, the debate's tonight," I piped up at Brett.

"We have a couple of hours to prepare." He looked pointedly at Milo. "And to bathe."

Milo cut a panicked glance at me. "I'm going to the debate tonight." His tone said he'd forgotten.

"Of course you are." Damn. Trudy and I would be on our own. Which is how we ended up in a mess to begin with.

"Since it's going to be held at the college, I was hoping Trudy's husband would be there to introduce me to some of his colleagues," Brett said, "but Laird's not answering my emails."

"No—he wouldn't. He's . . ."

For a moment it looked like Milo was too flustered to come up with an answer, so I blurted out, "On a trip," at the same time Milo finished by saying, "On sabbatical."

"On a sabbatical research trip," Milo amended quickly.

I nodded. "Even Trudy hasn't heard from him lately."

"So he's out of pocket?" Brett asked.

"Totally," Milo said, but to my ears it sounded like *toadily*.

"Totally," I corrected.

Milo scowled. "That's what I said."

Brett's brow scrunched. "Is everything okay?"

"Of course. Gwen was just dropping by to—" Milo's face went blank again.

"To loan Milo a pair of pliers. He said one of the faucets was leaking." I held out my hand. "I'll need them back, if you don't mind. They're my best pair."

He slapped them in my hand. I felt something else, too. Something hard and loose. The tooth!

"Okay." I didn't dare look at my hand as I began edging toward the door. "Welp, I'd better get going now. Good luck tonight, Brett. I'm sure you'll do great."

"Thanks, Gwen." He aimed his million-watt smile at me. How could he lose?

I was out the door and in the driveway before I realized I didn't have my car with me. I called Trudy. "I need a ride. I've got the bear tooth, but Brett walked in on us. We didn't have time to go to a nursery." I informed her that we would be spell-casting without Milo this evening.

"It'll be okay," she said. "Where are you?"

She collected me down the street from Milo's as soon as she'd left a pet shop with the thirteen doomed snails.

She also informed me that she'd found most of the plants on the list, except rue. "I think I know where we can find some, though," she said. "The college has a bunch of greenhouses—it's part of the state agricultural system. They grow all sorts of things, including herbs."

The college gardens were a series of fields and greenhouses several miles outside town. Trudy parked down the road and we walked up a path that was marked PERSONNEL AND AUTHORIZED VISITORS ONLY.

"It'll be fine," Trudy said when I pointed out the sign.

"Please don't hex anyone."

She looked annoyed. "Would you please stop saying that to me? I've only had two accidents."

"*Only?*"

"Well, pestering me about it doesn't help. It just makes me nervous."

"Okay," I promised. "I won't mention it again."

As we approached, Trudy frowned in concentration. "I came here once before. I know that one of these was reserved for vegetables and herbs."

I gawked like a tourist at the massive structures. I'd lived here all my life and had attended the university, and I'd never heard of this place. "What's it all for?"

"They cultivate old native species and also experiment with seeds and things." She stopped in front of a door that had another AUTHORIZED PERSONNEL ONLY warning in large black stenciled letters.

Before I could say anything, Trudy pushed the door open. An alarm like you'd expect from a nuclear reactor in meltdown went off right above our heads. Trudy pivoted, glaring at the red metal disk above the door. Then she raised her hand. Terrified of what might happen next, I lifted my own arms. *Silence*, I thought. Or maybe I yelled it. In the same instant, an electric flash shocked my fingertips.

Drawing in my hands took effort, but I blew on them, wondering what the hell I'd just done.

Whatever it was, the result was silence.

Eerie silence.

I blinked.

Trudy rounded on me. "What did you do?"

"I'm . . . not sure." I laced my fingers together into a double fist. Had I actually done anything? "Maybe it just stopped on its own."

Trudy looked doubtful, but that was nothing compared to what I felt. My fingers were still stinging. If I had done that, it had been all instinct and no skill. Which, gauging from Trudy's experience, wasn't always for the best.

"Let's just hope we can find what we're looking for and get out of here quickly," I said.

We were lucky. Among the rows of tomatoes, squash, and peppers, herbs were also growing. Trudy and I studied all the plastic markers until we found rue. There were several varieties, so I picked up a pot of the type that seemed the most plentiful.

"We don't need to take the whole thing." She reached forward, pinched off a few stems, and dropped them into her purse. "Put it back and let's go."

We hurried back the way we came. I was still halfway expecting another alarm blast, but we made it out without setting off anything. I heaved a sigh of relief. Then Trudy jabbed me in the side.

A cop in a blue uniform was staring straight at us. He was black with hair just starting to go gray at the temples. He wasn't terribly tall but he had an athletic build. Plus he was carrying a gun. Making a run for it wasn't an option.

Trudy smiled in greeting. "Hello, Officer." Her gaze searched beyond him, taking in his vehicle. "You're Zenobia PD, not campus police."

"That's right." The man's voice was deep, his words measured. "The alarm here triggers an automatic call to the campus police and the ZPD."

She tilted toward him, as if this were the most fascinating thing she'd heard all day. "To both! Isn't that interesting?"

The policeman's expression indicated he saw through her, but he still managed a smile. I was just glad he wasn't slapping cuffs on us. "All right, who are you and what are you up to?"

Trudy let out a slight laugh. "At the moment, I'm more confused than anything. I was supposed to meet someone here. Professor Webster, of the university."

"Uh-huh." The cop didn't appear impressed by this news.

Trudy continued, "But he never showed up. And now he's not even answering my texts."

"You had an appointment to meet here because why?"

"I'm not sure. We"—Trudy nodded her head toward me—"have a cousin, who's in landscaping, and Laird—Professor Webster—mentioned something about showing us a variety of tree our cousin should know about. But he's a no-show, so we decided to give up on him."

"Professor Webster's with the university?"

She nodded. "Yes. He's also my husband. *Was* my husband. We're separated, actually." She shook her head. "I shouldn't have agreed to come here. He's never been reliable. That's why we're getting divorced. One of the reasons."

I couldn't believe Trudy was announcing the end of her marriage to a complete stranger.

"Split up, have you?" the cop asked, sizing her up with more interest.

"Everything headed south just as soon as our two girls went off to college."

The cop shifted his stance. "I'm an empty nester myself. But me and my missus split up before our son left. I didn't think I'd miss him so much, but I do."

"I know what you mean. It's like the house has a black hole in it."

He nodded. "I try to pretend his room isn't even there now. Back in September I'd tear up every time I walked past it and glimpsed his poster of Ariana Grande."

Trudy nodded sympathetically. "They say it gets better eventually."

"Eventually."

She smiled at him. He grinned back. I was still frozen in panic that he was going to ask us why we set off the greenhouse alarm.

"All right," he said with a sigh. "Just give me your names and addresses. And promise you aren't some kind of plant burglars."

We scrawled our names and addresses across a clipboard.

"Thank you for being so understanding," Trudy said. "I didn't realize going in would be such a big deal."

He let out a long breath. "You wouldn't think there would be such a fuss over a bunch of plants. I imagine they're just worried about vandalism and such."

She handed the clipboard back to him. "There are so many incidents of that kind. We get them at the school, too."

"I bet." He lifted a hand before turning back to his car. "You two ladies have a good afternoon." He smiled and pointed a finger at Trudy. "And don't go getting into any more trouble."

A laugh trilled out of her. "I've already reached my quota for the year."

When we were in Trudy's car and watching the policeman's taillights receding down the lane, we both exhaled in relief.

"I thought we were going to be hauled off to jail," I said.

"You should spend more time around high school students. You'd know how to finesse your way around authority figures."

"We gave him our real names, though. How stupid was that?"

She didn't seem concerned at all. "You think the college is going to file a complaint because a few rue leaves are missing? They won't even notice."

I hoped she was right. "Let's get back to Esme's and start boiling all this stuff up while it's fresh."

Halfway there, Trudy asked, "Officer Timmens was awfully good-looking, don't you think?"

"How did you catch his name?"

"It was on his badge, and he'd also written his name on the sheet of paper we signed. Marcus Timmens."

"He seemed good-natured for a cop interrogating burglars."

"Oh, he could see that we were innocent."

"We weren't, though." An idea occurred to me. "Did he seem like a Watcher to you?"

"He just looked like a police officer to me. And so handsome, like a guy I dated in college. Before I met Laird."

At Esme's house we got out of the car and were almost to the door when a voice hailed us. "Hi there!"

A woman in highlighter-yellow sneakers, shiny blue leggings, and a fleece zip-up jacket power walked toward us, her ponytail bobbing from side to side as she approached.

"Uh-oh," I said under my breath. "A neighbor."

She waved and stopped about ten feet away, smiling in greeting. "I'm Grace."

"Hi, Grace. I'm Gwen and this is my cousin Trudy. We're house-sitting for my aunt Esme."

"Your aunt! That explains it, I guess. We so rarely see people around here, but now lately there are people coming and going."

"Just me and my cousins." I frowned. "Have you seen anyone else?"

Her head shake sent her ponytail swishing again. "No, but it just seemed so odd. What happened to Miss Zimmer?"

"She went to visit relatives," Trudy said. "In Ohio."

Her deftness at lobbing fibs at people amazed me. I never knew she possessed this talent.

Grace smiled. "Everyone will be so amazed when I tell them that she has all this family."

"Everyone?" I asked.

"In the neighborhood. We're a pretty tight-knit bunch around here, except for your aunt. She never wants to participate in the block parties, cleanups, or neighborhood meetings we have. We always invite her, of course, but she . . ." Grace let out a mirthless laugh. "Well, let's just say she tells us to buzz off. But everybody says she's been around forever. I suppose not everyone can be a joiner."

"No one would ever accuse Aunt Esme of being a joiner," I agreed.

"How did she get to Ohio?"

The question threw me. "What?"

Grace nodded at the purple Gremlin. "Her vehicle's still parked here."

Stupid, Gwen. I should have anticipated questions about her car. "I drove her to the airport," I piped up. "Early in the morning. Yesterday."

"Well, this is a relief. People around here were worried she'd died or something. That would be so terrible." The insincere look of concern on Grace's face said otherwise. I imagined Aunt Esme's demise would have suited the neighbors just fine.

"It was nice to meet you," I said. *Please go now.* She didn't. "We'll probably be around for a few more days yet."

"Great!" She flashed another grin. "You'll grow to love this neighborhood. We're East Zenobia friendly."

"Have a great evening."

This time she took the hint.

"She seemed nice," Trudy said as we watched the ponytail swish away down the street.

"She could be a Watcher," I muttered under my breath.

"Please. You think everyone's a Watcher."

"We have to be vigilant." I turned the key in the lock and pushed open the door.

"We don't even know that there are Watchers around here. Who told you that?"

"Mom and Dad."

"You really think the Grand Council of Witches has people stationed outside the Buttered Biscuit, keeping an eye on our family?"

"Maybe not outside the café, but I do believe they keep tabs on us."

"They just want us to think that."

I finished securing all the locks and latches and turned to her. "If Watchers are a myth, then where's our cousin Odin? Aunt Esme said they just zapped him out of existence one day."

We hurried down to the basement. I was always nervous that we wouldn't be able to get into the lab, but the stone lever worked for us again. Hopefully we wouldn't have to come here too many more times.

Trudy was obviously thinking the same thing. She dropped all the items we'd found on a table. "If this stuff has to boil for three hours, let's get going ASAP. I'd dearly love not to have to spend many more evenings here. I'm already exhausted, and I'll still have to make cupcakes when I get home."

"We could always make them upstairs while we wait."

"I'm not sending anything made in this house to the Buttered Biscuit."

That was probably wise.

We found a cauldron in Esme's cupboards and lit a burner on the stove that stood in the far corner of the lab. No telling what Esme had cooked up on this appliance over the years. I glanced over at the rabbit sitting on her hind legs, watching us with interest.

"So far, so good, right?" I asked Esme.

She thumped.

We put all the ingredients in according to the instructions in her Book of Shadows. When it came time for the snails, I felt a qualm. "The ingredients are boiling," I said, holding back the little plastic baggie of slugs. They were disgusting, but they were alive.

Trudy grabbed the baggie. "We're talking about a human life versus a few slimy snails." She began flicking them in.

Esme, I couldn't help noticing, looked on approvingly.

The last thing we tossed in was one of Laird's socks Trudy had picked up at her house. "I hope that's personal enough," she said.

I peered at the book. "According to this, we just let this hell soup cook down for several hours and serve it up to Laird."

Trudy yawned. "I really didn't get much sleep."

I pointed to the pillows we'd belatedly brought down to sit on while reading. "Why don't you curl up over there for a while."

"What are you going to do?"

I nodded at the bookshelves. "I think I'll keep reading. See if I can dig up any interesting information."

What I didn't tell Trudy was that I'd felt a tug toward those bookshelves ever since we'd come into the laboratory. Something had happened to me this afternoon when I'd stopped that greenhouse alarm. I relived the jolt I'd felt in my hands, like my fingertips were charged. I'd forgotten what a thrill the manipulation of objects in the world could give me—the power rush.

I pulled out a new book, *Alchemy for Idiots*, and studied it for a long time. Even when the language was simple, I felt as if I were decoding Sanskrit. I should know this. This should have been my heritage.

Esme was looking at me, twitching with interest. *"Yes, it should have been, if you hadn't been such a biddable simp."*

I blinked. I had not just heard a rabbit thinking at me. That was not possible.

"Isn't it?"

"No."

I hadn't meant to speak aloud and glanced anxiously at Trudy to see if she'd heard. But she lay across a pillow, oblivious of my communicating with a rabbit.

I bit my lip. This was getting freaky. I got up and stirred the cauldron. The snails had dissolved, and more disturbing, it appeared the sock had, too. Only a few threads remained, floating around like noodles.

I went back to the books. Between the bubbling of the cauldron, the chirps and croaks coming from the many terrariums, and Trudy's soft snores from the cushions, it felt strangely peaceful down here. I glanced around at the lab. Whether she'd constructed it by the sweat of her brow or by witchcraft, the wonderful thing was that Esme had created a safe space for us to learn and practice.

"*Who is* us?" Esme said.

"For *you* to practice, I meant," I whispered back.

I didn't need a laboratory. I wasn't really a witch. I mean, I was by blood, but that very blood doomed me. I couldn't practice—not unless I wanted to take the risks that Esme had taken. Which I absolutely didn't. I wanted to have a real life. A normal life like Mom and Dad's.

With Daniel?

Holy moly. I'd forgotten about him. I pulled out my phone, but I couldn't receive any new messages from him down here. Just the old message I'd received last night: *Where are you?*

I wondered if he'd followed through on his bizarre intention to talk to Mom. What could he possibly need to ask her?

The most obvious answer was that he wanted to ask her something about me—something personal. I frowned. What could it be? Stuck in a Vermont forest, had Daniel suddenly become possessed with the desire to find out something about my past?

A terrible thought dawned on me. I was assuming that *I* was the focus of what he wanted to speak to Mom about. But Mom was also Tannith's mom. If he was contemplating running off with Tannith, maybe he was going to ask Mom something about Tannith's likes and dislikes.

I sank down. Should I warn Daniel? *This isn't about you. She's only interested in you because she can take you from me.* I should let him know that he was the victim of a hex.

But what if it wasn't true? I would either come off sounding like an egotist or a kook.

It shouldn't be this easy for a single mean-spirited letter to sandbag an entire relationship. At the very least, it showed that my relationship with Daniel was on shaky ground to begin with. I'd worried we were moving too fast. But Tannith was part of the reason I'd wanted to take the next step of moving in with Daniel. Given Tannith's history with my men, I'd suspected Daniel and I would never be safe until I staked a physical claim in his life.

Not to mention, I loved his house. I'd been living in the top floor of a drafty old house with bad plumbing and a landlord who was deaf to complaints. Daniel's house seemed warm and snug by comparison, especially in those first early months when the chill was still in the air outside. I believed that in the fortress of his house, Tannith would never come knocking.

I closed my eyes, taking myself back to that time of long weekend mornings snuggling under a comforter together. Just being wrapped up in another person, delighting in every new thing I learned about him, feeling amazed to have found someone at last. Every sensation was new—the way he kissed, the way he liked to drape one arm over my shoulder at night, the way his entire being was so relaxed and heavy while he slept, like he'd been given a full-body injection of Novocain.

I imagined being with him again, back under the comforters. Waking up to the eternal dilemma—get up and fix coffee, or stay in bed and snuggle? I smiled, imagining his face when his eyes just opened, thick black lashes against his cheeks. And then those soulful green eyes looking at me. I felt a rush of warmth, followed by an even stronger spike of confusion.

Daniel didn't have green eyes.

I sat up, confused, and touched my face. It felt feverish. Had I just been dreaming of *Jeremy?*

Trudy awoke with a snort and jolted up. "Why didn't you wake me up? The potion should be ready."

Rattled, I looked at my watch. She was right—three hours had passed. I couldn't believe how fast the hours had gone by. *Time flies when you're imagining sleeping with a guy you barely know. . . .*

We gathered at the cauldron and ladled up some of the concoction, using cheesecloth as a sieve as we poured the liquid into a bowl. While waiting for our magical broth to cool, we searched for a dropper to feed the stuff to the toad. To Laird. I needed to stop thinking of him as just a toad. Briefly, I wondered what exactly we were going to say to him when he was a human again. *Welcome back?*

Would he even be able to remember the last two days? Hopefully not too much. A thing like that could traumatize a person for life.

"I'm getting nervous," Trudy said.

"No need to be. We did everything by the book."

"That's what bothers me. If this doesn't work, what will we do?"

"It will work." Fingers crossed.

After the dropper was filled, she went to the terrarium table. Picking the top off one, she lifted toad-Laird out and put him on the counter. "You have to drink this," she told him. "It'll turn you back into your real self."

Eerily, the creature seemed to understand, and when she lifted the dropper, he put out one toad hand and helped steady the glass tube as he darted out his tongue to drink the contents.

When the dropper was empty, Trudy put it down and we stepped back. My heart was thwacking in my chest. I couldn't imagine how Trudy felt.

"Nothing's happening," she said, her voice cracking.

Neither of us could take our eyes off the toad sitting on the counter. He seemed to have gone inordinately still.

Please don't let us have killed him.

I'm not sure if some supernatural being heard my unspoken prayer, but in the next instant smoke seemed to pour out of the toad's skin, so much that its transformation could barely be seen by us. A revolting *squish* filled the room, followed by a guttural moan. Trudy's hand clamped around my arm, and while the smoking metamorphosis of flesh happened before our eyes, a frightened keening came out of both of us. I couldn't have stopped making the noise if I'd wanted to, any more than I could have stopped clinging to my cousin. I have no idea how long we cowered there. Time seemed to stretch, and each prolonged second was agony. I hadn't expected the spell to be so terrifying.

Or, in the end, so baffling.

When the smoke cleared, the naked man standing in front of

us bore no resemblance at all to Laird. This man was about six foot two, middle-aged, with a skull that was as bald as an egg. The colored lights of the lab played across his hairless dome like a disco ball. Gorgeous blue eyes blinked back at us. His muscular physique and chiseled jaw were as far from looking like Laird as I could imagine.

And as for the rest of his endowments, which were generous . . .

"*That* is definitely not Laird," Trudy declared.

Chapter 17

"Who are you?" I demanded.

The strange man tilted his head, birdlike, to inspect us. "I have to ask you the same question."

Trudy disentangled herself from me, stepped back, and flapped her hands in rising hysteria. "Something went wrong, Gwen. Very wrong."

No kidding. I scrambled over to the shelf where Esme stored towels and handed the man the largest one I could find, indicating he should wrap it around himself.

He did, twisting it around his waist to keep it in place. "You weren't expecting me?" he asked in a soft, slightly hurt voice.

"Of course we weren't, unless . . ." Bravely, Trudy marched right up to him and stood on tiptoe so she could look right into his eyes. *"Laird, is that you in there?"*

The man leaned as far away from her as possible without collapsing backward. "No, it's all me."

She crossed her arms. "Who are you?"

"You tell me."

Frustrated, Trudy asked me, "What went wrong?"

I edged closer to the strange man. "You don't recognize us?"

He blinked his startlingly blue eyes. "I'm a little muzzy headed, to be quite honest. There's a vague familiarity about you, but . . ." He shook his head, indicating his failure to connect any dots. "*Should* I know you?"

"Do the names Trudy, Molly, and Drew mean anything to you?" I asked.

"No . . ."

Trudy's anguished bleat rent the air. "That crazy old crone's stupid book—why did we ever trust it? I knew this would all go wrong."

"Just a minute," the man said. "From my perspective, something went very right. I'm not sure what you did, but I have a faint memory of being among toads and lizards. I just took a big evolutionary leap forward."

"You were a toad," I confirmed for him.

"The wrong toad." In frustration, Trudy rushed to the terrarium. "I obviously picked up the wrong toad."

How could that be? "Esme pointed him out to us," I said. "A red-spotted toad, she told us."

We inspected toads. Esme had mentioned red-spotted toads, but in the multicolored lighting of the lab, *half* of them seemed to have colored spots. Why had I not noticed this?

Trudy studied them frantically. "Laird?"

One of the frogs hopped against the glass, causing her to gasp. Then another joined him.

I groaned.

"Oh, dear." The bald man approached and peered curiously at his former brethren. "Was I one of those?"

Trudy rounded on him. "While you were in there, did one of the toads call himself Laird?"

He thought back. "As far as I can recall, we didn't really use names."

"You said Trudy and I looked familiar. Who do we remind you of?"

"I'm not sure." His face tensed in concentration. "Someone I knew once, maybe?"

Trudy let out a disgusted sigh. "We could hardly remind you of someone you never knew."

No, but he also reminded me of someone, too. I studied his face. It was my turn to make him feel uncomfortable. But those eyes.

Blue eyes like Paul Newman's. That's where I'd seen him before. *"Hud."*

"What?" Trudy asked.

"Your name is Odin."

He blinked. "You know, it might be." He frowned. "Then again, it might not be. How do you know?"

"Aunt Esme described you to me once." I looked at him closely. "Esme Zimmer. Does that name ring a bell?"

"It's a pretty name."

"You were in love with her," I said.

"That's right—Esme!" His face lit up. "Where is she?"

I was going to look around for Esme, but discovered that she was a mere foot away from him, staring intently up at the love of her life. *She* recognized him, although he surely didn't look the same as he had at twenty-one, when he disappeared. Even life in the ether aged a person, evidently.

I pointed to the rabbit looking adoringly at him. "There. That's Esme."

He took her in, and the eagerness in his expression faded. He sighed. "The course of true love never did run smooth, did it?"

"Do you recognize her?" I asked.

He tilted his head. "I'm assuming she looked a little different in the old days?"

An angry huff ripped out of Trudy. *"Who cares?* What does it matter whether he remembers Esme or us? He's not Laird." She glared at Esme. "You did this on purpose, didn't you? You knew all along we had the wrong toad!"

In answer, Esme hopped away and did a few bunny binkies, jumping and kicking her hind legs in a joyful burst.

Trudy was livid. "I'm going to kill that rabbit."

I grabbed her arm just as Odin threw himself between us and Esme to stop her. "Wait just a minute. No violence."

"Killing Esme would be a really bad idea," I agreed. "You need to calm down. You know what happens when you're angry."

Trudy closed her eyes and took several deep gulps of air. "We have to get Laird back. We've got the broth here. Let's just give it to all the toads. One of them must be him."

"Right," I said, "but in the meantime, who are all these others?" There was no telling whom Aunt Esme had been tossing into her terrariums. "We feed that soup to all those toads, and who knows what we'll end up with." The possibilities made me shudder. "We might be untoading more long-lost relations, or serial killers, or things that aren't even human. They might be wild animals, or demons."

"Demons?" Trudy snorted. "That's a little far-fetched, don't you think?"

"Well, considering that we just found a relation who was vaporized decades ago . . ."

She bit her lip. "Okay. But one of those creatures must be Laird, and we know we have a soup to reanimate him, or whatever you call it."

"Trans-speciate," Odin said.

I put my hands on my hips. "How did you know that?"

An astonished look appeared in his eyes. "I don't know. It just came to me."

I tried to remember everything I'd heard about Odin. Esme said he'd probably forgotten more magic than most witches ever knew. His brain might be muzzy now, but what if it cleared over time? Esme had indicated that he'd been working on something really big when the Council decided to punish him. Whatever knowledge was still rattling around in that head, lost, was worth protecting.

"We should put the broth in the fridge and come back tomorrow," I said. "Approach the problem from a fresh viewpoint." And hopefully with Odin more his old sharp self.

Trudy was not happy. "And what are we going to do with Uncle Fester here?"

"Odin," I corrected. He was one of our elders—we owed him a modicum of respect.

"If you're so paranoid about Watchers, we probably shouldn't call him that," she said.

He flinched. "Watchers? Here?"

That concept resonated with him. As well it might.

"Not here," I assured him. "Here is safe."

"I'll stay here, then."

I wasn't about to trust a half-gaga old cousin who'd just been reanimated from a toad to look after himself in Esme's laboratory. "That's not a good idea."

"He can't stay with me," Trudy declared.

"All right. Just hang on."

I hurried upstairs, where I could get a signal with my cell phone.

Milo picked up after five rings. "This better be important. I'm missing the big debate on sewer-line replacement schedules."

"Sorry."

He laughed. "Kidding. I shot out of that auditorium the minute the phone vibrated."

"I hope you won't mind shooting over to East Zenobia then. I know it's a big night for Brett, but we're having a crisis."

"Don't tell me Laird's half-toad/half-man."

"No, we've got a whole man."

"Seriously?" Milo asked, amazed. "Well done!"

"But it's not Laird. It's our long-lost cousin, Odin." I got Milo up to speed as quickly as I could.

"Who else does Aunt Esme have in those terrariums?" Milo asked. "Amelia Earhart? Jimmy Hoffa?"

"Let's just hope she still has Laird. In the meantime, could you please come help us? And maybe bring some clothes that would fit a man slightly over six feet tall?"

"Okay, sit tight. Brett and I came here together, so I'll have to

Uber over to my house to pick up my car. But I'll get there as soon as I can."

"Thank you, Milo. Also, we probably shouldn't call him Odin."

"Why not?"

"Watchers."

"What should we call him?"

"I don't know. He looks like Paul Newman."

"Butch Cassidy."

"Perfect," I said. "Although maybe just Butch would be better. We don't want people to think he's some kind of kook."

"Goodness, no." Milo laughed. "Definitely no kooks in this family."

Chapter 18

An hour later Milo was of a different mind. "You expect me to take this crazy cousin home with me? And explain that to Brett . . . how?"

"Just say you have a crazy cousin," I said.

"Like you, Trudy, and Tannith weren't proof of that already."

"I do feel a bit crazy," Odin admitted. He'd been getting dressed while we discussed him as if he weren't standing there listening to us. He now wore a BLAIR FOR MAYOR long-sleeve T-shirt. "I'm definitely not at my tack-sharpest, brainwise."

"It's only for a day," I told Milo. "Or two."

He gaped at me in disbelief. "How can you be sure of that? Do you have some foolproof plan for rehabilitating someone who's just undergone defrogging?"

"No," I confessed. "But once he's out and about in the world, he's bound to start remembering things again."

I held my breath as Milo thought this over.

"Okay." He looked over at Odin. "But you need to watch your p's and q's, man. My boyfriend's running for mayor. He's also very straitlaced."

"I'm straitlaced, too." Odin looked over at Trudy and me for confirmation. "Aren't I?"

"You can be anything you want to be," Trudy said. "It's like the beginning of a new school year. You've got a clean slate."

Odin's face broke out in a dazzling smile. "I like that!" In the next moment, though, the smile evaporated. "What's a slate?"

After Milo had left with his new charge, Trudy turned to me. "Would you mind coming back to the house with me? I don't want to be alone right now. To be honest, I'm still freaked out by what happened here tonight. That was terrifying. I'm not sure I'm cut out for witchcraft."

"You seem to be a natural."

"Only when I lose control. Otherwise it scares the pants off me."

I rounded up Esme and put her in her carrier, ignoring Trudy's grumbles. I doubted she and Esme would ever repair the rift this week had created.

"What about Laird?" I nodded toward the assortment of terrariums.

"I'm not taking all those toads home. He'll just have to hang out with his buds tonight." As we were leaving, Trudy cast a look back, obviously feeling guilt. "I'll try to find him and his friends some fresh flies tomorrow."

On the drive over to Trudy's, I kept wondering about Odin. Where had he come from? Esme must have been working on trying to get him back for years and years. Her life's work. Somehow, she'd retrieved him from the ether, either as a toad or as another being she'd turned into a toad for reasons known only to herself. But then why had she pulled the switch with Laird and Odin?

I decided to stay a while at Trudy's and help her make cupcakes. Baking usually soothed her nerves. Although it didn't do the same trick for me, tonight I didn't relish going home alone. Even alone with a rabbit.

Trudy hunted through her cupboard, then opened her fridge and inspected its contents with displeasure. "I had such great plans for the cupcakes for tomorrow. I was going to make them really special."

"Special how?"

"For Halloween! That's tomorrow, remember?"

It hadn't been foremost in my mind.

"I had ideas for icing some with little marshmallow ghosts, but . . ."

She didn't need to finish. We'd been too busy with our shopping list of teeth, socks, and snails to think about holiday cupcakes. She pursed her lips as she surveyed the fridge's contents. "We'll have to do a batch of lemon, and a batch of peanut butter–chocolate."

"Those both sound delicious."

"But not spooky."

"This week has been spooky enough to me without marshmallow ghosts."

"They would have been so cute." She pushed a cutting board, knife, and a grater toward me. "You can start zesting lemons."

"Oh, grate," I said, earning a groan. I grinned.

She handed me a net bag of lemons. "At least ten. Nothing worse than wimpy lemon flavor. Watch your knuckles."

I started zesting. Trudy had cupcake baking down to a science, and with me helping, the lemon cupcakes were out of the oven and cooling before too long. They smelled heavenly.

I looked down at Griz, who was perched on the back of the couch, studying us intently. I went over and picked him up, which caused him to flip out. He yowled, leaped out of my arms, and streaked out of the room.

"I think he's warming up to me," I said.

Trudy shook her head. "I don't see why Tannith didn't just drop Griz off at your place."

"Daniel's allergic."

"I thought he just didn't like pets."

"That, too."

Trudy frowned. "Does Tannith know that about Daniel's allergies?"

Good question. "I don't know." Maybe I had complained about his dislike of house pets in front of her. Or maybe Tannith had a specific reason for wanting to inconvenience Trudy. What could that be?

She shut off the tap and turned to face me. "Don't worry about Daniel. You'll never get me to believe he plans on leaving you for Tannith."

"Maybe not under normal circumstances. In fact, I heard from Daniel this morning. He seemed . . . odd. He said he had something *very important* to talk about when he got home, and he wanted to ask Mom about something."

Trudy's eyes blinked open wide. "That was this morning and you didn't tell me?"

"Tell you what? I don't know what he's up to."

She leaned against the counter, marveling at my dim-wittedness. "He's going to pop the question, obviously."

I shook my head. "You think he wants to ask for my mom's permission first?"

"No, he's going to buy you an engagement ring and he wants to know your ring size. That's something a mom would know."

"How? I don't even know it myself."

"Okay, maybe it's just something a guy would think a mom would know." Trudy bobbed with impatience. "When's he coming back?"

"No idea. It all depends on the beetle situation."

"What are you going to say to him when he asks you?"

"I don't think he will."

She rolled her eyes impatiently. "But if he does."

I frowned. "I don't know."

Excitement leached out of her. "But you were crazy in love. You moved in with him."

It was so easy to forget the crazy-in-love part, wasn't it? Those weeks when I walked around barely able to believe my luck, feeling as if I had more happiness than my heart was able to contain. I had more fun in a few weeks than I'd had for the past two decades. Daniel and I were together all the time—we took weekend biking trips, went camping, or simply stayed in at his place, cooked, and watched nature documentaries.

We complemented each other. I loved the way he fussed over his old house, the pride he took in it, and I was able to snap things up by making a few weekend repairs. Though I'd worried that I wouldn't be brainy and academic enough for him, he was delighted by my skill and boasted about me to his friends. I took a deep dive into vegan baking—with mixed results—and even enjoyed learning about insects. When I felt more secure, I introduced Daniel to my family and was relieved when he didn't seem to like Tannith. It was as if our fledgling relationship had passed the final test.

When my lease expired in the summer, it seemed a perfect time to take that next step. Why not?

Not until I'd sold all my stuff that wouldn't go in Daniel's house—practically everything—and had tucked away the contents of my last moving box, did it become clear that we might have been too hasty. What had once seemed a charming pride of home in Daniel became persnickety micromanaging. His cozy bungalow suddenly felt crowded. Opening a closet door could set off an avalanche, which drove Daniel crazy. "Can't you find another place for this?" he would ask, holding whatever possession of mine had just crashed to the floor. Too much "stuff" seemed excessive to him, and it was always my stuff that counted as too much.

Daniel felt strongly about buying organic, not owning pets, and not wasting energy. Unfortunately, he was one of those people who walked the walk. Certain television shows were deemed a waste of brain cells; I found myself sneaking out of bed at night to binge-watch in secret. I was starting to feel like a houseguest in my own home.

These were just minor things, I told myself. Details.

But wasn't a lot of life in the details?

"Right," I said. "I was crazy in love. And then I moved in with him."

"What does that mean?"

"It means being crazy in love while you're dating is one thing, but staying crazy in love with someone who freaks out when the butter dish ends up on the wrong shelf in the refrigerator is something else."

Her brows knit. "Daniel freaks out over where the butter dish is?"

"Well, maybe not *freaks out*. But it matters to him."

"Oh."

If there was one thing Trudy could understand, it was the importance of not having clashes over who controlled the kitchen. She controlled hers completely, which was probably why she'd let Laird keep his uncomfortable living room furniture for so long.

"How do you know if you're in a long-term, opposites-attract situation that requires give-and-take, or just involved in a slow-motion train wreck?" I wondered aloud. Although maybe the best person to ask wasn't a woman whose erstwhile husband was living with a bunch of lizards in a witch's basement.

Trudy was plopping a fat bag of icing sugar down on the countertop when the doorbell rang. She lunged to turn down the stereo—as if that would somehow change that someone was here. We stared at the door, then at each other.

"If this is that Jeremy character," I said, "I give you permission to turn him into a rabbit."

"Don't even joke about it." Her voice was a stage whisper. She wiped her hands on her apron. "Maybe I should just pretend I'm not here."

"Half your lights are on." Also, whoever it was had probably heard the radio.

An impatient knock on the door made us both jump.

"Mrs. Webster," a voice called out. "It's the Zenobia police."

I tried to take a breath, but a huge lump clotted my breathing passage.

Trudy mouthed, *Oh. My. God.* "What do I do?"

"Answer the door. We're making cupcakes. It's not illegal."

"Right." She made pushing motions with her hands to calm herself. "Not illegal. We haven't done anything wrong."

Except breaking and entering, lying, performing dodgy amateur witchcraft . . .

She hurried to the door, unlatched it, and swung it open. I prepared myself to hear something like dialogue on a cop show. Instead, the ensuing exchange was like a sitcom when an old friend drops by.

"Oh my gosh, it's you!" Trudy exclaimed.

"I thought this was probably your place," a strangely familiar male voice said.

"Come in."

"Should I take off my shoes?"

"Not unless you feel like it. I don't have carpet."

I was staring at the door, still trying to place the voice, when the policeman from this afternoon crossed the threshold.

"Gwen, look who's here." Trudy beamed as if I would be thrilled at the sight of Officer Marcus Timmens again. Strangely, she did seem to be thrilled.

I, on the other hand, was panic-stricken, not only by Officer Timmens's showing up this way, but also by how happy Trudy seemed to see him. Had she taken leave of her senses? There was no way a policeman showing up at her house at this hour could be a good thing.

"What's going on?" He inspected the mess on the kitchen island.

"Making cupcakes," she said. "Lemon. If you stick around, you might be able to sample one."

No, no, no, I screamed internally. *Don't ask him to stick around.*

I could see the gears in his brain whirring. "Kind of late for baking, isn't it?"

"It's my side hustle. I supply cupcakes to a local café. You probably know it—the Buttered Biscuit?"

His jaw dropped. "Get out. You make the cupcakes there?" He surveyed her mixing bowls—and her—with even more interest. "Those are just the best damned cupcakes in town. That's *you?*"

Unable to hold back a smile, she pushed one of her unfolded Enchanted Cupcakes boxes toward him. "I was just about to start making the icing for them."

"Don't let me stop you. I love the lemon-flavored ones."

"Can I get you something to drink?"

That question—finally—seemed to remind Timmens that he hadn't come here to learn about Trudy's baking operation. His smile faded and he cleared his throat. "Actually, I'm here on business. We received a call earlier this evening at the station."

"Not about the greenhouse kerfuffle this afternoon?"

"No . . ." He pulled out a pad of paper and frowned at what he'd written down on it. "It was a call from someone who wanted to report your husband missing."

My heart thudded in my chest.

"Laird?" Trudy swallowed. "Missing?"

"Laird Webster. Professor Laird Webster."

"Well . . ." Trudy looked at me for help, but I still had that throat clot. "That's . . . odd."

I managed to swallow. "Who called?"

"That's confidential, ma'am. The thing is, I just need to verify that he's not a misper."

"Missing person?" Trudy translated. "Of course not."

"That you know of," I said, trying to alert her that we might need wiggle room.

"Yes," she added quickly. "That we know of. The truth is, he did stand me up this afternoon, as you know. So . . ."

Timmens frowned. "You never did hear from him after that?"

"No. But honestly, I've been so busy that I haven't given Laird a lot of thought since I saw you. Like I said, we're separated."

"And you don't know where he's staying?"

"Not since he walked earlier this week. It's been a difficult time, as you can imagine. I just assumed . . ." She sniffed. "I guessed there was another woman in the picture."

His mouth turned down in sympathy. "I see."

"Was it a woman who called you?" she asked.

"I really can't say."

Of course it wasn't a woman. I knew exactly who it had been. Jeremy. He'd even warned me that he was going to do this, the creep. And just when I'd started to believe that he was a decent human being. He'd wanted me to think that, probably, so he could get me off my guard and trip me up.

Now Trudy was unwittingly handing Officer Timmens information that conflicted with what I'd been telling Jeremy. If the two men ever compared notes, we'd be sunk.

"Excuse me," I said.

I took off the apron Trudy had given me and went downstairs to the basement. Griz, who'd crept back up to the living room, shot down the stairs in front of me. He was the strangest cat.

Laird, old-school academic that he was, still kept a Rolodex in his basement office. I flipped through it until I found Jeremy Westerman, then I punched the number into my phone.

The line rang and then went to voice mail. I left a short message, barely able to restrain my anger. "Jeremy, this is Gwen. I know what you did, you fink. And just as I was beginning to like you!"

I hung up, then kicked myself. What a stupid message. There needed to be a ten-second window when you could delete a voice mail, the same way Google allowed you to unsend an email.

I looked over at the old couch and saw Griz huddled in the corner. Poor guy. The mixer noise and the unfamiliar voices were probably traumatizing him. I threw myself onto the couch and gathered him in my lap. He growled but, for once, didn't claw himself out of my grasp.

"It's okay," I cooed in a low voice. "This, too, shall pass, Grizzle-friend. Next time Tannith has to drop you off somewhere, I'll ask her to leave you with me and we'll play with Ping-Pong balls and eat salmon for a week. Would you like that?"

He looked up at me, and his growls changed to purrs. Almost like he understood.

I stared into his eyes. This afternoon, I'd imagined Esme talking to me, I'd cast a stop spell on a ringing alarm, and now I was communicating with a cat.

You're not communicating with a cat, Gwen, I scolded myself. You're just exhausted. Also, if I was communicating, I was also lying. Because there was no way Tannith could drop Griz at Daniel's—fur played havoc with his mucous membranes—or that we'd be feasting on salmon there.

"Just hang in there, Griz."

I went back upstairs, Griz at my heels. Officer Timmens had been put to work. He was wearing one of Trudy's aprons with EAT, DRINK, AND WEAR STRETCH PANTS emblazoned across the bib and was perched on my old spot on a stool at the kitchen island. He'd taken over my lemon-zesting operation. Neither he nor Trudy looked up when I came back in. I doubt they'd noticed that I'd been gone.

"My wife never could get into it," he was saying.

"It's only one of the best shows ever." Catching what must have been a confused expression on my face, Trudy explained, *"Great British Bake Off."*

That wasn't what was confusing me. "Everything under control here? Do you need my help?" *Do you need me to rescue you?*

"No, we're fine. Officer Timmens said he's never made a cupcake. Can you believe it?"

"I've *eaten* plenty of them." He laughed. "I'm more of a grill cooker, myself."

Trudy nodded. *"BBQ with Franklin.* It's inspired me to get more serious next summer."

They continued talking as Trudy iced a lemon cupcake and then showed Marcus how. Evidently this required standing so close she was practically giving him a lap dance. You'd think the man had never held a butter knife before.

My phone rang and I glanced at it. Jeremy, of course. I slapped the cover closed again and dropped it into my pocket. I wasn't going to talk to him now—especially not in front of the police officer he'd ratted us out to.

Not that anyone was paying the slightest bit of attention to me. I could have been doing Simone Biles–level gymnastic routines across the living room and I doubt either of them would have done more than flick a glance my way.

By the time Trudy fired up her KitchenAid mixer to make the peanut butter–chocolate batter, the Marcus-Trudy party didn't look as if it would be breaking up anytime soon.

"I better get home," I announced over the mixer's insistent whir. "Another busy day tomorrow."

I half expected Trudy to beg me to stay, but instead she smiled her biggest smile and said, "Usual time in the morning?"

The thought of having to get up early made me want to cry, but I nodded and bent down to pick up Esme's carrier.

"What's that?" Timmens asked.

"My rabbit."

A dark eyebrow arched at me. "You always lug a rabbit around with you?"

"This is a special rabbit. So close she feels like family."

"Whatever floats your boat." Timmens and Trudy laughed as if he'd said something hilarious.

My face must have shown my dismay because Trudy came forward with a box of the cupcakes they had just frosted. "I promised you food and we forgot to eat. Take these."

I couldn't help glancing over at Marcus and then meeting her eyes again. "You sure you don't want me to stay and help you finish up the last batch?"

"Not necessary." She patted my shoulder.

The cop nodded and lifted a spatula. "We've got this."

I hovered uneasily, not liking this scenario at all. "I thought you might have to go back to work."

"Nope. End of my shift."

I tried to send Trudy a meaningful look. *Don't talk too much.* It could be that Officer Timmens was just pulling a Columbo on her, trying to get her to let her guard down.

"Get some sleep," Trudy said. "I'll see you tomorrow. Same bat time, same bat channel."

No matter how chipper she seemed, I could not bring myself to approve of this flirtation. The cop's popping up was ill-timed, and Trudy was so lust-struck that she seemed completely oblivious of the pitfalls that having a cop in her house under the current circumstances represented.

By the time I got back to my house, I'd stress-eaten half a lemon cupcake—they really were good—and felt a kind of ache at being so disapproving of Trudy's dalliance with the good-looking cop. Love was a wonderful thing. Why shouldn't she embrace it if it came along? Maybe I was just jealous. What wouldn't I do to have a guy lust after me that much?

Sighing, I pushed open my car door. As I moved to stand, a tall figure emerged from the shadows.

Chapter 19

After letting out a shriek that terrified both myself and Jeremy, I sank back down on the driver's seat, with my feet hanging out the door. My heart punched against my ribs. "You've got to stop doing this."

"What's wrong?" he asked, as if my fear were totally misplaced.

"Oh, nothing—it's great when strange men unexpectedly jump out of the dark at me."

"How could you not have expected me? You left me that message."

"It wasn't an invitation to come over."

He took the cupcake box from me and helped me out of the car as if I were an old lady—or just a lady, actually. I wasn't used to being helped out of cars. Did normal men do that anymore?

He's not normal. He wanted something. "Why are you here?"

"Your message confused me. And when I called you back, you didn't pick up your phone."

I slammed the car door. "Are you saying you didn't call the cops?"

"The police?" His eyes widened in confusion. "Why would I do that?"

"You said you were going to." I circled to the passenger side of the Kia to retrieve Esme.

The corners of his mouth tucked downward. "I forgot about that."

I pulled out the carrier and nudged the passenger door shut. "I didn't. And tonight a cop showed up at Trudy's."

"To ask about Laird?"

"Yes."

"So he really is missing."

"No, he's not."

He traipsed after me to the porch. I needed to get rid of him. After unlocking the front door, I turned around. "Thanks for carrying the cupcakes. I'll take them from here."

"I thought you picked those up in the morning."

"How did you know that?"

"I saw you delivering them, remember?"

I doubt Daniel knew my schedule as well as Jeremy did.

"Don't you want me to come in?"

A flashback to the daydream I'd had this afternoon flitted through my mind. I frowned. I shouldn't be thinking of Daniel while talking to Jeremy. Or maybe I shouldn't be talking to Jeremy and comparing him to Daniel.

"I'm worried about what happened with your cousin and the police," he said. "She's not in jail, is she?"

I remembered how I'd left Trudy and Officer Timmens, yukking it up in her kitchen. "Not in jail." But not safe, either.

"I also wouldn't mind sampling one of these cupcakes. They smell delicious."

I looked into those green eyes and my resistance wavered. He was staring at me the way Trudy looked at Marcus. A voice in my head egged me on. *A cupcake. What could it hurt?*

"Okay, but I can't stay up too late tonight. It was an exhausting day."

"What did you do?" He trailed me to the kitchen.

Helped transform a toad cousin I'd never met back into a human. I shrugged. "The usual."

In the kitchen, he set the box down on the Formica counter and opened it. "Mm. Lemon. That's what I thought—I love lemony things."

"Me, too." My half-eaten cupcake was testament to that.

"Mind if I try one?"

"Be my guest." I rustled up a plate and a napkin and handed them to him to catch the crumbs.

"What's this flavor called? I always love the names I see on the cards at the Buttered Biscuit."

"I don't know. Usually Trudy names them, but sometimes my parents will do it."

"Must have been nice growing up in a family like yours."

It was a puzzling thing to say. "What was your family like?"

He shifted feet. "Nonexistent."

Did this mean his family was emotionally distant? That his parents were jet-setters? "What did your parents do?"

"They owned a video store. At least, that's what I'm told. They died in a car accident when I was just a year and a half old. I was in the back seat, but I lived. It was flukish. I looked up a newspaper story on the accident once—it sounds as if I was inches away from being killed, too."

What a terrible story. My resolve to kick him out as soon as possible evaporated. I filled the teakettle and thumped it onto a burner. "What happened to you after that?"

"Foster homes. Lots of foster homes for the first few years. I guess I wasn't the easiest little kid to handle."

"After what happened to you, who would expect you to be?"

"More than you might imagine. Most people trying to adopt kids don't yearn for a toddler with PTSD. So I was shuffled around for a couple of years until I ended up with a nice couple who had several other fosters living with them."

"Good people?"

"They were great, but they'd taken a lot on themselves. A teenager they were also fostering had a lot of problems and kept running away, or getting caught with drugs. That part was chaotic and took a lot of their attention, so I just flew under their radar most of the time. But it was the most stable family I lived with, and I was able to go to a good school."

"And somewhere along the way you discovered a love of history."

He leaned against the counter. "Mostly, I loved libraries—the quiet, the endless books to escape into. I fell in love with researching and spending time working in library carrels."

"I can see that."

He'd made himself right at home and had pulled out another plate for me while I made tea. His being here seemed normal. Strangely normal.

"Sorry I've been so long-winded." He put my half cupcake on the plate and slid it toward me. "I assume this is yours?"

I reached over and picked at a crumb. "You haven't been long-winded. I asked you a question and you answered it."

"Most people have a hard time understanding what it's like to grow up without real parents. Not many people have much experience with orphans, except from movies and Dickens books."

"I do. My parents took in a girl whose parents had died." In the same kind of accident that had taken Jeremy's parents from him, which was a coincidence. But I supposed car accidents were a common denominator of many family tragedies.

"You have a sister?" he asked.

"Well, a distant cousin who was raised like a sister. Tannith. My parents were appointed her guardians, but she's never used my family's name and they never officially adopted her."

"I wonder why."

"I think it was her choice."

I bit into my cupcake and chewed. Lemon exploded on my tongue. Trudy truly was a wizard in the kitchen.

"Where does Tannith live?"

"That's sort of up in the air at the moment."

His gaze was intense, and it was difficult for me to drag my attention elsewhere. I couldn't let a sob story about his background seduce me into trusting him. If anything, his story's similarity to Tannith's should have put me on my guard. For all I knew, every word was a lie.

But why would he make up something like that? He sounded so sincere. And understanding. Maybe that was part of what attracted me to him. The longer our gazes remained locked, the further the possibility of Watchers strayed from my thoughts. I felt myself leaning toward him, just as I had in the daydream.

He cleared his throat, bringing me up short. "I really shouldn't be eating this cupcake." He demolished the last of it in a bite. "It's late."

Thank goodness one of us seemed capable of rational thought. "I'm sorry you wasted your time coming all this way if you just wanted to find out about Laird."

"I didn't really come here to find out about Laird. I mean, sure, I was curious, but"—two blotches of red appeared in his cheeks—"what really drew me here was when you said in your message that you were beginning to like me."

I'd forgotten blurting that out.

Heat climbed from my toes to my scalp, and for a moment it felt as if I were floating. In my mind's eye, Jeremy leaned across the table to kiss me. A long, lingering kiss.

For God's sake, stop. I gave my head a sharp shake. What was wrong with me? Probably the result of watching Trudy flirting with Officer Timmens over the cupcake icing. But Trudy saw herself as a soon-to-be divorcée, while I was still involved with Daniel. Probably. If Little Orphan Tannith hadn't charmed him away from me.

Regardless, I was living in his house.

I picked up my plate and cupcake. "I'm going to take this into the living room." There was more room in there, and the atmosphere wasn't as intimate as sitting around the little dinette.

Or it wasn't until Jeremy sat down on the couch next to me. Too close. Thoughts about Daniel flashed through my head. I

felt almost as if I were betraying him, sitting here and eating cupcakes on the couch with this near stranger. Daniel didn't approve
of eating on the living room furniture.

"Please don't bring up Daniel," Jeremy said, almost as if he
could read my mind.

I dropped the plate on the coffee table, spooked. "Why did
you bring him up?"

"Because he's your boyfriend. It's the elephant in the room,
isn't it? You haven't mentioned him all evening."

"Why would I? I take him for granted. I mean, in a good way—
the way couples take each other for granted when they feel perfect confidence."

I heard the words coming out of my mouth and writhed with
shame at what a liar I was. *I'm so sure of Daniel, I've spent days worrying he's been love-hexed by Tannith.*

"Well, where is he?"

"I told you—in Vermont, studying beetles." *I think.*

Jeremy's eyes narrowed, and he reached out and pushed a
stray lock of hair out of my eyes. "Beetles."

"Studying beetles is important." I swallowed. "The wrong
beetle in the wrong place can mean the end of civilization."

"And here I've spent all this time studying history, when
everything hinges on bugs."

We laughed, and I made the mistake of looking into his eyes
again. They were even more mesmerizing now than when I'd
first met him. They almost seemed to sparkle.

His smile faded. "I can't imagine ever taking you for granted,
Gwen."

My heart did a somersault. *Ludicrous.* I tried to scoot over, but
the couch's arm didn't let me go far.

"I mean, if we were a couple," he added.

"That's a big hypothetical."

"Is it?" He reached over and touched my arm.

That simple contact, even through my thick cardigan and my
flannel shirt, scorched something inside me. It wasn't warm in
the house—Daniel had the thermostats set to an energy-saving

sixty-eight degrees—but I felt warm all over. I intended to shrug my arm away, but my movement was languorous and heavy. I now saw Jeremy's eyes through a blur. I was viewing the world through an old Hallmark-card-commercial glow, as though someone had put Vaseline on the lens.

The first time I saw Jeremy I'd noticed his eyes, but I hadn't noticed that he had surprisingly broad shoulders. On the couch next to me, he seemed more substantial than he had in the kitchen. Moving to the living room had obviously been a mistake, but getting up and crossing back to the kitchen would require more energy than I possessed in that moment. I hadn't been drunk in a long time, but this feeling approached it.

"Gwen." He leaned toward me. He was about to kiss me.

And I just sat there like a bump on a pickle. This was crazy.

His lips touched mine. *Maybe not so crazy after all.* He might be a man full of doubts and questions, but nothing about his kiss was tentative. His hands moved up my arms, and one curled around my nape, drawing me closer, deepening the kiss. In that little space, in his arms, I forgot to think about what was at stake. Daniel, domesticity, Death Valley vacations . . . it all vanished, as did my worries about Watchers and hexes. All I could think about was the languidness in my limbs, the warmth inside me, and Jeremy.

He was stronger than I expected, solid. But he wasn't pushy. The kiss tasted of tea, and citrus.

Lemon.

Luscious lemon cupcakes. Lusty lemon.

Oh. God.

I pushed away. "We can't do this," I said, practically gasping.

He collapsed against the couch cushions. "Is it Daniel?"

"No, it's the cupcakes." When his bemused gaze met mine, I shook my head. "And Daniel. But the cupcakes . . ." I still felt almost drunk. What had Trudy done to those cupcakes? Whatever she'd been feeling for that cop must have spilled over into that icing the two had mixed up. Lust-Drunk Lemon, Mom could call them.

Those were dangerous cupcakes.

"I don't want to rush things," Jeremy said, "but I think it's only fair to say that I'm in love with you."

"No, you're not." I forced myself to sit up straight, my hands folded primly in my lap. "Believe me, this is something else." Cupcake alchemy.

"You're thinking about Daniel?"

"No—" I could have slapped my hand over my mouth. "I mean, *yes*. Of course. But that's not all."

"I can't get you out of my mind, Gwen. I've never met anyone like you."

"You don't know me. I have . . . issues. Especially right now."

"Everyone has issues." He took my hand. "I told you about myself tonight. You think growing up as a foster kid didn't affect my personality?"

Damn it, I did not want to hurt this guy. I liked him. Under different circumstances . . .

No, scrap that. The circumstances would have to be entirely different. I would have to not be me, basically. "Honestly, Jeremy, you're a nice guy, but I don't think—"

"Stop." He held up both hands in surrender. "When anyone says, 'You're a nice guy,' it's doom tolling."

"Don't say that. It's a myth that women are looking for jerks." The flicker of hope I saw in his eyes made me add, "I mean, yes, *this* is doomed." I pointed between him and me. "Romantically. The circumstances are all wrong. But I like you, and I'm sure there's a woman out there—"

"Please!" He stood abruptly, I assumed to head for the door. He didn't make it. "Don't—oh."

He swayed, staggered back, then crumpled and fell back onto the couch, landing exactly where he had been. He leaned his head against the backrest cushions and closed his eyes. "I feel woozy."

I wasn't feeling much better myself. This was terrible. That entire batch of cupcakes would need to be pitched. No telling the havoc they could wreak on relationships—not to mention the menace they posed to traffic safety. "Just rest for a moment. It'll pass."

"Rest, yeah," he echoed sleepily.

Exhausted and feeling the same physical effects from the cupcakes that he did, I leaned back and closed my eyes. A kaleidoscope of images danced in my mind. My cousins' faces. Rabbits. The foil inside the card Tannith had given me. Cousin Odin. Tannith, laughing. The cop. For one long psychedelic moment, these visions hung suspended in front of me, like the charms on Tannith's infernal mobile—cupcakes, a rabbit, a toad, Griz . . . They twisted and bobbed in the wind, making no sense. I tried to blink the mental picture away, and it was replaced by Jeremy's eyes. . . .

And this was all accompanied by a subtle swishing sound. What was it?

Oh, yes, the sound the Kit-Kat Klock made as its tail swept back and forth with the seconds. It was relentless, and the seconds piled on one another, even as I slept. Minutes of seconds, then hours.

"What the hell is going on?"

My eyes snapped open. Everything had changed. Morning sunlight poured through the windows. During the night I had jackknifed sideways, and though my legs were hanging off the couch, my torso was horizontal. My gaze was level with the coffee table, and my right cheek lay against warm denim. On Jeremy's thigh. Only it wasn't Jeremy's voice I'd heard.

I shot up to sitting again. "Daniel!"

Chapter 20

He stood in the center of the living room, his arms tensed at his sides. His unshaven jaw was clenched so tight I could see the skin under his unshaven stubble twitch. He was still wearing his field gear—faded jeans, Columbia hiking boots, green flannel shirt, puffy vest.

Next to me, Jeremy snorted awake. "Gwen?" he asked, as if worried I'd disappeared during the night.

If only.

"Gwen?" Daniel also asked, to remind me he was still waiting for an explanation.

Hearing the strange voice, Jeremy fumbled for his glasses, which had slid off onto the couch cushion. He found them and pushed them back in place, taking in the six feet of outraged boyfriend in front of him. "You must be Daniel."

"Yes." Daniel's voice was curt.

Jeremy cleared his throat. "Gwen was telling me about you."

"This isn't how it looks," I said.

"Not exactly how it looks," Jeremy put in, to be specific.

I flicked an annoyed glance his way. "Not *at all* how it looks."

Daniel shifted, crossing his arms, but something about Jeremy's manner seemed to tamp down his anger a notch. As if he'd taken Jeremy's measure and didn't detect a real threat. Daniel's next words were addressed to me. "You know, I drove all night to get here."

His manner was ticking me off. "How could I know that? I just woke up."

"Woke up on a couch with a stranger you picked up somewhere."

"Wait just a minute," Jeremy objected. "She didn't pick me up. We've known each other for two days."

"Oh, two whole days!" Daniel clapped his hands in mock surprise. "Forgive me—I didn't know. I've been away for . . . three whole days."

"Don't be melodramatic, Daniel. Nothing happened."

"Nothing much," Jeremy added.

Was he trying to make things worse? I sent him a warning glare. "Nothing important."

"That kiss meant something to me," he said.

Daniel spluttered.

"That kiss was a mistake," I said. "It wasn't even real. It was just the cupcakes."

Jeremy's gaze narrowed to a perplexed squint. "You said that last night. It didn't make sense then, either."

"None of this makes sense," Daniel said, livid. "Gwen, do you understand that when you didn't answer your phone or respond to my messages, I was worried as hell? I abandoned a colleague to drive all night to get here and check on you." He gestured at Jeremy. "And I find you with this . . ."

"Jeremy Westerman," Jeremy said.

"He's an adjunct at the college."

"History department."

"He knows Laird."

Daniel tossed up his hands. "I guess everything's okay then."

"Of course it's okay," I said calmly, just as Esme hopped into the room.

Crap.

Daniel looked over at the rabbit, whose presence seemed to annoy him as much as Jeremy's did. "What is *that?*"

"I'm bunny-sitting for Trudy for a few nights."

"You know how I feel about owning animals," Daniel said.

"Believe me, I don't own Esme."

Jeremy shook his head at me. "Is he always like this?"

"Like what?"

"A domestic Mussolini."

"I resent—" Before Daniel could finish, he drew back, puzzled. "Wait. Don't you have an aunt named Esme?"

I got to my feet. I was too tired to be having this conversation. "I need some coffee." I scooped up Esme. "There's no point in arguing about any of this. You're making a mountain out of a molehill," I told Daniel as I passed him. "I'm surprised at you."

He marched after me. "*You're* surprised? You've got lines on your cheek from sleeping on the crotch of some guy's jeans all night."

"We conked out on the couch and I just happened to flop over."

I yanked out the box of coffee pods, and when I saw Daniel's barely restrained irritation, it gave me extra pleasure to slam one into the slot. "I'm sorry my life didn't stop while you were away."

Although it might have been better for everyone if it had.

"Did I say anything about stopping your life? Just not cheating on me would be appreciated."

"I didn't cheat."

"She didn't cheat," Jeremy said from the doorway. "And she mentioned you several times."

Both Daniel and I rounded on him.

"You're not helping," I said.

Jeremy pushed his glasses up and looked from my face to Daniel's. "Maybe I should go."

"I think you'd better," I said.

He cast a glance at the pastry box on the table. "Can I grab a cupcake?"

Good grief. The cupcakes. "No."

But Daniel was already handing over the box. "Take them all. Those things are nothing but sugary, fat-laden junk."

Jeremy eyed me. "He's insulting your family's cupcakes. Think about that."

"Just go," I said. "And please don't eat those. Seriously. Throw them away."

"Will I see you later?"

I blew out a breath as the coffee maker belched its last blasts of steam into my cup. "No."

"I'll call you."

After the front door had closed behind Jeremy, I shook my head at Daniel. "You shouldn't have given him those cupcakes."

"Would you stop talking like cupcakes are the problem here? What's going on? I leave my house for a couple of days, and suddenly you're dragging in strange men and rabbits, and not answering your phone, and"—he glared at the verboten, wasteful one-cup coffee maker—"why are you using that thing?"

"Because it's convenient. And as for Jeremy, he's just worried about Laird."

"What does worry about Laird have to do with kissing you?"

I took a gulp of coffee. God, I needed that. "Jeremy got a little . . . tipsy, made a pass, and that was the end of it."

"Except for the sleeping together on the couch part."

"Fully clothed! I told you, I just flopped over. Like when you fall asleep on an airline seat and fall too far over into the neighboring seat."

He planted his fists on his hips.

"You're acting like an angry dad." *And a domestic Mussolini.*

"And you're acting like it's outrageous for me to feel angry that I rushed home worried about you only to find you—"

"Don't say it," I warned.

He ran a hand through his hair. "I don't get why you couldn't have just called me. I was worried. Thank goodness I talked to Tannith."

I put my cup down. "You talked to Tannith? When?"

"Last night. She called me."

My eyes narrowed on the linoleum underfoot. Why would she have called Daniel? "What did she say?"

"She was worried. She said she'd dropped Griz off at Trudy's but wasn't sure he was being taken care of."

An odd suspicion scratched at the back of my mind. "What time did she call you?"

"Last night, late. Almost midnight."

After Jeremy had arrived here, then. "And she told you that you should go home and check things out?"

"Not in so many words, but I was already worried, so . . ."

I tried to put the events in sequence. Jeremy had sworn he had nothing to do with the call to the Zenobia police about Laird. As annoying as Jeremy could be, he didn't strike me as a liar. If anything, he was too honest for his own good, or mine. Could Tannith have placed that call to the police?

But how would Tannith have known anything about Laird? Unless she was driving around peeking in windows . . .

"Did Tannith say where she was?"

"She's moving to Manhattan. She told me you all knew that."

She was supposed to move Friday. Tomorrow. But right now she could be anywhere. Or everywhere.

What was she up to?

I glanced at my watch. It was already after eight. "I'm so late. I've got to run."

I headed to the bathroom, flipped the tap onto full blast, and washed my face in cold water. Daniel stood at the door, watching me brush my teeth in double time.

"I just got here. I thought we could have a serious talk."

"Now?" I asked through a mouthful of foam. Whatever was on Daniel's mind, I wasn't sure I could face it in yesterday's clothes, with a cupcake hangover.

"There's something I've been wanting to ask you. Even after what's happened this morning, I think now's the time." He followed me to the bedroom, where I yanked a different flannel shirt off a closet hanger. "I'll take your word about that Jeremy character. Whatever your faults, I know you're not promiscuous."

I hooted. "What are my faults?"

"Maybe I worded that wrong." He frowned. "Please don't get sidetracked. This is important. This is life changing."

As I did up my buttons, my hands began to shake. So Trudy had been right. He wasn't running off with Tannith. He was going to pop the question. And I'd been so consumed with rabbits, toads, cupcakes, and paranoia, I hadn't given two minutes' thought to what would probably be the most important decision of my life.

"Daniel, are you . . . ?"

"Yes." He reached around to pick up a box from the dresser. A *very large* box. It was a double-size shoebox. He passed it reverently to me. "I went to the store yesterday after calling your mom for your size."

The possibility that this was just some humorous gag-wrapping job flashed across my mind. But when I flipped the top open and pulled the tissue back, I was looking at a pair of calf-high, insulated boots. The sharp smell of rubber, leather, and treated waterproof nylon wafted up at me. This was definitely not a De Beers commercial moment. "Boots?"

He nodded eagerly. "It's sudden, I know, but I just got the news the day before yesterday. I've been approved for a research position in Whitehorse, Yukon, to study spruce and pine borers."

"Wow. Congrats." *The Yukon?*

"I want you to come with me."

"Oh." The significance of the boots sank in. "I get it."

"I know it's a big change, but it would really suck to go up there all by myself. Obviously, I thought the job was a long shot when I applied for it. That's why I was making other plans, like our trip to Death Valley, which I know you had your heart set on. But believe me, this will be better. Just think of it—a cozy wintry cabin, the northern lights, and so many opportunities to study how migrating beetles are affecting boreal forests in some of the northernmost latitudes."

"Cozy firesides and invasive insects. Sounds almost too good to be true. How long do you intend to be there?"

"Two years. The grant comes with a teaching position at the university in Whitehorse."

Two years? "What about my family, and Abracadabra?"

"I'm sure you can do odd jobs in the Yukon."

"Yeah, but I've built up my business here. I have employees, not to mention regular clients counting on me."

He blew out a breath. "You think those old geezers won't be able to find somebody else to drive them to the drugstore?"

He's insulting your family's cupcakes.

Now my clients.

I put the boots back on the dresser and closed the box. "I'm sorry, I'm running late. We'll have to talk about all this later. I'm really happy for you, though."

He didn't bother to hide his astonishment. "You're going out?"

"Of course. I have to deliver the cupcakes"—come to think of it, I needed to *not* deliver the cupcakes, at least the lemon ones—"and then I need to get the guys set up for work for the day."

"You say that as if you won't be with them."

"I might have other things to tend to."

His jaw tightened. His disappointment was palpable. "I thought we could make plans."

"We can. Later." I needed time to process all this. He currently had no intention of running off with Tannith—that was the good news. But apparently he expected me to drop everything and move with him to the frozen north.

"I guess I might as well go to the college then." He looked over at Esme, who was staring at us from the doorway. "What am I supposed to do with the rabbit?"

"I'm taking her with me."

"You're taking a rabbit with you to do handyman work?"

"Not exactly."

His gaze narrowed on me. "Is something wrong, Gwen?"

"No." The answer came out too quickly. "Things have just been hectic." And hex-ic.

"All right." He blew out a long breath. "It's a good thing you're taking her. My eyes are already itching from the fur."

"I meant to vacuum before you got back."

"I'll do that before I go to the college. I'll have to pop a Benadryl, too."

I left, feeling guilty for dragging fur into the house and making him resort to drugs. I sat in the car, wondering what the hell I was going to do. I tapped out a text to Kyle telling him to meet me at Mrs. Caputo's again this morning.

He replied almost instantly: *Sure thing. Happy Halloween!*

Halloween was already off to a gruesome start.

Something in the trees caught my eye. It was a mirror hanging down from the center of Tannith's mobile, the one that had appeared in my nightmares. The medallion reminded me of the reflective disk on Griz's collar.

A little mirror. Reflective. Like the Kit-Kat Klock.

Holy . . .

I understood now. My cousins and I had a problem. A big one. Her name was Tannith, and she was watching our every move.

Chapter 21

When I arrived at Trudy's, Officer Timmens was parked on a stool at the kitchen island in a bathrobe that I could only assume was one of Laird's. The sight made me raise a brow, but who was I to judge? I'd just spent the night with Jeremy. For all I knew, this setup was equally innocent. Except that there was nothing chaste about the way the police officer's dark eyes drank in Trudy's movements as she bustled around the kitchen.

"We were expecting you thirty minutes ago." She gestured to the usual stack of boxes.

I sent her what I hoped was an urgent look. "Can we talk for a minute?"

"Sure."

I scoped the room for Griz. Officer Timmens must have thought that my hesitation to speak openly was all about him because he pushed off the stool. "I'll go take a shower while you ladies have your talk."

He and Trudy brushed hands as he passed. If I'd harbored any doubts, that single intimate gesture would have convinced me that they'd had more fun last night than Jeremy and I had.

When the bathroom door closed, Trudy turned back to me. "I hope you're not going to deliver a lecture."

As if. I cleared my throat, noting Griz perched on the arm of the sofa, watching us intently. I lowered my voice. "Come out onto the porch. There's something you should see."

Trudy eyed me warily. "Marcus can't hear us through the bathroom door when the shower's running."

"Come outside," I repeated more forcefully. "For just a moment."

Reluctantly, she followed me out to the porch, where only the jack-o'-lanterns could hear us. Trudy surveyed her yard and the surrounding houses as if expecting to see some obvious reason for me to have lured her out here.

Griz, I noticed, had sauntered after us. I shut the front door before he could dart out to the porch. He yowled and clawed the other side of the door in protest.

"What's going on?"

Even if it was no longer necessary, I kept my voice low. "It's Tannith."

Trudy waved a hand. "Oh, I don't care about her anymore. She can have Laird if she wants him so badly."

"That's not what I meant. Tannith is watching us."

Trudy took a step back and scanned the street again. "How?"

"I think she's using mirrors."

"What mirrors?"

"Those gifts she gave us—the hanging things—had mirrors. And those letters she sent to us had a foil *T* on the stationery."

"So what? I tore up my letter, and I tossed that hanging contraption in a drawer."

"Right. And so she dropped Griz off at your door—his collar has that weird reflective disk, remember?"

Realization dawned. If Tannith had been watching us, she not only knew some of what we were up to, she was also a more adept witch than we'd guessed. And how had she gotten away with this for so long without the Council catching up to her? On the drive over, I'd reached one conclusion about this.

"What could she have seen?" Trudy wondered aloud.

"Enough to know that Laird isn't here anymore. She's the one who called the police."

She laughed. "That might be the first thing she's done that I've wanted to thank her for."

I obviously hadn't conveyed how serious this was. "Trudy, I think Tannith might be a Watcher."

Her head jerked back, and all humor drained from her expression. "Surely not."

"Right, she could be messing with us all on her own. But I've been thinking. Tannith hasn't done a lick of work since she graduated six years ago, when she came into her mysterious inheritance."

"What's the mystery? Her parents left her money."

"So she said. But knowing Tannith, if she had all that money, why did she choose to stay here? Why has she spent so much time hanging out with us? That letter was all the proof you need of the contempt she feels for us."

Trudy didn't have a response.

"I think she's snitching on us to the Council," I said, "and that letter was meant to stir us up enough to give her something big to snitch about. She knew we'd be tempted to break out our underdeveloped powers."

Trudy's laugh was a raspy sound this time. "If she'd just stuck around for a day or two, she could have caught me at it."

"We're lucky she left when she did."

Trudy's eyes went round as the implications became clear. In the past few days, we'd all performed enough witchcraft—inept as it was—to cook our goose as far as the Council was concerned. I don't know what Odin had been working on before they zapped him out of existence, but was there any reason to believe they'd show us any more mercy than they'd shown him?

"We have to be very careful," I said. "Especially when we're in our houses."

Trudy looked troubled. "What about at Esme's?"

"I think it's okay over there—Esme seems to have fooled them so far. Tannith has such contempt for her, I don't think she ever took her seriously. But you've got to assume that Griz is watching your every move while you're here." Poor Griz, forced to be Tannith's unwitting spy. "Hopefully we haven't already given her too much ammunition to use against us."

"I haven't been doing anything too witchy at home since Griz arrived."

"Except for those lemon cupcakes you made last night."

Her face fell. "What's the matter with them?"

"Nothing, if you want your food to hit like an aphrodisiac."

Her eyes blinked open wide. "Really? Is *that* what happened?"

"Well, I assume Officer Timmens liked you before the cupcakes."

She laughed. "What went on at your house?"

"Jeremy came over."

"You said we needed to stay away from him."

"Right. Which made it very unhelpful when he started scarfing down your cupcakes and decided he's in love with me."

"That's kind of sweet, though." She smiled, clearly in love with love this morning, even the supernaturally imposed kind.

"Daniel didn't think so when he walked in this morning and we were piled on top of each other on the couch."

"Oh."

Remembering that scene made me squirm. What was I going to do? Whether to chuck everything for the Yukon wasn't even my biggest problem right now.

"The thing is, we need to get Laird back, and then we have to figure out a way to shut Laird up about everything that's happened."

"That shouldn't be a problem. Even if Laird remembers being an amphibian, he won't want to admit it. You know what he thinks about witchcraft."

"Good. Then all we have to do is get him back to normal."

Sure, that was all.

Trudy cast a regretful glance back at her front door. "As soon as Marcus leaves, I'll meet you over at Esme's."

I nodded. "I'll come back in and get the cupcakes. Act natural in front of the cat."

In the house, we made loud small talk for Tannith's benefit, via Griz, then I left for the Buttered Biscuit, as usual.

At Trudy's front door, though, I stopped to ask, "Have you tried the peanut butter–chocolate cupcakes?" It would be good to know of any side effects before distributing them.

"I finished one before bed last night. They seemed fine to me. I slept like a baby."

They were probably safe.

I found a city garbage can and tossed out the lemon cupcakes. Maybe the rodents would find them and there'd be a hot time in the old town tonight.

"We expected you an hour ago." Dad eyed me as I rushed through the door with the cupcakes. I must have looked as frenzied as I felt. "What's wrong?"

Nothing except that I was running further behind every stop I made, and that I desperately needed to get a curse reversed, and my relationship with the man I'd moved in with just three months earlier seemed to be entering a literal deep freeze.

"Everything's fine," I lied, because this was my dad and I didn't want him to worry that the Grand Council of Witches was going to obliterate his daughter. I had to make sure I didn't say too much to my parents now. Tannith's mobile had been hung right in the middle of the restaurant, amid the piñata pumpkins and spiders with pipe-cleaner legs that Mom had strung from the ceiling in honor of Halloween.

Dad gave me a hug. "We're always here, Gwendle-bug. If you're worried about what your mom was talking to you about the other day—"

"I'm not. Everything's great. Just in a mad rush. I'm late to meet Kyle and Taj."

I hurried back out the door, nearly slamming into Milo on the way in. Right behind him stood Odin. Our recycled cousin was dressed in high-water jeans, old sneakers, and another BLAIR FOR MAYOR T-shirt under a black jacket.

Was Milo nuts? I took hold of both their arms and dragged them away from the door and around the corner of the building. The last thing we needed was for Tannith to get a glimpse of Odin. Hopefully the mobile in the restaurant hadn't yet transmitted their presence to her.

"You can't take him in there," I told Milo. "My parents would completely flip out if they saw their long-vanished cousin walk in the door."

"Well, what am I supposed to do? I'm at my wit's end. Have you ever tried to explain to your boyfriend why you've brought a strange guy home with you?"

"Unfortunately, yes."

"And was your boyfriend already boiling with anger because he'd discovered his polar bear had a tooth missing?"

Damn. "What was he doing, giving the rug a dental exam?"

"It's pretty obvious when you look at it. Also, Brett just notices things. He's detail oriented. It's why he works in a bank, and why he wants to be mayor. He'll be on top of everything."

"You don't have to sell me. I voted early."

"He was already in a mood last night when I came through the door with Odin, who, I don't know if you realize this, isn't the greatest conversationalist."

"I'm just rusty." Odin smiled affably. "I haven't been myself for a while. I'll get the knack of things soon."

Milo shot me an exasperated look. "I'm due to meet a client in fifteen minutes. I needed to drop him somewhere, and nobody was at Esme's."

Thank goodness Milo hadn't sauntered into Trudy's house with Odin. But where could we stow him for the day?

"I'm not sure he would do us much good at Esme's." I glanced over at him. If he minded people talking about him in the third person, he didn't show it. "Can you remember anything about witchcraft today, Odin?"

"Not a durn thing," he said, unfazed.

No telling what kind of interference having yet another non-functioning witch in Esme's basement laboratory would cause. I couldn't leave him with my parents, and I'd have a hard time explaining him to Daniel. Plus, Tannith was watching all our houses. The thought made my heart sink.

"Never mind, I'll take him," I said, as if we were deciding who would dog-sit for the day. "But you're coming to the laboratory after your meeting, aren't you?"

Milo nodded. "I'll have the rest of the day free. If you don't count the work I *should* be doing instead of playing Dr. Frankenstein in Esme's basement."

"Thank you, Milo. The sooner we get this figured out, the sooner we'll all be free." We needed all hands on deck. All hands that might prove useful, that is.

Milo was already backing away, eager to get to his car and his meeting.

"Wait." I closed the distance between us and lowered my voice. "You need to be wary of what you say around anything that Tannith has given you."

He tilted his head. "Why?"

"She's spying on us."

"How?"

"The mobiles she gave us."

"Mine went straight to Goodwill."

"Beware of *anything* she's given you. Especially anything that looks reflective. Did you throw away the letter she sent you?"

"I'm not sure." He frowned. "I'll have to hunt for it next time I'm home—but right now I've really got to run."

He hurried off to his appointment, which left just me and Odin. He was gazing curiously at the building. "Have I been here before?"

Odin had been disappeared before my parents had opened their restaurant. They were just adolescents when he'd been cursed.

"I don't think so."

"Something about it feels . . ."

I waited for him to finish the sentence, thinking he was groping for the right words. Instead, he was distracted. The café's dumpster around the corner attracted flies, and he suddenly reached out his hands and clapped them together, killing one. Then, before I could react, he licked the fly off his hand and swallowed.

"Gross!"

The criticism didn't register with him. Instead, he smiled in satisfaction. "It was a plump one."

I took his arm and dragged him to the Kia parked on the street. "Don't do that. You don't need to eat bugs now. Didn't you have breakfast?"

"Sure. Milo made oatmeal."

"Good. Eat things like that now." We got into the car and I drove toward Mrs. Caputo's. "In fact, try to forget about your frog days . . . however long they lasted." It must have been longer than I'd assumed. "Do you remember what you were doing before you ended up in that terrarium?"

"Not exactly. It feels like I've been gone a long time, though."

I nodded. "Decades, probably."

"Nothing seems quite real to me." He stared at Zenobia's quaint main drag with the same amazement of someone driving through Times Square for the first time. "It's great here. There's so much of everything."

To someone used to living in a glassed-in box, maybe that was true. Zenobia wasn't exactly the Big Apple.

"I thought you might like to spend the day with my two workers. They're cleaning an attic."

"Fantastic."

When I pulled into Mrs. Caputo's, Kyle and Taj were standing by the dumpster. At least, I assumed it was them. Kyle had a puzzling contraption on his head that turned out to be a Styrofoam mock-up of a helmet, covered in foil. It was festooned with a snarling bat on the crest. The other helmet, which was perched on Taj's head, was a dragon with a tail that draped down to his nape. Taj removed his quickly.

"What do you think?" Kyle asked.

"Well, as tinfoil hats go, those are pretty elaborate."

"I wanted to made a model before I did the real metalwork."

"Good idea."

"Are those part of our uniforms?" Odin asked.

Kyle took off his bat headdress and eyed Odin distrustfully. "You hired someone new?" Kyle saw himself as second-in-command and didn't welcome interlopers.

"Just for a day or two, to get this job done. This is Butch." I introduced Kyle and Taj to him.

"Do I get a hat?" Odin asked.

"Maybe later." I pulled him toward the house. Let the guys get used to the idea of having a new coworker. "Come inside. I want to introduce you to Mrs. Caputo."

Mrs. Caputo was thrilled to see a new face—someone new to pamper. "Oh, and you brought cupcakes again. How nice!" she said, taking the box from me. "I'm just brewing a fresh pot of coffee for everyone, and making a mushroom frittata."

"You really don't have to cook for them."

"They can't work on empty stomachs," she insisted.

They didn't seem to be working on full ones, either. "Have they made any progress in the attic?"

"Oh, yes. But there's no hurry."

"Your food smells good," Odin said.

Mrs. Caputo beamed up at him. "We'll fix you a big plate."

He looked around the kitchen in open admiration, as if he'd never seen anything like it before. "You have such nice things." He eyed a bowl of fruit. I saw the attraction immediately. Fruit flies were buzzing around the ripe bananas. For Odin, they were a flying smorgasbord.

I poked him and gave a sharp shake of my head. Then I gestured for him to follow me. "I'm going to show Butch up to the attic."

"Breakfast will be ready soon," Mrs. Caputo tootled.

Up in the attic, I began to despair. The area looked just as filthy and cluttered as it had days before. Did Mrs. Caputo have a secret store of old boxes that replaced the things Kyle and Taj brought down every day? It was starting to seem like one of those Grimms' fairy tales where the poor spinner had to face the same pile of flax every night.

I explained the game plan to Odin. "The job is to empty this place out. Mrs. Caputo will tell you whether items should be stacked neatly in the garage or taken down to that dumpster-pod thing where Taj and Kyle were standing."

He nodded eagerly. "I can do that."

"And if you have any questions, just check with Kyle. He's sort of my deputy."

"Like *Gunsmoke*."

I drew back in surprise. "You remember *Gunsmoke*?"

He looked amazed himself. "I guess so."

That had to be a good sign. If we could get him to remember his pre-terrarium life, maybe he would be able to let us know exactly what had happened to him, and why. "Esme hinted that you were working on something important before you . . . got into trouble."

"Really? That's so cool." He tilted his head. "I wonder what it was."

"Well, think about it in your spare time."

I escorted him back down to the kitchen, where the others were starting to gather around the table. Mrs. Caputo had the bat helmet on. I needed to get out of there.

"Would you like a cupcake to go?" she asked me.

"No thanks." After last night, I was considering laying off the cupcakes forever.

Back in the Kia, Esme was sitting forward in her carrier, her nose twitching close to the cage door. "Everything okay?"

She thumped.

What a world. My newly transformed cousin had bug cravings and my aunt spoke in leg thumps. I'd always known my family was unusual, but we were well into freak-show territory here. I could only hope that today would be the day that my cousins and I figured out how to get us back into normal-land.

It was time for us to flex our witch muscles.

Chapter 22

Griz

"Close your eyes and try to remember a time you were happy," the soothing voice of Dr. Tim instructs me from the television screen, and I dutifully obey. I picture myself in our old house, stretched out on the warm tiles of the kitchen, where the sun shone through the patio's long windows. Luxurious warmth. I didn't have a care in the world.

"What would it take to recreate that happiness?"

A miracle. I need Tannith to come get me away from here.

"Or do you need to forge a new happiness?"

My skin twitches at that suggestion. I don't like it.

At other times, Dr. Tim uses terms I've never heard, yet seem to describe what I'm going through. It's as if he knows me. "Maybe you think you don't deserve happiness," he says, looking out through the screen.

My throat catches. I always thought of myself as such a clever cat—a cut above. Because of Tannith. But now I wonder if I'm not up to her standard—even maybe that I do belong back at the SPCA with all the common alley cats, couch shredders, and other losers. I was given the perfect person, and I simply didn't measure up.

Worse, when Gwen came in and cuddled with me on the basement couch, I *purred*. That's how desperate I've become for cheap affirmation. The memory makes me cringe in shame.

Although Gwen also has a pleasing voice, like Dr. Tim's.

"Griz!"

I jump. I *hate* it when Tannith does this. Imagine having someone yelling at you from your own neck.

"I didn't send you over there to watch television."

"How do you know I am?" I ask guiltily.

Her reply is withering. "I can see through your tag, idiot. It's been pointed at the screen for the past hour."

That's right. I keep forgetting. "I can't help it if Trudy leaves the TV on. It's very loud."

"Especially when you're sitting right in front of it." Tannith releases a huff, and I imagine the black curtain of her hair swishing from one shoulder to the other.

Strange. It doesn't have the usual effect on me.

"What have you found out?"

I shift my front paws anxiously. "If you're watching, don't you know?"

I must be out of my mind to talk to her this way. If she were in the room with me, my reply would have earned me a swat. Her livid silence is enough to make me shrink back, anticipating a verbal smackdown.

"Where did they go?"

"I don't know."

"Where is Laird?"

Abashed, I repeat, "I don't know."

"You must have noticed *something*. Just from looking through your collar, I've witnessed some mighty strange goings-on."

"There's a man . . ."

"The policeman."

"He appeared out of nowhere. It surprised them."

"Of course he did. *I* called the police station and gave them a tip about Laird's disappearance."

"That was clever of you."

"That guy of Gwen's gave me the idea. If he'd been as concerned about Laird as he was about Gwen, I wouldn't have had to take the trouble."

I don't think her action reaped the outcome she intended, as with many things this week. I know more about the police now from a 911 show that comes on in the evenings. "This man doesn't behave like the policemen on television."

"What's the difference?"

"On television, they don't stay the night."

I hear an intake of her breath. I've said something right at last. But there's no word of praise.

Communicating is a two-way street, Dr. Tim advises us. I decide to take the initiative. "Have you ever heard of codependency?"

She laughs. "What the hell are you gibbering about?"

"It's when two individuals are locked in an unhealthy relationship, with one feeling as if he's making sacrifices but not being appreciated."

"Okay . . ." She sounds as if she doesn't see a problem with that.

"I'm trying to help, but I'm unhappy here."

She sighs. "Oh, Griz. Do you know what hearing you say that makes me feel?"

"No, what?"

"*Irritation!* This isn't about you, fleabag."

I'm stunned. What a horrible name to call me. "I only had fleas that once. It wasn't my fault."

She laughs, and I bristle. As if I couldn't point out some embarrassing things that would humiliate her.

Oh, yes. We cats see things. We don't demand access to bathrooms while you're in them for nothing.

She reads my mind, and her voice grows harsh. "You'd better

wipe those thoughts from your feeble brain and tell me what happened with that cop overnight."

"Nothing. At least, not that I could see. They talked about television shows, ate that nauseating food she bakes, and closed the door to her bedroom."

Tannith laughs delightedly. "Cheating on Laird! Trudy, I never thought you had it in you." There's a pause. "Maybe she really did bury him beneath the begonias."

At least I've pleased her. This gives me hope.

"Can I come home now?"

"No."

"When can I?"

"I'll come get you when I'm ready. It shouldn't be long now."

"I was just thinking about how happy we were back—"

"Wow, I'm so not interested in your emotional wittering, Griz. Just keep your eyes open. And stop watching television. It'll rot what's left of your pea-sized brain."

I can tell by the sudden silence coming from my collar that she'd shut me off.

I felt stung. She wasn't *listening.* I needed to find some way— some last-ditch effort—for her to see how much better it would be if we tried to start over. Back where we were happy. I just need to wait for my chance.

Chapter 23

Gwen

"Not to be negative, but this day has the stench of failure," Milo said.

Our combined efforts at witchcraft had not produced optimal results. Reheating yesterday's potion had left a pungent, puzzling scent of gardenia permeating the laboratory all day. To build our confidence, we attempted what one grimoire called an elementary doubling spell. Our test run on a small newt, instead of creating a clone, had resulted only in slightly enlarging the newt and creating a strange tuft of black fur on its head. We put our Elvis lizard into his own terrarium and sank onto the floor by the bookcases, unsettled and exhausted.

I checked my watch. "It's only two in the afternoon."

"Terrific," Milo said. "That leaves us plenty of time to create at least one more mutant by dinner."

Trudy regarded our creation in a different light. "I think he's kind of cute."

She wasn't wrong, but still. "Reptile grooming shouldn't require hair clippers."

"What now?" Milo asked. "Even if we pinpoint which of those toads is Laird, the most we'll be able to do for him with any certainty at this point is unrecede his hairline."

"I'm not sure we should try," Trudy said. "It's too dangerous."

Given our limited skills, I was absolutely sure we shouldn't. "What we need is Esme. If we could just get her back . . ."

Esme, who had been watching our progress, thumped her back leg twice. *No.* She obviously didn't want to be our guinea pig. Who could blame her?

Milo pushed up to his feet. "I don't know about you two, but it smells like someone set off a Lush bomb in here. I'm going to go outside to gulp in some fresh air and check my messages."

We all trouped upstairs, spent minutes unlocking ourselves, and stepped out into a windy fall afternoon. So cut off was Esme's basement laboratory that a cyclone could have hit Zenobia and we would never have known it.

I breathed deeply just as my phone started vibrating and hooting at me to let me know that messages were waiting for me.

I peeked at my phone, as Trudy and Milo did with theirs. Trudy was grinning, which made me suspect that she and her policeman had exchanged numbers.

Given how Daniel and I had parted, I doubted there would be anything in my messages to make me smile. There was, however, plenty to puzzle me.

MOM: *Call me.*

And later . . .

MOM: *Where are you? I must talk to you about Trudy. She's enchanting her cupcakes again. People are falling asleep in the restaurant.*

That didn't sound good.

One person who wasn't texting me was Daniel. Another was Kyle. Radio silence about how things were at Mrs. Caputo's. He usually checked in at lunch to let me know what was up, or to complain about Taj. With Butch there, I'd assumed he would have twice as much to grouse about.

"Trudy, are you sure you didn't do anything to those cup-cakes?"

She looked up from her screen, her smile fading. "As far as I know. Is there a problem?"

"You said you were tired by the time you iced those peanut butter cupcakes?"

Her face fell. "Oh, dear."

"I'm going to head over to my job site for a few minutes to check on everyone."

Milo glanced up, remembering that he had a passing interest in my company finishing on time this week. Otherwise we wouldn't be available to help him next week. "You aren't running behind, are you?"

"No, everything's fine." I'm not sure how convincing I made that sound, though. "When you go back in, tell Esme I'll return as fast as I can." I didn't want her to get nervous that I was going to leave her with Trudy and Milo forever.

"What should we do while you're gone?" Trudy asked.

Nothing, I wanted to say, remembering the Elvis lizard. In-stead, I suggested, "Read a little more. We need to find out where we fell short."

"Given the fact that we could have ended up with a Godzilla with a pompadour, we should be glad we fell short," Milo said.

He had a point. "I won't be long."

On the way over, I pulled over into a convenience store's lot and dialed my mom. She picked up right away.

"What's going on, Gwen?" Her voice lacked its usual Zen calmness. "It's like we've dosed half our customers with Valium. They're zonked out on the tables. One poor man face-planted into his meat loaf."

"I guess that's one argument against eating dessert first."

Chilly disapproval-disappointment crackled over the line. "Kidding aside, what is happening? Should we be warning our customers about these?"

"Trudy wouldn't put drugs in her cupcakes."

"That's what frightens me. What is she doing over there? Sorcery?"

I chuckled nervously. "Not on purpose."

"I warned you—"

"I know, I'm on it. Just pitch out the rest of those cupcakes. Unless you need a sleeping pill tonight, that is."

"This is no laughing matter, Gwen."

"I know."

"No, you don't know. The Council can get hold of you and do terrible things for transgressions like this. They can disintegrate you just as easily as pouring salt on a slug. Please tell me that you kids aren't dabbling?"

A laugh burbled in my throat, both at calling the purposeful, terrifying things we were up to in that laboratory "dabbling," and that Mom was referring to both me and thirty-nine-year-old Trudy as "kids." As if we were the *Scooby-Doo* gang.

Big difference: The *Scooby-Doo* gang actually solved their problems every episode, while we . . .

"It's fine, Mom." I wanted to tell her that, if nothing else, she could rest assured that Odin hadn't been vaporized permanently. But if I told her that, I'd have to let her in on everything. My parents had protected me the best they could for my whole life. The least I could do was try to keep them out of this catastrophic cock-up my cousins and I were in.

"I have to go. By the way, if you see Tannith, don't tell her about the cupcakes. Try not to talk to her at all. I think she's a Watcher."

Mom's throat hitched. "I don't want you to have friction with her, Gwen."

Would Mom ever not stick up for Tannith? It was so annoying.

"I've got to go, Mom."

She sighed. "Well, at the very least we have plenty of coffee here to perk the cupcake casualties back up again."

I hung up and hurried on to Mrs. Caputo's. Everything

seemed tidy in the yard when I parked and got out, but I didn't detect much activity. The side door was ajar, so I let myself in. The house was silent. Too silent. I tiptoed down a short hallway to the kitchen, where I found Taj asleep at the table, using his open textbook as a pillow. An empty plate with cupcake crumbs lay by his head. Two other plates similarly crumbed were also still on the table.

I continued on to the living room. Kyle was lying on his stomach on the floral-upholstered couch curled up with a dragon helmet and Binky the dog, who was also out for the count. In a recliner chair nearby slept Mrs. Caputo, her mouth open, snoring softly. This was not good.

Where was Odin? I remembered the door standing open and shuddered in dread. He could have taken off—off on a bug hunt that might have taken him all the way out of town by now. I imagined him halfway to Lake Placid. No telling what he was capable of.

A creak overhead made impossible hope jump in my chest. Could Odin still be here? Maybe he had eaten a cupcake, too, and had fallen asleep in the attic.

I ran up the narrow wood steps. When my eyes were able to peek over the attic floor, there was Odin, looking over a copy of a yellowed, brittle paperback copy of a John Jakes book. He shook his head. "I think I read this once, but I don't remember how it turns out. It's pretty good."

I finished climbing the stairs and stepped into the attic. The immaculate attic. Everything but that last box of books had been cleared out. It even appeared that the floor had been thoroughly swept and perhaps even mopped, although it was perfectly dry. I shook my head in amazement. Everyone downstairs was asleep, and from the looks of things they had been since breakfast.

"Did you clear this entire attic by yourself?"

"Of course."

"How?"

"I did what you told me to. It was a snap."

I turned in a circle. I couldn't get over it. "This is amazing. This space probably hasn't seemed this clean in sixty years. All it lacks is a coat of paint to look brand-new."

"That's a good idea." Before I could register what was happening, Odin lifted his hands like a maestro sans baton and snapped his fingers twice. For an instant, the atmosphere in the attic quavered like heat rising off asphalt on a blazing-hot summer day. It was the briefest hiccup of a moment, and when I focused again, the walls of the attic were a clean, soft white. Another snap, another shimmer, and the overhead beams had the appearance of fresh-cut cedar timber. He looked down at the pine boards at our feet, and with another snap, they were varnished.

"Better?"

My jaw was nearly touching the newly finished floors. "You . . . just did that." I'd thought his comment about cleaning being "a snap" was just a figure of speech.

His skill seemed to have caught him unawares, too. "Handy, isn't it?"

Handy, and amazing. *He had more talent in his fingers than the entire Council possessed,* Esme told me two days ago. She wasn't kidding. Excitement rose in me, and even a little envy. What I could do with powers like that! Abracadabra Odd Job could annihilate the handyman competition. I wouldn't even need employees. Oh, maybe one or two, just for show . . .

I gave myself a shake and trained my mind away from avaricious thoughts. Obviously, I was not Odin. The only talent I'd manifested so far was for shutting off alarms and putting hair on newts. The most important takeaway from this demonstration was that Odin, disintegrated and then regenerated though he had been, still had *it*. If it was possible for a talent for sorcery to have muscle memory, his had just rebounded with a vengeance.

"Can you control that?" I nodded at his hands. After all, if he was just another Trudy . . . There were enough toads and rabbits hopping around that laboratory already.

He studied his hands in wonder. "I think so. It's hard to say for sure, but they got the job done today."

Yes, they had. This would wrap up my work for Mrs. Caputo. I could give the guys a day off. If I ever managed to wake them up.

Most of all, I could concentrate on getting Esme and Laird back to normal.

I took Odin's arm. "I have another job for you."

Chapter 24

I wrote the others a note explaining that Odin and I had finished up and that they could take tomorrow off. Whatever confusion Kyle and Taj felt about the amazing job that had been done while they slept would be overridden by their joy at having an unexpected holiday.

Just as I was finishing the note, my phone rang. Daniel. Taking a deep breath, I swiped.

"I've made a decision," he announced. "The rabbit can stay for a week. But he can't come to the Yukon."

"It's a she, and she has no intention of going to the Yukon."

He half laughed. "You seem pretty confident about speaking for the rabbit."

"I am. Because I have no intention of going, either."

I hadn't known for sure, but as soon as the words slipped out, I knew they were the right ones.

A second of hesitation crackled over the line. "Just because I won't allow the rabbit to go?"

"It has nothing to do with the rabbit. It's because *I* can't go. I have a business. You didn't even consult me about any of this."

He sighed heavily. "Do you want an engraved invitation? I thought for sure you'd be happy for me."

"I am, but it seems like you've just assumed I'll trundle along after you. Like I'm your valet."

"A valet? You're not making any sense."

I closed my eyes. How could this relationship I'd been clinging to for six months be unraveling so quickly?

Almost as if someone had snapped their fingers . . .

"Have you talked to Tannith again since this morning?" I asked.

"Why, has something happened to her?" He actually sounded worried. About Tannith.

"You two seem closer than I realized."

"You're not jealous of her, are you?"

"Don't be ridiculous. Should I be?"

"Come on. You honestly think I'd be interested in someone like her?"

"Beautiful? Self-sufficient? Together?"

"High-maintenance."

I suppose that made me low-maintenance. Which didn't sound exactly like a compliment.

Stop being paranoid. The week had begun with Tannith trying to undermine my relationship. Now I seemed to be doing a good job of that all on my own. With my thoughts on a negative loop, I couldn't help feeling like one of those cartoon characters sawing off the branch I was perching on in the crazed belief that I was freeing myself.

Odin hovered near, noting the strain in my expression. "Is something wrong?"

I shook my head reflexively while over the line Daniel asked, "Is that Jeremy guy with you?"

Talk about being paranoid. "It's my cousin. Butch."

"Who?"

"My cousin Butch. He just popped into town."

"Another cousin. Am I going to meet him?"

Odin had drifted over to the bananas again. Significantly fewer fruit flies buzzed around that bowl than there had been this morning. No mystery what had happened to them. I jerked my gaze away before I could catching him eating one.

"Maybe some other time," I said. "Today's been difficult."

"What do you want for dinner?"

"I still have a lot of unfinished business to do. Just go ahead and eat without me."

"Hm." The disgruntled tone of that one syllable came through loud and clear. "I guess I'll see you when I see you, then."

I had too much on my mind now—Odin, Esme, mutant newts—to deal with my Daniel conundrum. "I'll call you later."

I hung up before his response, eager to get going.

Odin and I closed up the house and headed back to Esme's. As I parked, Grace, the neighbor with the ponytail, was making another power lap around the neighborhood. I had a feeling she was being more health conscious than usual today. Her head swung around to watch us get out of the Kia. I hustled Odin to the door, knocked loudly, and then rang the bell three times.

I felt so conspicuous standing there with my tall, bald relation, it seemed to take an eternity for Trudy or Milo to let me in. Odin unselfconsciously gawped at the neighborhood around him, and at Grace. I elbowed him a little, but unfortunately he took that as a signal to be polite and wave to the passerby.

I groaned in frustration and then held my breath, sending up a prayer that she wouldn't come over again. No such luck.

"Helloooo!" she called out.

I smiled half-heartedly. "Hi, Grace."

"I thought I'd warn you all that we do trick-or-treating in a big way around here." She gave Esme's barren porch a distasteful once-over. "Your aunt doesn't take part usually, and we all warn the kids"—she stopped, then smiled tightly—"I mean, the children don't normally come over here. But if you were thinking of giving out candy, you need to keep your porch light on. A few decorations wouldn't hurt, either. Not that the HOA has strict regulations about that. We just forbid anything inflatable, obscene, higher than twelve feet, or noise emitting. You know, the talking ghosts and motion-activated stuff."

"Right." It crossed my mind that at least some of those critters in the basement might be missing HOA members. "Well, I'm not sure we'll have trick-or-treaters. We're so busy."

Her curious gaze sharpened on Odin. "Doing what?"

"Oh, just . . ." Obviously I couldn't tell her we were doing experiments down in the basement. "A few home-improvement projects, to surprise Aunt Esme when she gets back."

At that moment, the sound of someone on the other side of the door undoing all the locks and chains could be heard. I cleared my throat, trying to cover the sound of Esme's home-defense overkill, but Ms. Ponytail's eyes were wide as she stared over my shoulder.

I chuckled anxiously. "Aunt Esme's a little bit of a security freak."

Her lips flattened into the thinnest of smiles. "Your cousins are still here, I take it?" She gave Odin a speculative up-and-down gaze.

"Yes."

Odin stuck out a hand to her. "I'm—"

"Butch," I said over him. "Another cousin."

She looked at his hand and recoiled.

"You know Esme?" he asked, undeterred by her reaction. Picking up social cues seemed to be one of those things that hadn't transferred when he'd been switched back from amphibianism.

"I do," she said tightly.

"She's wonderful, isn't she? I don't think anyone ever made me laugh as much as Es."

I gasped. "You remember her now."

The woman's eyes widened at my outburst.

I could have kicked myself. I bit the inside of my lip. *Hurry, Milo.*

"It's been a while since Butch has seen Aunt Esme," I explained. "It'll be a big surprise when they meet again."

"I'll bet." Grace gave Odin another sharp look, probably committing his face to memory in case she ever ran across it in a police lineup.

The door behind us opened and Milo poked his head out. When he caught sight of Grace, he registered alarm for a split second before breaking into a dazzling smile. "Oh, hi."

"I'm just leaving," she said. "Good talking to you all again. And meeting you, Mr. . . . ." She frowned. "I didn't catch your last name."

Odin turned to me. "What is it?"

"Zimmer?" I said, unsure.

Unfortunately, Milo blurted out, "Blumquist," at the same time.

Odin seemed pleased as punch to have two names to claim as his own. "Zimmer-Blumquist," he proclaimed.

Grace's tight smile remained firmly in place as she backed away.

When she was gone, we yanked Odin inside and didn't breathe again until all the locks had been shoved back into place.

After I paused to appreciate the relief of having a locked door between us and the outside world, I noted Trudy scowling at Odin. "What is *he* doing here? I thought we'd agreed you'd keep him busy today."

"That was when we were assuming he would be a liability to our work here, not an asset." I took Odin's arm and steered him toward Aunt Esme's living room. "Room looks a little tired, doesn't it, Odin?"

"I like it," he said. "It's homey."

"Homey to Ma and Pa Kettle, maybe," Milo muttered.

"You wouldn't like sitting on that lumpy couch," I told Odin. "It needs fixing up."

"Oh, I get it." Odin eyed the old davenport with such intensity that I half expected rays to shoot out of his eyeballs. Instead, the air shivered in that same unnerving time-quake I'd experienced in Mrs. Caputo's attic. Feeling the same jolt, Trudy and Milo stiffened. Then their mouths gaped in wonder at the instant makeover Odin had given the couch, whose upholstery was both bright as new and restuffed.

"See?" I said. "Odin has more magic in his muscle memory than most witches have after a lifetime of study."

He shuffled his feet in an aw-shucks way. "I don't know about that."

"You certainly couldn't do any worse than we have."

Milo's words made me wonder if further experimentation had taken place in my absence. But once we got downstairs, I was relieved to see no additional mutant creatures hopping around underfoot. The laboratory was in the same shape I'd left it in.

"Smells nice in here," Odin said, taking a luxurious sniff. "Gardenia!" He turned in a circle like a gawking tourist. "Look at this place! Was I ever here before?"

Dear God. "You were just here last night," Trudy said tightly, sending me a pointed look. *This is an asset?*

I sympathized with her, until something in Odin's tone made my brain double back. Surely he remembered last night. Maybe he was referring to something else. "Are you asking if you were here *before* last night?"

"I think I must have been."

We knew he'd been living here as a toad—although we had no idea for how long. But what if he hadn't been a toad when Esme had conjured him out of the ether? For all we knew, he might have been living in this house in his current form for years, hidden away from prying eyes of neighbors and whatever Watchers the Council had occasionally sent around. Maybe Esme had only turned him into a terrarium dweller when she'd sensed a heightened danger of his being caught. Perhaps she even knew about Tannith—she'd certainly expressed a dislike of her.

But if Esme had known, I think she would have warned us.

"Were you here working on a big project once?" I asked. When Esme said he'd been on the verge of an earth-shattering discovery, I'd assumed she'd been talking about what he'd been working on *before* the Council had hexed him. Maybe his vital experiments were of a more recent vintage.

From his vacant stare, it was hard to believe he'd ever been a sorcerer to be reckoned with. "I'm not sure. I'm not sure about anything."

Trudy put her hands on her hips. "Look, he might be great at renovating sofas, but I don't think he's the right witch to reverse the hex on the father of my children."

"He's not going to reverse the hex on Laird," I said.

"Then what was the point of bringing him here?" Trudy asked.

Milo looked at me and understood. "Odin's going to bring Esme back."

"And Esme will change Laird back into Laird," I finished. Given that Odin seemed to be working on instinct, the spell reversal would probably be more likely to work on someone he had an affinity for. Odin had never met Laird, but he knew Esme. She was less skilled than Odin, but she seemed to work more mindfully.

Odin's face brightened. "Do you all know Esme?"

Trudy, Milo, and I exchanged anxious stares.

"She's our aunt," I reminded him. "We're all related, remember?"

"Oh, right, I forgot." He nodded somberly. "That makes sense."

"I don't know if this is going to work," Milo said under his breath.

I gave him a gentle kick.

"Is Esme here?" Odin asked.

"She sure is." I pointed to the beige bunny with the smoky-tipped ears perched near his feet.

"Es!" he exclaimed delightedly.

She rose onto her hind legs, and he lifted her up and set her gently down on the lab table nearest us.

"We need you to make her human again," I said.

He straightened. "Are you sure? Maybe one of you would be better suited to the task. I haven't been myself lately."

"You don't have to be hasty," I told Odin. "You might want to browse through the library, if you can think of a book that might help you brush up on your conjuring skills."

He pivoted toward the bookcases. "Books." His voice held no enthusiasm.

"Or maybe you were always more of a hands-on, instinctive witch," I said.

He tilted his head, thinking about it. "Yes, I might have been."

Nothing about his manner inspired confidence. Yet I'd seen him work wonders. Obviously an attic wasn't the same thing as a person, but he'd transformed it without thinking, as if it were second nature to him.

I skirted around to his side of the table to give him a pep talk. "You must possess amazing powers, or the Council of Witches wouldn't have bothered punishing you. I'll bet in your heyday you could have brought Esme back in your sleep." I turned toward her. "Just look at her. You said you could see her. What we need you to do is turn that vision you hold of her in your imagination into a flesh-and-blood human again."

I didn't expect fast action, but his gaze locked onto the rabbit as if he were hypnotized. The rest of us braced for an impact that wasn't long in coming. It didn't take potions, or smoke. This time, Odin's shimmering felt intensified by a thousand times more force, as if the molecules around us were all being disassembled and reassembled, quickly and violently. The pressure was painful, like being in a plane whose cabin had depressurized all at once. I squeezed my eyes closed and heard a shriek. It might have come from me, or from all of us.

When I opened my eyes, Aunt Esme was standing on the table.

Except it wasn't the Esme I'd known since I was a girl, the caustic old crone to be avoided if at all possible. Nor was she the flamboyant woman she'd turned herself into when she first showed me this laboratory. This Esme was my age or younger, and her red hair spilled over her shoulders in a spiral perm. She was wearing clothes I'd never seen her, or anyone else, wear, except maybe in a John Hughes teen movie from thirty years ago. The dress had a square-cut black velvet bodice with a wine-colored taffeta skirt and puffy taffeta sleeves. It looked like a prom dress. She seemed amazed by it, too.

I'd told Odin to conjure the Esme of his imagination. He must have spent all of these decades imagining her as she was before he'd been zapped into nonexistence by the Council.

It definitely was Aunt Esme, though. Just as Odin had been able to see his old love in a rabbit, I could now see my cantankerous aunt in this gorgeous creature.

When she spoke, I could hear her, too.

"Damn," she proclaimed in her distinctive rasp. "That was seriously messed up."

Chapter 25

Esme looked down at Milo, Trudy, and me and laughed. "What's the matter? You all seem more mouth breathery than usual."

"They gaped at me the same way when I came back," Odin said.

At the sound of his voice, Esme looked toward him, astounded. As she drank him in, for once her face wasn't in the least guarded. The cynical set to her mouth disappeared, and she flew off the table, into his arms. He caught her and swung her around as gracefully as if they were Astaire and Rogers.

"You're back," she said.

He grinned. "Not even a toad anymore."

She cupped her hand over his scalp. "What happened to your beautiful hair?"

"I'm not sure. When I changed back, this is how my head looked."

She laughed. "Well, don't worry. We can fix it. Although the Captain Picard thing is kind of sexy."

"You're just as beautiful as you ever were, Esme."

As if he weren't responsible for that.

"But how . . . ?" Esme pivoted toward me. "Did *you* do this?"

I crooked my head toward the others. "It was a group effort."

"Because we thought he was Laird," Trudy added bitterly.

Esme snorted in understanding. "Bet you were surprised."

Could she not remember last night? "You were here," I reminded her.

"Hon, when you're a rabbit, you don't exactly have a lot of gray cells dedicated to short-term memory."

Odin nodded in sympathy. "It's even worse when you're a toad."

She gave him a few pinches to test that he really was flesh and blood, then she looked up into his face, drinking him in. She pivoted back toward us. "I would never have guessed you numbskulls were so capable."

"And I never thought you would be so treacherous," Trudy said angrily. "You knew we had the wrong toad. You could have done something to let us know."

"And ruin my chance of having the most able witch in the world on hand to bring me back?"

"Odin is the most able witch in the world?" Milo asked skeptically.

Odin hadn't even been paying attention to our conversation. He couldn't take his eyes off Esme. "I'm older than you are now."

My aunt laughed, and for once it wasn't a cackle. "You always were, old man."

He bent down and kissed her. Their smooching went on so long that Milo, Trudy, and I shifted uncomfortably. We would have headed for the exit, but there was still work to be done. Trudy was growing more irritated—never a good sign.

Her breath hitched in her throat. "This reunion is sweet and all, but you do remember we're here?"

I also had questions for my aunt. "Why was Odin a toad?" I asked when they broke apart for air. "And who else do you have in those terrariums?"

"One of them better be Laird," Trudy said.

Esme clucked in disgust. "Don't worry about your precious

Laird. He's there." She went over to a terrarium. "At least, he was."

She bent over the opening, picked up one of the toads, and looked deep into its eyes. "Yup. This is the one."

She held him out to Trudy, who stepped back. "For better or for worse" apparently ended when Laird had announced he was moving into the basement. Or maybe when he'd transformed into something with moist, warty skin.

"Squeamish, still?" Esme chuckled. "He's your husband."

"Soon-to-be ex-husband," Trudy corrected.

The doorbell sounded. We all froze, until Esme rounded on us, furious. "Who did you bring here?"

"Nobody," I swore.

Esme hurried to a tiny spy camera monitor none of us had realized was there. It was set up so she could watch the porch.

"Nobody, my shapely new butt! Why are the police standing on my doorstep, then?"

"The police!" Hyperalert now, Trudy peered over Esme's shoulder at the grainy black-and-white image. She gasped and turned to me. "It's Marcus."

"Who's Marcus?" Esme asked.

Trudy shot a nervous glance at the toad. She lowered her voice. "A man I know."

"Know in the biblical sense, I gather." Esme planted her hands on her hips. "What have you kids been up to while I was a lagomorph?"

"I swear, Officer Timmens has never been here," I said. "I don't know what he's doing here now."

Trudy added, "I never told Marcus about this place."

Milo cleared his throat. "Well, since all our cars are parked outside, it might be a good idea to find out what he wants."

Milo was right. Pretending no one was home wouldn't fly. The neighbors had seen me and Odin come inside less than an hour ago.

"I'll go," Trudy said.

Milo and I followed her.

By the time we'd unlocked the door, Officer Timmens's face was fixed in an impatient expression. Dusk had fallen, and in the distance we could hear the shouts of trick-or-treating children. The police cruiser hadn't gone unnoticed, though. Down the street, several neighbors stood in their yards, looking our way. Their flashlights were pinpoints of light in the distance.

Timmens's partner, a skinny younger guy with the kind of red hair that was almost orange, was standing next to him, one leg jogging restlessly.

Marcus's expression did a complete 180 when Trudy appeared on the other side of the threshold. "Trudy?" He spoke her name as if he half believed she were an apparition.

"Hi, Marcus." Though nervous, she couldn't help smiling. "What are you doing here?"

His face whiplashed from baffled to ecstatic to confused again. "We were called out because someone reported suspicious activity."

I didn't have to ask who that someone was. *Grace strikes again.*

"The caller said that the homeowner had disappeared, and that there were a lot of strange people coming and going." He grinned at Trudy. "Not that I think you're strange."

"If it's the neighbor lady that called you out here, you should warn her about harassing people on no evidence," I said. "We already told her what we're doing here."

"Okay." Marcus nodded.

"What *are* you doing here?" his partner asked.

None of us spoke.

Marcus cleared his throat. "This is my partner, Officer Kerry."

"Hello." Trudy smiled as if she were meeting one of Marcus's relations.

"What *are* you doing here?" Marcus repeated.

"House-sitting," Milo said. "Our aunt went out of town—"

"We explained that to the neighbor," I said.

"—and now we're just here looking after things."

Kerry asked, "Do you have a phone number where your aunt can be reached?"

I gulped and turned to Trudy and Milo. "Do either of you have a phone number for her?"

They shook their heads, both bearing the same shell-shocked look in their eyes. We should have planned our story better before answering the door.

"Email?" Marcus asked. "Or even a snail-mail address?"

"Why, do you intend to drive to Ohio to verify our story?" Milo asked.

Too snarky, I wanted to warn him.

Officer Timmens's patient tone let us know that he'd dealt with snark before. "Anything that could help us verify your story is all we're looking for here."

Anything. Yet my mind was drawing a blank.

"You don't need to call me, for heaven's sake," came my aunt's throaty voice behind us. "I'm right here."

Trudy, Milo, and I gave way as Esme sashayed forward, followed by Odin, who still had Laird cupped in his hands.

Marcus looked at Esme in surprise. "*You're* Esme Zimmer?"

"I sure am. I just got back tonight."

Officer Kerry wasn't pleased with us. "They just said you were in Ohio."

"I was."

"But you're here now."

Esme's lips twisted. "Obviously."

"You might have told us that right away," Kerry said to Milo, Trudy, and me.

"My nieces and nephew aren't used to having to tell the cops my whereabouts," Esme said. "But I see my busybody neighbors have escalated their nosiness during my absence. There's no reason why I should have to answer questions about what's going on in my own home. Ask anyone around here. I like my privacy."

Marcus nodded. "Like I said, we just got a report . . ." His voice died away as he gave Esme a doubtful once-over. "Wait, you're *their* aunt?"

"Yes." *Want to make something of it?* her voice said.

I understood his confusion. Esme now looked younger than

the rest of us, and I doubt Grace Ponytail's description of Esme Zimmer would have led them to expect a nubile creature wearing Molly Ringwald's prom dress.

Trudy stepped forward. "Aunt Esme's ageless."

"Really?" Kerry still seemed skeptical. "She looks about twenty-six to me."

"Got myself a vacation makeover," Esme said, primping her voluminous hair.

"So you see, everything's fine," I interjected, trying not to sound anxious, or pushy, no matter how much I wanted the cops to go away. *Nothing to see here. Move along, folks.*

A series of loud pops jolted us all. The policemen swiveled. The explosions had come from a neighboring block.

"Teenagers setting off firecrackers," Marcus guessed.

"They're not supposed to be doing that," his partner said, as eager as Barney Fife at the thought of catching the miscreants.

I sent out a silent thank-you to the firecracker hooligans. The distraction was a godsend. "That's terrible," I declared. "Especially when there are little kids out trick-or-treating. This might scare them back into their houses."

Kerry was already headed in the direction the sound had come from as a Roman candle exploded over neighboring rooftops. Marcus sent us an apologetic glance. "You all have a pleasant evening." With a last wink at Trudy, he followed his partner to their patrol car.

My jittering purse returned to normal. Hopefully we would no longer be the focus of the neighborhood's curiosity.

The relief was short-lived. As the patrol car's headlights swept across the yard when they pulled away, their beams illuminated Odin's tall figure on the lawn, staring at the leaf-strewn ground as intently as a kid hunting Easter eggs.

"Odin, what are you doing?" Milo called out to him.

"The bang scared the toad. He leapt away before I could stop him. I didn't see where he landed."

Trudy rushed to the edge of the porch, her hands on her cheeks. "Laird?"

Milo opened the front door, reached inside, and flipped on the porch light.

"Are you sure he hopped in that direction?" Esme asked.

"Pretty sure," Odin said in a tone that failed to convey confidence.

With little light, and with the unraked leaves fluttering in the night breeze and more leaves drifting down from the trees on the crisp night air, it was going to be hard to find one small, frigid toad. We spread out, dividing up the yard and each taking a quadrant to search. Milo, Trudy, and I used the flashlights on our cell phones to supplement the illumination put out by the porch light.

That light, however, came with unintended consequences. Within minutes, a contingent of sharp-eyed children dressed as a witch, a robot, and a cowboy were making a beeline for Esme's house.

"There's no candy here," my aunt barked to shoo them away.

The costumed trio wasn't so easily put off. There were trick-or-treating rules, and we were violating them.

"Your light's on," the cowboy pointed out.

The witch nodded. "If you don't want trick-or-treaters, you're supposed to sit in your dark house."

"We need to have the lights on right now," I said.

By this time, the kids had noticed the flashlights in the yard. "What are you looking for?" the robot asked.

"A toad," Milo said.

It would have been smarter to make up a lie. If there was one thing that might distract kids from begging for candy door-to-door, it was a toad hunt. They immediately joined the search, leaning over like the rest of us, their eyes on the ground.

"Be careful where you step," Trudy admonished as they crunched across the leaves. "Laird's very small."

"That's a weird name for a frog," the witch said.

"Do we get to keep him if we find him?" the cowboy asked.

Trudy straightened, horrified. "No."

"He's a pet," I explained. "She's . . . attached to him."

"If she likes him so much, you'd think she'd have thought of a better name," the girl grumbled, pulling her cape around her. "And taken better care of him. It's cold."

No kidding. How long could a toad survive out in this?

More flashlight beams shone our way from down the street and grew brighter as they approached. My heart sank. These were adults, probably coming to make sure that the weird lady didn't kidnap their child. We were all out in the front yard, though, so it was hardly as if anything clandestine was going on here. *Just a family of witches searching for their enchanted toad.*

The robot, a budding naturalist, informed us, "Our first-grade class had a frog and it escaped and froze to death."

"It didn't escape," the witch reminded him. "Jason let it out."

"So? It was still dead. I found it by the playground. It was like a frog Popsicle."

Trudy emitted a nervous cry.

"Here he is!" the cowboy called out. "I found him!"

Just in time. The parental delegation was arriving just as the cowboy captured the toad. Laird looked slightly bigger when overspilling the confines of the child's small hands.

"I'll trade some of my candy for him," he offered.

A horrified woman appeared in the yard, her flashlight shining on Laird's startled, shiny toad eyes. "Nathan! What are you holding?"

"A toad."

"Give him to me." Trudy looked ready to wrestle the kid to the ground if he didn't relinquish Laird.

"Mom, would it be okay—?"

Trudy put her hands out. *"Now."*

"Well!" The mother's voice was as indignant as her expression was relieved. "I guess you need to give the toad back to the rude lady, Nathan."

The handover was made, reluctantly. "Thank you," Trudy said.

Nathan glared at her. "You ought to give it a better name."

As soon as we could, we all retreated indoors and turned off the porch light.

Trudy looked more traumatized than she had all week. Of course, she was holding her husband's compact, warty body in her cupped hands, so maybe that was understandable.

"We need to switch him back now," I said. "Otherwise things like this will keep happening."

"Are you insane?" Trudy nodded toward our aunt. "I'm not entrusting Laird's future to Esme. She was the one who caused all these problems to begin with."

"*I* didn't turn my husband into a rabbit," Esme said.

"No, toads are more your speed," Trudy fired back. "But I didn't notice you changing the love of your life from a toad to a human again. How can we be sure you even know how?"

"I kept him in that terrarium on purpose," Esme explained. "It's dangerous for him to be like this now. I'm thrilled to have him here, but if the Council gets wind that Odin's out and about, it will bring doom down on our heads. I tried my best to keep him hidden. But you amateurs just took matters in your own hands."

"We thought he was Laird," Trudy reminded her. "Our bringing him back was *your* doing."

"Yeah, well, you'd changed me into a rabbit. Rabbits aren't great at long-term planning."

Milo frowned. "So did you intend to keep Odin in that terrarium forever?"

"No. Just until I found a solution."

This is what puzzled me. "To what?"

"To how we could carry on his important work, which would allow us to be together."

The way my parents told it, the Council was never going to reverse the Edict in their lifetimes, so it would never be safe for Odin and Esme, especially not if they wanted to continue practicing witchcraft. And probably not even if they didn't. They'd been cursed, and the Council wouldn't take kindly to having their judgments flouted.

"I still haven't seen evidence that you can reverse a spell," Trudy said. "We were the ones who got Odin back."

"Did you?" Esme asked. "Or did you just blunder into it, like you blundered into your rabbit spells?"

Milo and I exchanged anxious glances as the hostility escalated between Trudy and Esme. If the last few days were anything to go by, mounting anger was bound to end with someone in a cage. A time-out seemed essential.

"Maybe we should wait until tomorrow before we take any rash actions," I suggested.

Esme crossed her arms. "Tomorrow's a long time. I have to think about Odin."

"What about him?" Milo asked.

Odin seemed curious about this, too.

"He's a wanted warlock," Esme said. "The terrestrial plane isn't safe for him as a human. Not for long, anyway."

It was hard to know where he would be safe. Unless she wanted to keep transforming him, which . . . didn't seem like a good idea. He already showed signs of that too-often-recycled old-sock syndrome.

But it was finally agreed that tempers were too frazzled to do any more spellcasting this evening. We left Esme and Odin together in the house. They seemed eager to be rid of us. This time, Trudy insisted on taking Toad Laird—the real one, Esme assured her—home with her.

After waving Trudy off, Milo and I lingered by our cars. I didn't relish returning home to another confrontation with Daniel.

"Want to go for a drink?" Milo suggested.

I'd never wanted something so much in my life. We agreed to meet at our old college haunt, the Night Owl, which was on the pedestrian commons downtown. The Night Owl hadn't changed in decades. It smelled of stale beer, played the same music that had been dated when we were in college, and served food that featured melted cheese, bacon, or both. We ordered beers, settled into a booth in the back, and read the Trivial Pursuit cards stacked next to the salt and pepper shakers while an R.E.M. song played on the speakers overhead.

"So you're avoiding going home," Milo said, filing his card away.

"How did you know?"

"Because I'm avoiding going home. Even if I'm not dragging Cousin Odin home again, I'll still have to deal with Brett's tacit disapproval."

I nodded in sympathy. "Daniel is incensed that he walked in on me sleeping with Jeremy on the couch this morning."

Milo's eyes bugged. "Excuse me?"

"We really were sleeping. Fully clothed. But before I could explain that, Esme hopped in, and Daniel got upset about that, too."

"Never trust guys who don't like animals."

"He likes them, he's just allergic to some of them. Also, he considers owning a pet to be a form of slavery."

"You don't think that's weird?"

"I always thought it was just because he'd never had a pet. I thought . . ."

Milo groaned. "You thought you were going to change him."

"Not that I was going to change him. Just that he might . . . unbend."

Milo looked at me with pity. "Unbending is changing."

He was right. How stupid could I have been? "Anyway, he did get over the rabbit thing—mostly because I assured him Esme wouldn't be there long. But now he's upset that I don't want to move to the Yukon."

"Whoa. When did this come up?"

"This morning. After Jeremy and the rabbit. Trudy had me convinced that Daniel was going to pop the question. Instead of presenting me with a ring, though, he produced a pair of insulated hiking boots."

One of Milo's dark eyebrows darted up.

"They're high-quality boots."

He took a drink of his beer before responding. "Well, on the upside, it doesn't sound as if his plan is to run off with Tannith. I can't see *her* embracing the Nanook of the North lifestyle." He frowned. "But that leaves either Laird—and I'm assuming she *really* doesn't want to have a romance with a frog—or Brett."

"She could still plan on hexing Daniel."

"What fun will that be for her if you don't want him anymore?"

Did I really not want Daniel? "I wouldn't have moved in with him if I hadn't intended for us to go on forever."

Milo looked at me with the same concern he might have if I'd just sustained a head injury. "You weren't thinking. You were in lust, and you needed a place to live."

"I had a perfectly good apartment."

"No, you had a studio with pipes that leached *Creature from the Black Lagoon* odors and sounds."

The plumbing situation hadn't been ideal. But the apartment had been affordable, and in the attic of a charming old Victorian. Despite its defects, I'd felt at home there, and at ease. In retrospect, I couldn't remember why I'd been in such a hurry to leave . . . aside from the plumbing. I'd just been impatient to move on—and to grab Daniel before Tannith took him. I thought being part of a couple would make me complete. But in the past days I'd begun to realize that what my life was missing was something more fundamental than a partner. It was missing the me I wanted to be.

I shook my head. That sounded so trite—like something a TV psychologist would say.

"Daniel's great, he really is," I insisted.

I was on the receiving end of that pitying look again. "If you really believed that, you wouldn't be sitting here drinking beer and eating bad nachos."

I leaned back. "You're here, too. Why do you think you're avoiding Brett?"

"Because it's a pressure cooker over there. Everything's about this election. It seemed so great at first. Now I'm not so sure I want to be Zenobia's answer to Chasten Buttigieg."

I laughed. "I like that guy."

Milo wasn't laughing with me. "The trouble is, I feel like this whole relationship is playing out like a Greek tragedy. Not that I'm going to gouge out my eyeballs, but you foretold it all and I screwed everything up anyway. You said I shouldn't spy on Brett, but I did. And now I have this secret information about the jewelry store that's driving me crazy. But I can't let him know it's driving me crazy, because then I have to fess up that I found it through devious means. And so it's all going to fall apart."

"No, it's not. You'll work things out. This has just been a tense week. But after the election next week, and after this whole situation with Tannith is over—"

"How will that ever be over?"

Good question.

My phone vibrated across the tabletop. My stomach somersaulted in dread, then I flipped the cover to see who it was. Trudy.

When I picked up, her hysterical voice was almost unrecognizable. "He's gone."

"Laird?" I couldn't believe he'd hopped away again so soon after the mishap in Esme's yard. You'd think even a toad would have more sense.

"Not Laird. Griz."

Alarm must have been written all over my face because Milo reached out for my hand. "What is it?" he whispered.

"Who's that?" Trudy asked. "Is that Duran Duran I hear in the background?"

Guilt pierced me. Trudy liked this place, too. "Milo and I are at the Night Owl."

"You went out without me?"

"It was spur-of-the-moment," I assured her. "How could Griz have gotten out? And when?" Trudy would have left the house locked up.

"He dashed out the door as I was unloading Laird and his terrarium from the car." The despair in her voice tore through me.

So did worry for Griz. It was Halloween, he was a black cat in an unfamiliar neighborhood, and people could be cruel to animals. Including their owners.

"Are you sure Tannith didn't retrieve him at some point today?"

"No, he was there, and now he isn't. He ran away."

I still had a strange feeling about Tannith. She had to be involved in all this somehow. She'd planted that cat to spy on us. Maybe he'd completed his mission. "I've got an idea. On our way to your place, Milo and I can swing by Tannith's to see if Griz made his way back over there. Cats like to go back to territory they know, right?"

Trudy clutched at that hope. "That would be great, Gwen. Thank you."

Milo and I got into our respective vehicles and drove to Tannith's. The first, fun stage of Halloween night was petering out. The little trick-or-treaters had all gone home to inspect their loot, and now it was just the occasional band of costumed teenagers loitering on the streets. The farther I drove from the university, the fewer people were out and about.

Tannith's house was completely dark when we both pulled up. Dark and deserted. Other houses on her street had turned their porch lights off—the candy bowls were empty—but showed signs of life in their windows, or had jack-o'-lanterns still blazing on the porch. Nothing but inky black draped the front of Tannith's one-story wood-frame house, which I could barely make out against a sky in which the stars and the moon were hiding behind a scrim of wispy clouds.

"At least we can be sure she's not here," Milo said when we both got out and stood on the sidewalk. "Her house has seemed abandoned like this every time I've driven past this week."

"Maybe she just wants us to think it's abandoned."

"A trap?"

I sent him a look. "Don't act so incredulous. This is Tannith we're talking about. She's spent her whole life sandbagging me.

Didn't I tell you that I was supposed to be salutatorian? And then, in the last week of high school, her GPA magically surpassed mine?" I frowned at the house. "Gluing the mortarboard to my head was just icing on the cake for her in that instance."

"You're right. I always thought that time I got the call from a talent scout for *American Idol* was probably Tannith's doing. Nothing like practicing 'Proud of Your Boy' from *Aladdin* for a week straight and then showing up for a big audition only to find out that you've been directed to a Walmart parking lot." Milo sighed.

"She's diabolical."

He frowned. "But in this instance she'd have to foresee that Griz would escape from Trudy's."

"Or ensure he escaped." I thought about this some more and shook my head. "But surely she wouldn't put Griz in danger, even to mess with us."

Milo pinned his dark gaze on me. "I don't want to frighten you, but you just sounded like your mom when she talks about Tannith."

It was true. That last sentiment reeked of the kind of wishful thinking Mom always engaged in. The hoping that Tannith was actually better than she seemed, the turning of a blind eye to her worst faults. The desperate attempt to make people see positive attributes that were figments of her maternal imagination.

Milo put his hand on mine. "Okay, let's go see if your furry friend is around."

I stumbled on the uneven walkway before I thought to turn on my phone's flashlight. "The trouble is, I have the unsettling feeling that she's nearby."

"I thought Griz was a he."

"Not the cat. Tannith."

Milo uplit his face with his phone flashlight and hummed *Twilight Zone* music. "Are we psychically connected to Tannith now?"

"Haven't you felt it, too? She's watching us."

As I was saying the words, a glint from one of the windows

caught my eye. I turned and aimed the beam, weak as it was, at the window. It created more glare than anything else, but I thought I could just glimpse a feline outline. "Griz is inside."

"How could he be? Unless Tannith is here. And if Tannith is here, why are we here?"

"She's not here."

He shook his head. "Then what was all your woo-woo nonsense about feeling her close by?"

"Close, but not here."

"Okay, Uri Geller. Explain how a cat can walk through walls."

That didn't take magic. I went through the gate to the backyard and checked the cat flap on the back door. It was open. "Tannith forgot to lock the cat flap. You'd be surprised how many people do this when they go away on vacation. Then they come back and discover that squirrels or groundhogs have moved in."

"How do you know this?"

"Because last year I was called to repair squirrel damage from a rental unit. They can really trash a place."

"Okay, so Griz got inside his house. Now what? Do you know if Tannith keeps a spare key hidden around here?"

I shook my head.

"I guess we'll just have to text her, then."

"I'm not leaving Griz behind."

"This isn't *Saving Private Ryan*, Gwen. He'll be okay for one night."

"She already dumped him on a porch. I don't even know if he has food or water."

"He's got the whole outdoors."

"But that's why we're here—to keep him from being out wandering the streets."

All I could think was that he must have been under severe stress to come back here. That couldn't be good for any animal. "I just need half a sec."

"To do what?"

"Break in."

He let out a sputtering sound.

"It's okay. I'm handy, remember? I'll come right back and patch the hole and get a piece of replacement glass tomorrow morning. No one but us will ever know."

Famous last words.

I grabbed my toolbox from the Kia. I was quick and did a tidy job, especially given the dim cell-phone light that I was working with. Tannith, however, wasn't the person I should have been worried about. Just after I found Griz and rounded up a cardboard carrier box for him with I'M GOING HOME emblazoned above the air holes, a loud knock at the door was followed by a shouted command to stop what I was doing and put my hands up.

"Zenobia Police," a voice announced.

Chapter 26

Even in Zenobia, Halloween was a busy night for the cops. By the time we arrived at the police station, it was full of people who'd been celebrating Halloween a little too boisterously. As we waited in a hallway of the old downtown building where Officer Kerry—it would be Kerry who'd answered the call—deposited us momentarily, two college-age girls dressed as a zombie nurse and Snow White were frog-marched past us.

"At least they haven't arrested us," I whispered to Milo.

"Oh, sure, that's great," he shot back. "Wait till Karen Morrow's team gets wind that their opponent's partner and campaign manager is in jail for breaking and entering. Wait till it's on the front page of the *Zenobia Bee*!"

I writhed in guilt. I hadn't considered how this would affect Brett's electoral chances.

Officer Kerry appeared again and beckoned us to a room. Interrogation time.

You wouldn't think rescuing a cat from an abandoned house would be considered that big a deal. After all, if it had been a dog or a cat stuck in a hot car, breaking a window to get the animal out would have been considered the only humane thing to do. Unfortunately, it hadn't helped our case that Officer Kerry had recognized us right away from the earlier report of suspicious activity at Esme's house. Part of the drawback of living in a small city—there were only so many cops to go around.

Kerry—Marcus Timmens was attending to another matter, we were told—had all sorts of questions, like how I knew Tannith wasn't coming back, and why I hadn't tried to call her, and what exactly my relationship was to her.

"She's my sister," I said, not for the first time. More like the hundredth time.

Kerry looked down at the clipboard he'd been taking notes on. He pointed to my last name, then Tannith's, and asked me to explain.

"*Practically* my sister. She was an orphan. My parents raised her."

"Uh-huh."

Milo, who had been trying to keep a low profile throughout this discussion, finally piped up in my defense, "It's the truth."

"You were also there when we followed up on Ms. Engel's suspicious activity across town."

"That was my—our—aunt's house."

"And this place tonight was your cousin's house?"

Milo nodded. "We're a very tight-knit family."

"No so tight-knit that this cousin didn't give you a key." Kerry tapped his pen. "Instead, you had to commit breaking and entering."

"It wasn't a break-in," I insisted. "It was a cat rescue."

The interview seemed to go on for an hour—not that he got much information out of us. We repeated the same details and finally provided Kerry with a few names for references. I had to cough up Daniel's number. I'd been avoiding calling him, reluctant to involve anyone else in this situation. But Kerry seemed to think it incriminating that I wouldn't want him to contact my boyfriend. Milo dragged his feet even more before providing Brett's name.

The moment he said it, Kerry's red brows rose to the middle of his forehead. "Brett Blair, the candidate for mayor?"

Milo smiled ruefully. "That's the one."

We were left alone in the room for another half hour while Kerry either checked on our stories or just let us sit there stewing for his own enjoyment. Finally, he came back and announced that everything we'd told him had checked out. We were free to go.

He deposited us at the front room of the police station, where the receiving-desk sergeant handed me my cat carrier. I hadn't wanted to leave Griz behind, but Kerry hadn't allowed us to take him into the interrogation room. "That's a cranky cat." The desk officer hoisted the I'M GOING HOME box across the desk. I peered through the air holes and was rewarded with a hiss. "He's had a rough night."

Griz wasn't the only one.

While I was collecting the cat, Milo wandered out to the station foyer. Brett had arrived. The two were in a heated discussion, so I slowed my steps. On a bench next to them, two guys sat dressed in green long-sleeved T-shirts, jeans, and foam tubing with crudely drawn beer logos across their chests. It took me a few seconds to realize that the two guys were supposed to be beer koozies. They were also watching Milo and Brett.

"I'm not mad," Brett insisted. "I just don't know why you've been acting so strange—so furtive."

"*I'm* being furtive?" Milo asked, his voice rising. "What about your sudden trip to New York during the last week of the campaign?"

"That was for work."

Hurt made Milo rash. "Did the bank also send you to Tiffany's?"

Brett went still, his face red. "How did you find out about that?"

Milo at least had enough shame to duck his head. "It was on your credit card bill. You left your password file right there for anyone to see."

"I can't believe you're spying on me."

"I can't believe you're cheating on me."

Brett looked around. The koozies and I were all wide-eyed. He took Milo's arm. "We should talk about this at home." Brett glanced back at me. "Can we give you a ride, Gwen?"

No way did I want to be a part of that car ride home. "Thanks, but I think Daniel's coming to get me."

I'd felt my phone vibrate several times but hadn't had the nerve to look. I flipped the cover open now and keyed in my password. A string of messages popped up.

DANIEL: *WTF?*

DANIEL: *You're not answering, so I assume this means you really are in jail.*

DANIEL: *On my way. I hope you have an explanation.*

"Yup. On his way." I closed the cover and stuck the phone in my pocket, feeling queasy. To Milo, I said, "I'll see you tomorrow."

He nodded. "That's right. We've still got the thing." The Laird thing, I assumed he meant.

"There's also the other thing."

He frowned. "What thing is that?"

"Tomorrow's Friday." The deadline day in Tannith's poisonous letter. "You know—the end-of-the-week thing? Moving day?"

"What are you two talking about?" Brett said.

"Nothing," we replied in unison.

He rolled his eyes in exasperation. "It's like you guys speak in code."

"Talk to you tomorrow," I told Milo.

I watched them go, then remembered how tired I was. A little room was left on the koozie bench. I made the two occupants scoot over and sat down. They might be dressed as beer koozies, but they didn't seem drunk. "What are you in for?" I asked.

"We're not. We're waiting for them to decide if they're going to press charges against my girlfriend."

"Snow White?"

"No, she's the zombie."

"What did she do?"

"Nothing," said the boyfriend. Then he backed up. "Well, they're *calling* it arson, but that's jacked up. It was an accident."

"Then I'm sure it will work out," I assured them, feeling kinship to the wrongly accused everywhere.

"Gwen?"

Jeremy stood in front of me. He'd showered and changed since this morning, but he was still in his work clothes. I recognized his jacket as the one I'd seen him in that first morning we'd talked outside Trudy's house. This time, though, I remembered what it felt like to be pressed against him, his lips on mine.

That wasn't a good place for my thoughts to be traveling at the moment.

"What are you doing here?" he asked.

"I had a little difficulty this evening," I said, deciding to keep it vague. "You?"

His gaze strayed toward the door, as if he were contemplating the feasibility of escaping without answering. "You're not going to like this, but I can't lie to you. I came here to file a complaint against Trudy Webster."

I jumped to my feet, and he was trying to calm me down before any words had issued from my mouth. "I couldn't help it. Trudy—well, she lied. I had a friend who works in IT at the college trace the IP address attached to the email Laird sent me the other day. It was Trudy who sent it."

I swallowed. "How can you be sure? Laird and Trudy live together. They have the same internet provider."

"Yes, but at the time it was sent, Trudy was the only one who would be using that router."

My brain scrabbled frantically for some way to make this go away. "It's not a crime to send an email from a fake account, is it?"

"Not necessarily. But it looks bad. Especially since someone reported Laird as missing earlier this week."

"Damn it—she didn't do anything like what you're imagining. Why did you have to come here?"

"After someone reported him missing, I had to tell the police what I found out. What if I held back and something really terrible has happened to him?"

"Nothing has." I shuddered at how blithely I was dismissing the situation poor Laird was in. "Are they going to arrest Trudy?"

"I don't think so—not right away, at least. The officer I talked to said they were going to look into it." He shrugged. "He was a real nice guy, but you know the police around here. Officer Timmens didn't strike me as the brightest light in the law enforcement firmament. In fact, he looked pretty tired."

This new wrinkle made me breathe easier. Surely Marcus wouldn't drag Trudy off to the hoosegow on the basis of one questionable email.

The outside door's opening drew my attention. Daniel was steaming toward us. He stopped, glancing accusingly between Jeremy and me.

"What's *he* doing here?" Daniel asked by way of greeting. Before I could answer, he added, "You called this guy instead of me to help you out?"

Jeremy's face collapsed in concern. "Help you out of what? Are you in trouble?"

Daniel laughed. "She didn't explain that part?"

"I didn't explain anything because I didn't call him," I said. "Jeremy just happened to be here."

"Oh, sure—you both just happened to be here at the Zenobia police station at eleven at night on Halloween?"

"Yes," Jeremy said.

"You must think I'm an idiot."

"Not an idiot," I replied. "At the moment you're just being a distrustful, judgmental jerk."

Daniel's face reddened. "I came here to help you."

"And proceeded to throw accusations around before you'd even said hello. Thanks."

"Because you started lying to my face again."

"Dude, she wasn't lying."

Daniel scowled down at the koozie bench.

Koozie Two agreed. "She was just sitting here with us talking when this other guy appeared and they were all, 'Hey—what are you doing here?' Like, it was totally a coincidence."

I turned back to Daniel, but he wasn't at all soothed. He jerked a thumb at the bench. "Who are those guys?"

"They're waiting on a zombie accused of arson."

"You shouldn't talk to Gwen that way," Jeremy said. "She hasn't done anything wrong."

"Breaking and entering isn't wrong?"

"It wasn't breaking and entering," I assured Jeremy. "I was just rescuing a cat from my cousin Tannith's place." I nodded toward the carrier.

"Oh." Jeremy leaned down to inspect Griz. "I like black cats."

"I'm not taking a cat into my house," Daniel said. "I'm allergic, you know that. The rabbit was bad enough."

"*Your* house?" Jeremy said. "Doesn't Gwen live there, too?"

"Of course—" Daniel shook his head. "I don't have to explain myself to you."

"The cat's not going home, and neither am I," I told Daniel. "I'll stay at Trudy's."

Daniel's jaw dropped in shock. "You're just walking out?"

"I'm responsible for Griz."

"Fine—drop off the cat."

Except that I wanted to talk to Trudy. And I wasn't wild to spend any more time explaining myself. I was exhausted. "I want to stay with Trudy."

Daniel looked mistrustfully from me to Jeremy as if piecing something together. Daniel nodded. "I get it."

"No, you don't," I said. "I'll call an Uber and get to Trudy's."

"I'll take you," Jeremy said.

Daniel's lips flattened. "Of course you will."

"No, he won't," I said.

"I'd be glad to," Jeremy insisted.

"After you've just reported Trudy for suspicion of killing her husband?" I reminded him. "I'm not sure you'll be the most welcome person over there right now."

"Maybe she has an honest explanation," Jeremy said.

"Of course she does." Weird, but honest.

Daniel snorted in derision. "It's interesting to hear you two concerned about honesty."

I sucked in a breath, my mind struggling to find a retort. But Jeremy didn't give me time. In the next moment, he hauled back and punched Daniel square in the nose.

Chapter 27

"He had it coming."

"But in a police station," I lamented.

"It all worked out."

I wasn't sure what he meant by working out. That Daniel's nose finally stopped bleeding? That Daniel didn't press charges? That Jeremy had gotten his wish and we'd left the police station together?

"Just take me to get my car," I said. "It's at my cousin Tannith's."

"Probably better if you just go to Trudy's. I can take you over to get the car tomorrow morning."

He made it sound as if he was expecting to stay over at Trudy's, too. I sent him a look.

"I mean, I can pick you up tomorrow morning," he elaborated, reading my thoughts. "Or meet you at the Buttered Biscuit. Whatever. I'll be there for you."

"You probably have a class to teach."

He shook his head. "No classes on Friday till noon."

I relented. "Okay, drop me off at Trudy's. But don't worry about tomorrow morning. Trudy can take me."

"Oh. Okay."

His audible disappointment made me laugh. "What else do you like to do? Drive people to the airport? Attend office team-building seminars? Get that seven-year tetanus booster?"

He didn't take offense. "Am I hopeless?"

I trained my eyes on the street. "Too kind for your own good."

"Gwen, you must remember what I told you last night, about how I feel about you. Before I met you I never believed in love at first sight."

"You didn't even remember me the morning after we first saw each other."

"Okay, but the second time I saw you. That's when I knew."

I kept my eyes trained on the street. "Cupcakes."

"You keep saying that, and I still don't know what the heck it means."

"Part of what it means is that you don't know me, or anything about me."

"That's where you're wrong. I know you like to help people, and animals, and that you don't tell people to buzz off even if they show up on your doorstep at midnight."

"I did tell you to buzz off. You just didn't listen."

"I know that you want a family to belong to, a world to belong to, as much as I do, even."

"If there's one thing I have already, it's a family."

"Then why would you settle for living with a person who's anything less than head over heels in love with you?"

I bit my lip.

"Look," he said, "I know what it's like to want to be a part of something so much that you're willing to try to jam yourself in, like a kid trying to mash the wrong piece into a jigsaw puzzle."

He'd put his finger on it. For three months, I'd been trying to fit myself into Daniel's life. I hadn't wanted to admit it for all the reasons that Jeremy said—I wanted to take that next step. I wanted what my parents had. But I'd tried to convince myself that soul mate status was something you could will into being.

But Daniel's turning out to be Mr. Wrong didn't make Jeremy Mr. Right. Especially when I suspected he was still under the influence of Trudy's unintentional alchemy.

Bringing up the cupcakes again would probably just confuse him, though. "There are things you don't know about me. About who I am, fundamentally."

He sent me an anxious look. "Are you a flat-earther or something?"

"Or something."

"I grew up in families in two different religions and three different denominations. I'm pretty open-minded."

I took a deep breath. *Here goes nothing.* "How do you feel about witches?"

He broke into a grin. When I didn't respond, it faded. "That's a joke, right?"

"Not to my family. I come from a long line of witches."

"Gwen, your parents run a diner. They're the most down-to-earth people I've ever met."

"That's because we aren't allowed to practice witchcraft anymore."

We drove a block in silence before he spoke again. "Okay, I'll bite. What's stopping your family from practicing witchcraft?"

"The Grand Council of Witches."

In the darkness inside his car, I could feel his gaze burning into me. "Is there some kind of April Fools' equivalent on Halloween that I've never heard about? Because I'm not getting the humor here."

"The Grand Council of Witches doesn't allow my family to practice witchcraft because my great-great-grandfather had a spellcasting mishap that caused the Dust Bowl."

His mouth dropped open, then closed again. "When you were saying that the cupcakes were responsible for last night, was that your way of saying that Trudy's been lacing her baked goods with

some kind of hallucinogen? Because that's the only way I can interpret this crazy talk."

And there it was. "From head over heels to 'You're crazy on
drugs' in five minutes. That's why it won't work out between us,
Jeremy."

"I'm a historian. You realize there are valid, scientific expla-
nations for the Dust Bowl. Decades of soil erosion and lack of
crop rotation, years of drought, the plowing up of the grassland
prairies . . ." He shook his head. "It's all in the history books."

"Of course it is. If the Council hadn't planted a damn good
cover story, it would have been the Salem witch trials all over
again."

"That's—"

"Crazy talk. See? This was why I was hoping you'd take the
hint without my having to tell you. It's not going to work. It
never does. I need a person in my life who believes that magic is
more than a parlor trick."

"You're really not joking."

"No."

The following half minute of silence stretched like an eternity. I was never so relieved as when he pulled in front of the
BLAIR FOR MAYOR sign in Trudy's front yard.

"I don't know what to say," he confessed. "I'm stunned."

I closed my fingers around the door handle. "You don't have to
say anything. I understand. I really do." Impulsively, I leaned
over and kissed him on his cheek. "You're a good person, Jeremy,
and I wish you nothing but great things."

I got out of the car, then leaned back in to retrieve the cat carrier, which lay on the floor in front of the seat. *Not here again.*

I did a double take, lifting the box to look through the air
holes.

"Did you hear that?" I asked Jeremy.

"What?"

If he didn't believe the story about the Dust Bowl, I doubted
he'd be any more open to the idea of talking cats. Surely I'd just

imagined it. It had been a long day. "Never mind. Thanks for the ride."

I hipped the door closed, turned, and walked up to Trudy's porch without looking back. I'd meant what I said to Jeremy. Every word. Still, when I heard the engine turn over, my insides sagged. The sound of Jeremy's car retreating down the street hurt more than I anticipated. Not that I'd expected any other reaction from him. It was worse than that. I'd hoped.

Trudy's street was dark, and I stood for a moment at the bottom of the porch steps, swallowing disappointment. Which was ridiculous. I'd only known Jeremy for a few days—and using the word *known* was a stretch. We were strangers.

It was Halloween night, and I was beginning the witch's New Year in magnificent fashion—not only out with the old love, but also out with the new one. It was just me now.

No, that wasn't right. I had family. I had work. Daniel was wrong. My little business might not save the boreal forests, but it helped people. And I'd built it myself.

Maybe what I needed to do was find a nice witch to settle down with. I wondered if eCharmed would allow a witch from an Edict-restricted family to fill out a profile. *Nonpracticing witch seeks same.* I'd have to ask Milo the next time I saw him.

If he'd even be speaking to me again after tonight. Much would depend on whether our misadventure at Tannith's had sunk his relationship or Brett's shot at being mayor.

Wind made the dry leaves still clinging to their branches shiver, while their fallen friends danced across the grass and swirled on the walkway. In his box, Griz hissed. The next instant, I felt a presence behind me.

One possibility occurred to me—that this was Jeremy, remorseful about his reaction to what I'd told him. Even though it made no sense—I hadn't heard his car come back—I whirled like one of the airborne leaves, an expectant smile on my face.

It disappeared the moment I saw who it was. Not Jeremy. Tannith.

She was dressed in a deep purple sheath that hugged her figure from her coat-hanger shoulders to her stiletto-heeled black boots. Over her dress she wore a black velvet cape clasped with a medallion pin encrusted with jewels.

"Have you come to collect your cat, or to ruin our lives?"

She laughed and tossed her curtain of long black hair over one shoulder. "Do I have to choose?"

"Your letter promised us that you were moving. Or is that off?"

Her black lashes performed a slow blink over her green eyes. "We'll just have to see about that, won't we?" She nodded at the cat carrier I was still clutching. "You seem to have commandeered Griz."

"You know he ran away to—"

My words died as her chest rose and fell in an impatient sigh. "Yes, Gwen."

Of course she knew. She'd been watching.

Trudy's front door swung open and she stood in a rectangle of light. "I thought I heard voices out here. Gwen, what—" Her gaze fell on Tannith, who stepped out of the shadows. "Oh. You'd better come in."

I hugged Griz's box in my arms and climbed the steps. My gut churned. The unease I'd felt all week during Tannith's absence quadrupled now that she was back.

We made quite a trio. I was dressed in my Abracadabra work boots and jeans, Trudy was in navy blue yoga pants with an apron declaring THE BAKER RESERVES THE RIGHT TO LICK THE SPATULA across the bib, and Tannith looked, spectacularly, like a witch.

Tannith swirled her cape behind her and settled herself onto the armrest of Trudy's new couch. "Aren't either of you going to wish me a happy birthday?"

"Your birthday isn't till March," I said.

She smiled. "That was my fake birthday for my fake life with my fake family."

My heart gave a strange bound. "You mean we aren't related at all?"

Her lips flattened. "Well, maybe. Very distantly. But like your clan, my folks landed in the doghouse—posthumously. An accident of alchemy, but you know how the Council is. The sins of the father are visited upon the kids, et cetera—even when dear old dad and mom accidentally asphyxiate." She shrugged. "There may also have been a few people snuffed out in the next apartment. And for that, I was placed in the loving care of Mr. and Mrs. Buttered Biscuit."

"Gwen was right," Trudy said. "You're a Watcher." Fear crackled between us like an electric current. If Tannith had figured out a fraction of what had been going on here this week, we were well and truly screwed.

Tannith's voice dripped sarcasm. "And it only took her twenty years to figure it out. Well done, Gwendle-bug!"

I flushed. "Why are you telling us this now?"

"Because my time is almost up. My watch ends at midnight the night of my thirtieth birthday. Twenty-six minutes to go."

She could do a lot of damage in twenty-six minutes.

"And what then?" I asked. "You decide to steal one of our boyfriends and ride your broomstick off into the sunset?"

Tannith released a husky laugh. "That was the original plan, but you chowderheads messed it all up. For two decades you were all so predictable I wanted to weep. The Council might as well have assigned me to watch paint dry. And then what happens this week? I leave you on your own for a few days and everything starts to go haywire."

As if her poison letter hadn't been partially responsible for that.

Trudy, bless her, made a stab at brazening it out. "I don't know what you mean."

"Oh, give me a break." Tannith narrowed her eyes on us. "Where is Laird?"

I avoided Trudy's gaze.

A knock sounded, startling us all, and Milo burst in the front door. "I've had it." He dropped a leather overnight bag onto the floor. "Trudy, would it be okay if I stayed tonight in—" Belatedly, he caught sight of our visitor. "Tannith." He gave her a quick up and down. "Nice boots. You never looked witchier."

"I've never felt it, either." She preened. "Now that the gang's all here, you might as well know as much as Trudy and Gwen." In a few sentences, she got Milo up to speed on who she was and why she'd been placed in our family.

Now it was Milo's turn to look panicked. "If I've practiced witchcraft, it's only been in the most incompetent way. I'm sure the Council has bigger fish to fry."

"Indeed it does." Tannith crossed her arms. "I'll repeat my previous question. Where is Laird?"

My mouth was dry.

"H-he's on a research trip," Trudy said. "In Iowa."

Tannith rose to her feet, her face darkening. "Do not lie to me. Laird is no more in Iowa than I'm on the moon. Where is he?"

"He's right here." Trudy pushed his small plastic travel terrarium forward. "That's Laird."

The surprise in Tannith's eyes made me feel a little better. Our efforts to foil her surveillance must have worked in some small measure. She didn't know everything. She was intimidating, but not unbeatable. My brain raced. There must have been something in what I'd learned this week that could get her out of our lives.

"You turned your husband into a frog?" Tannith asked Trudy.

"Toad," the three of us chorused.

"*I* didn't—" Trudy had begun to speak, but at my panicked look, she swallowed her words. I was hoping against hope that we could get through whatever Tannith had in mind without involving anyone else.

Tannith pivoted toward me. "*You* did it?"

"I only meant to say that I didn't *mean* to," Trudy said. "It was a mistake. If I executed a spell, it was only accidentally."

Tannith paced across the room toward Milo. "Is she telling the truth?"

"That she didn't mean to?" He nodded. "Yes."

Tannith slunk over to inspect Laird more closely. "Why on earth didn't you change him back, then?"

"Because I don't know how." Here Trudy's voice took on the ring of truth. "I only hexed him by instinct, out of anger."

Tannith clucked. "That's never good."

Milo stepped forward. "So she tried to get us all to figure out how to reverse the spell, but we—well, we didn't have much luck."

Tannith drew back. "You couldn't figure out how to reverse a toad spell? Guys, that's basic spellcasting."

"Not when you've been forbidden to practice all your life."

Her crimson lips twisted. "So were you going to let Laird remain this way forever, or just for the term of his sabbatical, or what?"

We all said nothing.

"There was no Plan B?" The wry edge that crept into Tannith's voice scared me.

We shook our heads.

"Liars!" she bellowed.

Trudy, Milo, and I edged closer together, clustering instinctively, our collective fear ramping up. I'd been anxious about Tannith when I thought she was simply my bitchy adopted sister-cousin who dabbled in witchcraft. Now that I knew she was a Watcher, I held out little hope that this encounter would end well.

"Do you think I just fell off my first broomstick?" she asked. "I've been watching you. I can see into your lives. Even yours, Milo." She poked a long-nailed finger into his sternum.

He gulped. "How?"

"You don't make it easy when you send the presents I give to you to Goodwill. Although you might recall a certain fridge magnet I gave you."

"Oh." His Adam's apple bobbed over his collar as he swallowed.

I remembered the invisibility spells I'd read about and wondered for a moment if I could make Milo, Trudy, and myself disappear before some horrible curse was put on us. There had to be something we could do. We were three against one.

That one suddenly seemed more formidable than the rest of us combined, however.

"You know, my original plan was to barter away your partners for information," Tannith said, amused. "But you all seemed to have inadvertently double-crossed me by trashing your relationships in the course of a few days. How did you manage it?" We all remained dumb. "Of course, I now know what happened to the unfortunate Laird, but you really surprised me, Gwen. Cheating on that handsome bug guy with an inferior specimen."

"Jeremy isn't inferior."

Tannith sniffed and refocused her attention on Milo. "And you—causing all sorts of problems by bringing a guy who looks like Mr. Clean into your happy home with Brett. I couldn't understand it at all—until I heard you call him by his name after Brett left for work."

Cold fear clutched my heart.

Tannith stepped closer to us, smiling as she noticed the panic in my eyes. "That's right. Your miserable little tricks and love affairs have dwindled in interest to me. I want Odin Tiberius Klemperer."

It was the first time I'd heard his full name. I lifted my chin. "That's impossible."

She wasn't going to take no for an answer. "Maybe I haven't made myself clear. It's not I who wants Cousin Odin, it's the Council. They don't take it kindly when a witch they've exiled to oblivion manages to manifest himself back in our world."

"We don't know where he is anymore," Trudy declared, just before the doorbell rang.

Tannith turned toward the door with a frown. "It's like Grand Central Station here tonight."

"Probably just a late trick-or-treater," Trudy said, not making a move to answer it.

I knew she worried it was Marcus. That was my guess, too. But far from fearing him, I wondered if an armed cop could work to our advantage.

The doorbell sounded again.

Impatiently, Tannith strode to the door and yanked it open. But it wasn't Marcus standing at the threshold. It was Jeremy.

I felt as if I'd swallowed a boulder. *Why had he come back?*

"Is Gwen here?"

A toothless smile stretched across Tannith's face. "Of course. Jeremy, isn't it?"

He looked surprised—and, heartbreakingly, almost pleased. "Yes." Then he caught sight of me and scooted right past Tannith. "Gwen. Forgive me. I'm so sorry for being such a jerk. Just because you believe in something doesn't mean I have to."

I had to make him go away. Now.

I shook my head. "I don't forgive you." I willed myself to look as unrelenting as possible. "Get out of here."

My harsh tone hit him like a slap.

Then the front door clicked closed. "Jeremy's going to stay a while," Tannith said.

Oh, no. "Why did you have to come back?" I asked him.

He was still too focused on explaining himself to me to heed the danger around him. "I'm sorry I drove away like I did. I thought about what you said about wanting a man who believes magic is more than a parlor trick. Because I realized that man is me. What I feel for you *is* magical, Gwen."

I bit back a groan. Of all the times for him to go all supernatural and syrupy.

Tannith clapped her hands together. "This is *so sweet.*"

Jeremy turned to her. "I'm sorry. I should have introduced myself formally. I'm Jeremy Westerman."

"I'm Gwen's cousin Tannith."

"Oh! Gwen told me all about you. You were raised like sisters, she said."

Her dark brows arched with interest. "How touching that she was thinking of me this week. And now you've come here burning with the same love you were unable to control last night when you two had your little dalliance."

His face reddened and his gaze cut back to me in surprise. I shook my head, although kissing and telling was probably the least of his worries right now.

Tannith proved me right. "You look like you're on fire, poor man. I didn't mean to embarrass you. But don't worry—I'll cool you off."

Although it's doubtful I could have stopped her, before I thought to move a muscle, Tannith raised her hands and swept them from Jeremy's feet to the top of his curly brown hair. A huff went out of him, like the expelling of air when something is being vacuum sealed. In horror, I saw that his body had gone completely still, shock frozen in his wide-eyed expression. Within seconds, his glasses frosted over. I tentatively touched my hand to his. It was like ice.

I rounded on Tannith. "Release him!"

"Bring me Odin."

Trudy tried to intercede. "You know we aren't very adept, Tannith. How do you think we could possibly have any control over Odin?"

"Because if you don't exert some control over our wayward cousin, Sir Ice Cube here is going to remain frozen in your living room forever. And maybe one of you would like to join him?"

Milo shook his head. "I thought we were friends."

"You thought wrong," Tannith shot back. "I was a prisoner. You think I didn't miss my *real* family, my *real* friends? I was exiled to Zenobia. And you weren't even the slightest bit interesting. Any of you! You couldn't have performed witchcraft even if you'd wanted to. Barbie dolls and Warlock Holmes aside." Tannith smirked at Milo's surprise. "You were all pathetic—until this week! Maybe my letter shaking you up is the best thing that could have happened to the three of you. Odin's reappearance is the first noteworthy event to happen in Zenobia since *I've* been here. My swan song as a Watcher will result in one of the biggest collars in Council history."

"How exciting for you," I said.

Her face tensed in determination. "You bet it is. Now pick up the phone and get Odin here, or I'll turn Trudy into ice next."

Trudy let out a gasp. Her pleading gaze met mine.

There was no doubt in my mind that Tannith would make good on her threat.

I dug my phone out of my pocket and dialed Esme's house.

Chapter 28

Part of me hoped Aunt Esme wouldn't be home, but she answered her phone on the third ring.

"Kind of late to be calling, isn't it?" she growled over the line. "What do you want? Odin and I are just trying to make up for lost time, if you know what I mean."

Aunt Esme's love life wasn't something I wanted to ruminate on in too much detail, especially in this horrible moment. In as circumspect a manner as I could manage, given that Tannith was hovering right next to me, I told Esme that Odin was needed at Trudy's. I glanced over at poor frozen Jeremy. His skin was turning bluish. How long could he survive in a deep freeze?

"It's a matter of life or death." As I said the words, I cringed inside. I was setting up Odin to be turned in to the Council. No telling what would happen to him this time, or to Esme if they found out she had retrieved him from his punishment and had been harboring him.

But Esme and Odin were witches. They had a fighting chance against Tannith. Jeremy had simply been in the wrong place at the wrong time. I'd told him that he needed to believe in witch-craft, but being turned into a human icicle was a high price to pay to have one's skepticism disproved.

I couldn't let Tannith do the same thing to anyone else.

"I suppose Trudy has decided that she wants us to do some-thing about Laird after all," Esme said.

"Uh, yeah."

A long sigh blew through my phone. "Okay. I guess we can make a house call just this once."

"Just Odin," I said.

"What, I'm not invited?"

"Only Odin is needed."

"Please, We're talking toads here. I can do those spells."

"I know—Tannith says they're basic."

A slight hesitation crackled over the line. "Tannith? She's there?"

"Yes. We're all looking forward to seeing Odin again. We'll be *watching* for him."

"Hang tight. I'm firing up the Gremlin."

I ended the call, hoping I'd given Esme sufficient warning. I felt like a terrible niece, throwing my own aunt to the wolves. Aunt Esme had never been nice to me, but as Mom had said, she'd had her troubles. Now I was compounding them.

"Stop with the long face," Tannith said. "You're killing me."

I wish. "You can un-hex Jeremy now."

"Not a chance. I'll wait to see that I have Odin in hand before I thaw out your sweetheart."

I hated her more than I ever dreamed I could hate another person.

Trudy's unnaturally chipper voice broke the tense silence. "Would anyone like a cupcake?"

My stomach felt so queasy I doubted I could have kept any-thing down. Something about seeing a man's flesh frosting over took my appetite away. Besides, the last cupcakes Trudy had made had put my employees and half a restaurant to sleep.

A lightbulb went off in my head. "Cupcakes—good idea. What kind are there?"

"Autumn spice. For tomorrow."

"Any more peanut butter–chocolate?" I asked, sending Trudy a meaningful glance. "Those are your best ones."

Trudy's look was glazed until understanding dawned. "Oh! Yes! I have a few of those left over. I'll put one out for everybody."

"Not for me, thanks," Tannith said.

"You should try one," I said. "They're incredible."

"I'll take one," Milo said.

Trudy and I shot him a look—unfortunately, Tannith saw it, too.

She crossed her arms. "What did you do, lace them with cyanide?"

"No!" we chorused too quickly. Even Milo had finally caught on.

Tannith smirked. "Nice try."

The rest of us exchanged disappointed looks.

Griz, I remembered, was still in his cardboard box. I opened the top, extracted him, and gave him a hug. "I suppose you'll want to take him tonight."

"Oh, I'm not sure." Tannith stared at her cat, disgusted. Or maybe just bored. "He isn't much use to me. I might have to send him back to the SPCA."

Griz stiffened in my arms, and who could blame him? Tannith was a monster.

"I'm thinking about getting something a little more exotic for a pet," she said. "A hyacinth macaw, maybe."

Milo smiled. "No winged monkeys available?"

Griz jumped out of my arms and streaked toward the basement.

"See what I mean?" Tannith said. "Useless. I've been so good to him, too."

"Yeah, you've been a peach," I grumbled.

Tannith slid onto the couch and jogged one of her stiletto-booted legs lazily. "God, I can't wait to be out of this place for good." She shifted her glance to the kitchen clock. "Thirteen more minutes, and then it's goodbye, Zenobia, this stupid cupcake coven, and the idiotic Engels."

I scowled at her. Her insults didn't bother me for my own sake, but her sneering at Mom and Dad ticked me off. She'd been part of our family. They'd bent over backward never to anger her in any way. Every time we'd argued, they'd seemed pained, as if they were afraid—

No. Not *as if*.

They'd been afraid. Of Tannith.

They must have known about her—or at least suspected—all along.

It would have been like living with an unexploded bomb in their house for over twenty years. I wondered how much my mom knew about Esme, too. If they'd been aware of what was going on in Esme's basement, and what would happen if Tannith found out about it, they must have been on pins and needles for decades.

And now I'd undermined all their careful playacting in one night.

The rattle of the Gremlin's engine approaching rent the silence that had fallen over the room. I tensed. It wouldn't take Tannith long to put it together. Only one car in town sounded like the Gremlin.

Her eyes popped open wide. "Surely not."

Outside, the engine spluttered and died, and heavy steps came up the walkway. I tried to steady my nerves. Once Tannith got a look at the new Esme, it would be game over for my aunt.

When Trudy opened the door, though, it wasn't the new Esme that stood on the threshold. It was my old-crone aunt, hunched and scowling.

"I'd heard you were gone," she barked at Tannith. "I should have known it was too good to be true."

A dismissive sneer was all the greeting Tannith spared Esme. I doubt Tannith even noticed the pop-eyed wonder in the eyes of the rest of us as we gaped at my aunt, whom we'd last seen as a dazzling twentysomething. Tannith only had eyes for Odin.

I couldn't remember the last time I witnessed Tannith showing genuine astonishment. "*This* is the boy genius, the famous exiled sorcerer?"

"How do you do," he said in his kindly, befuddled tone. "I'm Odin."

The friendly yet strangely vacant look in his eyes made my heart sink. For some reason, I was hoping that his feats of the past few days would have sharpened him up and brought him back to his old self. We needed a witch at the top of his game. Instead, we still had a warmed-over former toad.

"What happened to this fellow?" Odin asked, studying Jeremy with a grave expression. "He seems to be chilled."

"He was my leverage," Tannith said.

Odin turned back to her. "And you are?"

"Your worst nightmare."

Esme chortled. "How's that for hubris?"

"Shut up, old woman." Tannith didn't even spare her a glance, but kept her gaze pinned on the prize that had just been dropped in her lap. By me. How would I ever live down the shame of this?

I stepped forward. "Tannith, please. No matter how distant, Odin is your flesh and blood. The mistakes he made, whatever they were, happened when he was younger than we are now. He's part of our family."

"Stop yammering at me about family!" Tannith snapped. "Did you ever consider me your sister, really?"

I opened my mouth to lie, but couldn't. "I tried to."

"That's right. Sometimes I could hear Jane giving you little talks: 'Treat Tannith like your sister, Gwen.' 'Share with Tannith, Gwen.' She's probably *still* giving you those little talks, and you know why? Because you never thought of me as anything but an intruder in your happy little domestic circle."

Milo crossed his arms. "Isn't that what you were?"

"*She* didn't know that," Tannith shot back at him. "And even if I was planted by the Council, I was also a kid. I had feelings. How would you like to have been orphaned at eight and shunted into a strange family, and to be told that you were stuck with these lamebrain people for the next twenty-two years? I wasn't even given time to grieve for my own parents!"

It was more genuine emotion than I'd ever seen her display. "Then honor them now by stopping whatever you're going to do. For decades you fulfilled the Council's instructions. You have your inheritance. At the stroke of midnight you can be free, and you won't have harmed anyone."

"Or I can go down in the books as the witch who found Odin Tiberius Klemperer."

Esme had been doing a good job of containing whatever she felt, but now she trembled in outrage. "*You* found him?" For a moment I worried she was going to spit, but she let out a contemptuous "Ha!" instead. "I spent a quarter of my life looking for Odin, and having to hide my search from the likes of you."

"Oh, really?" Tannith couldn't contain her amusement. "And this shell of a man is your handiwork?"

"This shell of a man could crush you like a bug, hon. And so could I." In a replay of what had happened back in the farmhouse basement, Esme transformed herself back into young, slinky Esme. The rest of us were almost used to these changes now, but the shock on Tannith's face was glorious to see. My aunt cocked a hip, Mae West style. "The only difference is that Odin wouldn't enjoy destroying you. But I'd love it."

I wanted to pump my fist.

Odin put a hand on her shoulder. "Not here, Es."

"What do you mean, not here?" she asked.

"The kids"—Odin gestured to Milo, Trudy, and me—"they would be implicated. We can't trade our safety for theirs."

My aunt's expression collapsed in confusion. "You're going to let this two-bit supernatural bounty hunter take you?"

"I don't want to. I'd rather appeal to her reason. I'd at least prefer to do this somewhere else."

"Don't be a fool. She'll snitch on her cousins anyway."

"All I have to do is snap my fingers," Tannith said, raising her hand.

In response, my aunt raised hers, but then Odin reached out and grabbed Esme. I stared in horror at Tannith's fingers. Her thumb rubbed her middle finger.

Would this be how it ended for all of us? Tannith could destroy us all—or the Council would. I envisioned all that might never happen. Milo and Brett reconciling, Jeremy coming unfrozen, Laird being untoaded. Maybe I wouldn't be allowed to tell my parents goodbye. My parents, who'd cared for Tannith under their own roof. They didn't deserve this betrayal.

Anger boiled up inside me like lava. Before Tannith could snap, *I* snapped. I'm not sure how it happened, but my voice cried out for her to stop—using words I'd never before voiced, although I must have seen them on the page of one of Esme's old grimoires. My hands thrust forward, and the electric charge that went through me dwarfed what I'd felt when I'd stopped the greenhouse alarm. My whole body was possessed, my mind centered on my erstwhile sister, my fingertips shooting bolts of rage.

I now understood Trudy and her rabbit spells. When the electricity left my body, I was limp and exhausted. The others were staring at me, bug-eyed with various levels of surprise or fear. All except Tannith. Tannith was nowhere to be seen.

"What just happened?"

Abruptly, everyone's attention shifted to Jeremy, standing behind us all, testing out his limbs. Other than his skin being on the blue side, he seemed to be okay. I could have wept with relief.

Milo turned to me. "How did you do that?"

Esme drew up proudly. "She's my niece, that's how."

I scanned the room. "Where's Tannith?"

"What just happened?" Jeremy repeated.

I reached out and took his hand. Still frigid, but it seemed to be warming up. I hoped his temporary ice suspension hadn't done him lasting harm. "I must have thawed you." God knows I felt as if enough heat had passed through my arms to melt what was left of the Arctic.

"I believe you performed an invisibility spell, similar to what was performed on me once," Odin said.

"It was a little bit of overkill," Esme allowed, patting my shoulder, "but inexperience can make things hard to control."

"Don't I know it," Trudy commiserated.

"But where is Tannith?" I asked. "What have I done?"

"It'll be okay," Odin said. "Someone will probably conjure her back eventually, and she'll be right as rain. Look at me."

That wasn't as reassuring as he'd intended. Not that I cared about Tannith herself. "What will I tell my parents? What if the Council comes searching for her?"

"Why would they do that?" Trudy asked.

"Look at the time," Milo told me. "It's just turned twelve. Tannith said her days as a Watcher ended at midnight. She's free—just like she wanted to be."

"I don't think this is what she meant."

Milo's tone sharpened as he reminded me, "She was going to narc on us all—if you hadn't done what you did, when you did, it'd be all of us floating around in the ether now."

"And I'd still be frozen." Still in disbelief, Jeremy cocked his head. "Was I really frozen?"

We all nodded.

Esme stepped toward me. "I'm glad your days in the laboratory taught you something. Maybe you can get some more use out of it. I can't believe I'm saying this, but you might have the makings of a good witch in you."

"You never told _me_ that," Trudy said.

Esme glared at her. "For good reason. Stick with cupcakes, cupcake." Before Trudy could do her worst, Esme raised a hand.

"Never mind tossing one of your bunny spells. Odin and I will be moseying along now. You might not have to lay eyes on us for a good long while." Esme took my hands and slapped a set of keys in them. "The house and the Gremlin are yours until I get back. Don't strip the clutch."

I frowned. "Won't you need your car?"

She smiled at Odin. "Not where we're going."

"The Gremlin would stick out a little in the 1920s," Odin said.

Milo drew back. "A time-travel spell?"

Time travel was not something easy to do. The powers that be didn't encourage even trying it. So much could go wrong, and witches were strictly forbidden to change past events.

"Wish us luck, kids," Odin said. "We're off to get the family curse reversed."

"You mean the Dust Bowl wasn't caused by witchcraft?" Trudy asked.

"It was," Esme said. "But the question is, which witch cast the spell? The punitive Edict reeks of classic deflection, and Odin said he once conjured the ghost of Elam Clancy, the great-great-grandfather of the Council's leader."

"A ne'er-do-well of the first water," Odin said. "He intimated that he'd been the real culprit."

"The next day the Council came down on Odin like a ton of bricks," Esme said. "Our hope is to bring Elam back so there can be a real accounting, and the true culprits can be punished."

"How long will you be gone?" I asked.

They looked at each other. "We've got the time spell figured out, but reversing it's going to be trickier," Esme said. "I sent an email to Jane explaining everything. Worse-case scenario, we get stuck in 1930. We'll suck it up, put on our best duds, and hit the Cotton Club."

They turned to go.

"Wait!" Trudy called out.

Esme and Odin stopped.

Trudy nodded to the terrarium. "Isn't there something you can do for Laird?"

Esme thought for a second, then relented. "You're all such babies." She lifted her hand and threw bolts as casually as someone tossing a ball. Nevertheless, hell broke loose. The terrarium exploded in pieces, the air's very molecules seemed to detonate, and a sound so terrifying ripped through the room that we clutched our ears to block it out.

When the dust settled, a dazed Laird stood before us, naked except for a pair of Kermit the Frog briefs. *Nice touch, Esme.*

I looked around for her, but she and Odin were gone. During the chaos, they'd vanished.

Trudy handed Laird her apron to cover himself. He was still pop-eyed in shock.

Even now that he was human Laird again, I couldn't unsee the toad. I worried I never would.

Jeremy edged closer to me and asked in a low voice, "Is your family always like this?"

"This has been an exceptional evening."

"At least everything's back to normal now," Trudy said.

Except for the small matter of Tannith's having vanished. I would have to concoct some explanation for my parents. Yet I sensed now that they would accept her disappearance and even welcome it.

"Does anyone have a hot beverage?" Jeremy asked. "I still feel a chill."

Trudy brightened. "Cocktails!"

I shook my head. "Maybe alcohol isn't the best idea right now."

"Speak for yourself," Milo said. "I could use a belt of something."

"I'll make tea, and those who want to spike it can," Trudy said. "Oh—and we have cupcakes. Autumn apple."

As she pushed a plate toward us, the doorbell rang. In her old hostess mode now, Trudy swept toward the door and pulled it open.

Brett Blair stood on the porch, smiling but anxious. "Hi, Trudy. Can I come in?"

She stepped back and he strode into the living room, smiling at us all in greeting. He was normally gregarious, but clearly he hadn't expected so many of us to be here. That smile faded and his gaze lingered for a moment on Laird, who was standing by the kitchen island in his apron and Kermit underwear, smashing a cupcake into his mouth as if he'd forgotten how food worked.

Milo stepped forward. "We have nothing to talk about, Brett."

"I just wanted to let you know that I explained to the editor of the *Zenobia Bee* that the incident tonight was all a mix-up. Since no charges were filed, it's a nonstory. So you don't have to feel defensive about messing up the campaign. Because you didn't."

"That's not the reason I left, though," Milo said. "You were right to be angry. I've been devious. I really did look at your credit card bill, and worse."

Brett frowned. "Worse?"

Milo took a deep breath. "Our whole relationship is based on a lie. The second time we met about the landscaping job, I put a spell on you to make you care for me."

"A spell?"

"A love spell."

Brett looked curiously around the rest of us. "Milo was talking wild about witches and Tannith earlier. Do any of you believe in that stuff?"

We all exchanged cautious glances.

"A few of us do," I answered.

Jeremy nodded. "Speaking for myself, I'm growing more convinced with each passing moment."

"Me, too." Brett turned back to Milo. "But I can't say I believe much in *your* magical abilities. The truth is, I fell in love with you at first sight—before we met about the landscaping job. We hadn't even been introduced. So you see, I was under your spell before you ever thought of casting a spell." Brett laughed. "Maybe *I'm* the wizard here."

A smile broke out across Milo's face, but it faded in the next moment. He crossed his arms. "There's still the small matter of the candidate who dashes off to New York in the last week of the campaign and spends thousands of dollars in jewelry stores. Why would you have done that?"

"Why do you think?" Brett took a deep breath. "I was going to wait until after the election, but I guess I'm going to have to do this now." He pulled out a box. "Because win or lose, Milo, I want you with me forever."

Brett flipped open the box's top, revealing two thick rings of braided silver. Aching hope shone in Brett's eyes as he looked into Milo's shocked face. "Maybe they're not what you would have chosen. I'm not the most imaginative guy. For one thing, I absolutely can't imagine a future without you. Will you marry me?"

Someone gasped. I wasn't sure if it was Milo, or Trudy, or maybe even me.

Tears stood in Milo's eyes. "For once in my life I can't think of anything to say."

Brett stepped closer. "Yes would be nice."

Milo rushed forward to embrace him. "Yes."

They leaned in and kissed, as Trudy clasped her hands together. She gave them a long moment before announcing, "The coven is now in session. Champagne cocktails!"

Trudy's champagne cocktails were as delicious as they were potent, and I only allowed myself a half of one to toast Milo and Brett before I set my glass down. Tomorrow was a day off for my employees, but I was scheduled to clean a client's patio furniture and haul the set down to her basement for the winter. I needed to get at least a little sleep.

I was just opening my mouth to announce my departure when flashing red and blue lights from a car in the driveway filled the living room, then turned off. I groaned. After a week like this one, I should have known our troubles weren't yet over.

"Why would the police be here?" Laird asked, blinking.

I could think of a couple of reasons, and no doubt there were probably more that I wasn't aware of. Trudy went red, and Jeremy and I exchanged glances. Up to now, I'd forgotten the small matter of his having reported Trudy to the police.

Marcus Timmens rapped briefly on the door and pushed it open, then paused in surprise. He obviously hadn't expected to encounter a party underway in Trudy's living room.

She rushed forward. "Hello, Marcus. I'm not sure if you know everyone." Holding his arm, she escorted him into our midst to show him off. "Everyone, this is Officer Marcus Timmens."

His reticence only grew. Unlike her, he kept his voice low and tried to address her alone—although of course we could hear. "Trudy, I'm afraid we've had a complaint made by—" He did a double take at Jeremy, standing next to me. Then Marcus turned quickly back to Trudy. "A citizen brought to our attention that an email sent from your account appears to be fraudulent."

Trudy's unflappable smile faded. "Oh."

Marcus looked pained. "Do you still insist that you have no idea where your husband is?"

"Laird?" All at once, she brightened. "Of course!" She pointed across the room, at the kitchen island. "He's right here."

Laird, food stained and standing by himself in his underwear, raised a champagne glass in greeting.

Marcus leveled a hard, assessing stare at him. "*You're* Professor Webster?"

The incredulous question tapped right into Laird's professorial core. He drew up to his full height, heedless of his wearing Muppet briefs. "Is there a problem?"

"We've, uh, had several reports that you were missing."

"I went away," Laird said curtly. "I'm back now."

Marcus looked sidewise at Jeremy. "That's the man you know as Laird Webster?"

Jeremy nodded. "I'm sorry to have wasted your time. That email must have been legitimate after all."

"Well. Good." Marcus cast a doubtful glance back toward Laird, then looked longingly at Trudy. "I suppose I should get going, then."

"But you just got here," she said. "Stay and have some champagne—my cousin Milo just got engaged to Brett Blair."

Marcus's eyes widened in surprise. "Brett Blair for mayor?"

"The one and only," Milo said.

The cop's face broke out in a grin. "Congratulations!"

"So you see, you have to stay." Trudy led Marcus over to the kitchen island, where she started mixing a drink for him.

"I don't know, Trudy. . . ." He tossed another anxious glance at Laird. "If I've come at an awkward time . . ."

She blinked at him. "Awkward? Not at all. The more the merrier. Right, Laird?"

Laird was caught in the middle of upending his glass and attempting to get the cherry out with his tongue.

It seemed as good a time as any to make my exit. "Good night, everybody. I need to go home now."

Jeremy stood.

"Me, too."

Weird. That hadn't sounded like Jeremy's voice. "What did you say?" I asked.

He stared blankly at me, confused. "Nothing. Yet." He turned and thanked Trudy and congratulated the engaged couple again and said he wished he could drink another champagne cocktail. "But I really do need to go now."

"You already said that," I told him.

He frowned. "No, I didn't."

"I could have sworn I heard—" Something furry brushed against my leg. I jumped back, but it was only Griz. I'd forgotten all about him. Now I stared down at him, spooked. "Did Griz say something?"

Marcus laughed. "Yeah, he said, 'Meow,' about a minute ago. You didn't hear him?"

I'd heard him, all right. But it hadn't been a meow.

Trudy came toward me, worry lining her brow. "Are you okay to drive?"

I forced myself to nod. "Come to think of it, I should take Griz with me."

I rounded up his carrier. Now that I wasn't going back to Daniel's, there was nothing to stop me from adopting a kitty. I wasn't sure how I was going to like staying at Aunt Esme's. Some feline companionship would be welcome in that place.

I cast a last look at Brett and Milo, sitting together on Trudy's new sofa. Happy. I was glad the week had turned out well for some of us. Trudy and Marcus—and Laird—might take a little more time to work the kinks out of their situation.

At the Gremlin, Jeremy held the door while I put Griz's box on the passenger seat. "Thank you for an extremely memorable night. And for saving me from being a life-size ice cube."

I wondered if I'd ever see him again. Something in my chest hollowed out at the thought of his walking entirely out of my life . . . but who could blame him? In his place, I would run as fast and far as my legs would carry me.

"I'm sorry about what happened." Even as I said it, it seemed like a woefully inadequate apology.

He laughed. *Laughed.* "Well, you made a believer out of me."

"I'll understand if you still feel like driving away and never looking back."

"I'm going to drive away, but I expect I'll see you very soon."

I frowned. "When?"

"How about in, oh . . ." He checked his watch. "Six hours? Breakfast at the Buttered Biscuit? I'll save us a table."

For some foolish reason—probably because it had been the longest day of my life—a lump gathered in my throat. Was he for real? He wanted to see me again?

"The charm hasn't worn off?" I asked. "After all you've been through tonight?"

"I'm not sure. Let's find out."

He leaned in and kissed me. The moment our lips touched, I felt all the rest of the world melt away. The chilly wind blew around us, but his arms drew me closer, warming me. A feeling of pure happiness coursed through me. After a week of craziness, the present seemed like a wonderful place to be, and the future? That now held all sorts of tantalizing possibilities.

Moonlight broke through the clouds, and Jeremy pulled away slowly, looking deeply into my eyes. "It wasn't the cupcakes," he said.

Epilogue

Griz

Change takes getting used to. My new mistress is disgustingly demonstrative and strangely democratic. Gwen asks me constantly what I would like—and she pays attention to the answers. I am fussed over by her and her relatives, who come in and out regularly. Some are important people—like Zenobia's new mayor. Yet he's one of the people relegated to the upstairs. Only the two cousins, and me, are allowed access to the laboratory.

Gwen is a much different witch from my raven-haired mistress. I have been witness to many sad failures in the basement. But with my own eyes, I saw her vanquish Tannith. Tannith, who assured me that she was cleverer than anyone. That has to mean something.

To her credit, Gwen has upgraded my food options. Non-pellet dinners appear every night. She doesn't bat me off tables, either. And she lets me sleep at the foot of her bed, even when she has Jeremy over, which is often. She tells him she prefers to have him stay at her house because she doesn't want to leave me alone all the time. It's ridiculous how happy this makes me, although it's beneath my dignity to show that I care one way or another.

Yet, I do care. Solitude has become my enemy. When I'm alone, I sometimes sense a haunting presence. Her voice comes to me when I'm half-asleep—that familiar, terrifying voice. Sometimes it's accompanied by her laugh, the one that used to make me purr with delight. I'm not purring now.

"Don't get too comfortable, hair ball," she whispers in my ear. "I'll be back."

Acknowledgments

I want to thank my editor, John Scognamiglio, for mentioning exactly the right title to start my imagination percolating. My hat's off to him and the entire team at Kensington, who all managed to keep everything up and running smoothly in 2020.

As always, big thanks to Annelise Robey for her help and encouragement, and to Joe Newman for being my first reader and principal cheerleader.

Connect with U s

Visit us online at
KensingtonBooks.com
to read more from your favorite authors, see books
by series, view reading group guides, and more.

Join us on social media

for sneak peeks, chances to win books and prize packs,
and to share your thoughts with other readers.

facebook.com/kensingtonpublishing
twitter.com/kensingtonbooks

Tell us what you think!

To share your thoughts, submit a review,
or sign up for our eNewsletters, please visit:
KensingtonBooks.com/TellUs.